THE CHALK CIRCLE

ANTONY TREW

The Chalk
Circle

St. Martin's Press
New York

Library of Congress Cataloging-in-Publication Data

Trew, Antony.
     The chalk circle / Antony Trew.
         p.   cm.
     ISBN 0-312-03301-X
     I. Title.
PR9369.3.T7C47   1989
823—dc20   89-30419
                                                 CIP

First published in Great Britain by William Collins Sons & Co., Ltd.

First U.S. Edition

10 9 8 7 6 5 4 3 2 1

With happy memories of Basil and Joan Le May, our hosts at the Vila da Pesca in those earlier, less troubled days when we went after big fish off Pomene

ONE

The distant speck glinting in sunlight above the Lebombo Mountains grew larger, came steadily closer. Soon the small aircraft was making its pre-landing circuit, over the harbour and bay and on past the red cliffs of Polana Beach. Flaps were lowered, the engine throttled back and the final approach began. With the skill of long experience the pilot put the Cessna down with a mild squeak of tyres, turned it on the runway and taxied across to the parking area where an African batman waved it to its berth. The letters on the buff and silver fuselage showed that the Cessna was registered in the Republic of South Africa. Most of the other parked aircraft belonged to Mozambique, among them those of Matavia Airlines and TTA, the state charter services. Some distance away a number of military aircraft stood on their own as if unwilling to rub shoulders with the common herd.

The Cessna's engine was switched off, the three-bladed propeller jerked to a stop and the batman put chocks under the wheels. The cabin door opened and three men stepped down. The last of them was a large, bearded man in a safari suit and a bush-hat with a leopardskin band. He shouted an African greeting to the batman. The man replied in English. 'Good to see you, Mr Johnson. You okay?'

'Fine thanks. How's that son of yours?'

'He been back in school yesterday. Bit sore. That's all.'

'Great. Tell him to *hamba gahli* – go carefully. Too many cowboys on the roads these days.'

7

'Yes. I tell him that. He be keeping a good look-out now. You can be sure.'

An African arrived with a trolley. The bearded man took off his sunglasses, unlocked the luggage compartment and handed out mailbags, an assortment of parcels and three luggage grips. Before re-locking the compartment he took from it a pilotcase. The African reached for it. Johnnie Johnson – JJ to his friends – waved him away. 'No thank you, José. You ought to know that pilots don't part with their pilotcases.'

José's broad, white-toothed grin suggested that he did know. 'I try to help, sir.'

Johnson turned to his passengers. 'Right. Let's get moving.' The three men headed for the airport buildings followed by José with the luggage trolley.

'They still know you here, JJ,' said the bigger of the two passengers. The deep voice issuing from below the ample moustache emphasised the Afrikaans accent.

'They bloody well ought to. I'm in and out of the place a lot of times each year.'

The other passenger, a man with narrow eyes and a lined face, said, 'The buildings look – ' he finished in Afrikaans, *'n bietjie afgeloop, né?'*

Johnson frowned. 'Run down? What d'you expect? Sub-tropical sun and a shattered economy.'

'Ja, I suppose so. They must miss the Portuguese.'

'I doubt it. But they have problems, including a war and years of drought.'

An aircraft was taking off as the trio made their way to the building, but other than airport staff and numbers of armed soldiers there were few people about. Shepherded by Johnson, who seemed to be known and liked by everyone, they completed the form-filling formalities, their passports and visas were checked and they passed through immigration and customs to the concourse. There a slight, dapper man with a military moustache came forward to greet them.

'Hello, JJ.' He shook hands with Johnson. 'You're bang on time.' He turned to the big passenger. 'Good to see you, Jan. All well on the farm?'

Jan Wessels, looming large over the slight man, took his hand, held it firmly. 'Fine, Charles. *Alles gaan goed.* Meet my pal, Piet Pienaar.' He motioned towards the balding man with the deeply-lined face. 'Piet, this is my old friend, Charles Scott. He's boss of the syndicate.' The two men shook hands.

'Welcome to Maputo, Mr Pienaar. Hope you're going to enjoy the trip.'

Pienaar said he was sure he would, adding in Afrikaans that he was looking forward to catching a big marlin. Having explained that Scott couldn't speak Afrikaans, Wessels translated. Scott smiled. 'The man who doesn't look forward to that isn't a fisherman.' He turned to Johnson. 'Well, JJ. If your people are ready I think we should be getting along.'

Johnson nodded. 'I'll join you later, Charles. Must file flight documents, hand in manifests, see to refuelling, etcetera. I'll take a taxi.' With his bush-hat pushed back on his head and the pilotcase wedged under his arm, he left them.

'There goes a good man,' remarked Scott quietly. 'And a fine pilot.'

With luggage grips slung over their shoulders the new arrivals walked over to the car park, led by their host.

The elderly man with his back against the Matavia Air lines' desk looked at his watch before lighting a cheroo Wearing a white seersucker suit, a Panama hat and da sunglasses, he had the calm, detached manner of someo to whom time was of little consequence. But that wa façade; Andrada Gouveia was a man to whom time wa consequence. But he measured it against objectives: if was patient, if one persisted, if one waited long enough, he believed, the desired objectives would be accomplished. The flight for which he was waiting was twenty minutes late, but he was not unduly concerned for it was his custom on such occasions to reflect and observe; airports were good places for reflection and even better for observation. It was while so engaged that he saw Johnnie Johnson with his leopardskin bush-hat coming from the flight offices. He waved a folded newspaper at him, calling, as he approached, '*Boa tarde.*'

Johnson came up, luggage grip in one hand, pilotcase in the other. 'The man himself,' he said with a grin. 'What brings you here so late, Andrada?' He took Gouveia's hand, shook it warmly.

'I'm meeting the Johannesburg flight.'

'What's she like? Blonde or brunette?'

'Neither, JJ. She's a man.'

For a few minutes they exchanged news, asked after friends, discussed the weather. There was a moment of silence; Johnson picked up his luggage grip, slung the strap over a shoulder and was about to go when Gouveia said, 'I saw you helping your passengers through customs and immigration.' He smiled, revealing gappy, yellow-stained teeth. 'Don't think I know them.'

'You must know Jan Wessels, the big chap. He farms at Dullstroom. Piet Pienaar's his chum. They're going up the coast with Charles Scott to fish. Wessels is a member of Scott's syndicate. He's been down here a good few times. Pienaar's on his first visit. Hasn't done any big-game fishing but he's dead keen to have a go. Both Afrikaners. I know Wessels pretty well. He's okay. Pienaar's a quiet chap. Met him today. Wessels wouldn't have brought him down if he wasn't okay.'

Gouveia's slow nods suggested that he was weighing what had been said. 'What's his job?'

'Sales rep, agricultural machinery. His territory takes in Dullstroom. That's how he came to know Wessels.'

10

'Good.' Gouveia looked at his watch, added, 'When are you off again?'

'Tomorrow, Monday.'

'Where to?'

'Mutare, then Quelimane maybe.'

'Passengers?'

'None yet.'

'Well, so long. Take care.'

Johnson straightened his bush-hat. *'Tot siens*, Andrada.'

'Até à vista, JJ.' Gouveia smiled distantly, mouthed his cheroot as he watched the departing figure until it had disappeared through the exit doors. He unfolded the newspaper but his thoughts were about Johnnie Johnson. The man was a good contact, a useful source of information, not only about the passengers he carried but about things that were happening in the countries bordering Mozambique. Johnson's company, Charter Couriers RSA (Pty) Ltd, a South African concern, small and independent, had a contract with the Mozambique Government to carry mail, parcels and sometimes passengers to neighbouring territories. It performed a useful function, filling gaps in the schedules of the regular carriers, particularly in flights to small, out-of-the-way places. The fact that Johnnie Johnson himself often did duty as pilot – although chairman, managing-director and principal shareholder of the charter company – belied his outward image of cheerful extrovert. He never failed to carry out both the letter and spirit of the contract; apart from this he was at times, perhaps unwittingly, a useful purveyor of intelligence. To Gouveia he was one of the few white South Africans he knew who appeared to understand the difficulties confronting the Mozambique Government and to sympathise with its aspirations.

Outside the building Johnson found a waiting taxi, asked the driver to take him to the Polana and climbed in. The tired old Chevrolet moved off on its noisy journey into

11

town. Johnson thought about Gouveia, wondering as he often did where the man figured in the government hierarchy. He had known him for some time, liked him, yet had never succeeded in really getting to know him. Andrada Gouveia was a very private person; intelligent, sophisticated, an *assimilado* half-caste, educated under the old régime in the days before Frelimo had defeated the Portuguese and seized power.

It was rumoured that he was important, some said high up in security. Since Maputo was a city of rumours, Johnson accepted the possibility but kept an open mind. It was unwise for white South Africans to be inquisitive about the country's internal affairs.

The Land Rover was leaving the airport when Wessels said, 'Piet hasn't been here before, Charles. How about showing him a bit of Maputo on our way to the Polana? The docks, say, and along the seafront. We'll be leaving first thing tomorrow. Unless we take this chance he won't see much of Maputo.'

Scott's eyebrows lifted. 'Well, yes,' he said without enthusiasm. 'But we haven't much time. It's past five and I have to get back to the office. We'll have to make it snappy.'

By way of streets lined with flamboyants and jacarandas he drove the Land Rover across town to a park on high ground over-looking the harbour. They got out and walked to the edge of the cliff. Below them lay the blue gums and casuarinas of the Aterro do Machaquene; to their right the faded reds, browns and greys of the town buildings, to the left the older buildings: the Port Captain's office and its precincts, the Old Fort, the dry dock and boat harbour, a few rusted dredgers and tugs, and the sheds and warehouses along the Gorjão Quay where the bent heads of cargo cranes hung like great birds feeding from the ships alongside. Beyond them the broad waters of the Rio

Espirito Santo shimmered in late sunlight, a mosaic of blues, browns and greys reaching across to sandy beaches and scrub on the far bank where rusted barges lay offshore. A few small boats moving on the water gave life to an otherwise inanimate scene.

'This used to be a thriving seaport,' said Scott. 'Look at it now. Richard's Bay has taken millions of tons of traffic away from the place. The railway system is old and decaying. Half the rolling stock is laid up or broken down. The guerrilla war, lack of overseas investment, of technicians, has devastated the economy and there's nothing coming in to restore it. Beira is as bad. With all the help in the world it's going to take years to get back to where we were before independence. God alone knows what the future holds. Not much, I'd say.'

'Well, they wanted a Marxist state. Now they've got one,' Pienaar said with a certain relish.

Chastened by Scott's gloom they went back to the Land Rover. He started the engine and they went down to the road skirting the foot of the cliffs, and along the seafront past the old Naval Club and bathing enclosure. They stopped there briefly before the Land Rover climbed again to the main road. Shortly afterwards Scott turned into the driveway of the hotel and parked in the shade of magnolia trees.

Late though it was, heat rose from the paving stones in unseen waves as they walked across a courtyard lined with palms. Under a blue sky crotons, geraniums and cannas threw splashes of colour against the white walls of the hotel. The Polana, Maputo's most famous hotel, had a colourful history reaching back to the days when Mozambique was the jewel in the crown of Portugal's vast colonial empire. The Mozambique Government, though acutely short of funds, had insisted that the Polana's lavish excellence should continue undiminished, thus making it an island of plenty in a sea of poverty.

The new arrivals registered at the reception desk – the

13

formalities there quickly completed since Scott was their sponsor – and were allocated their rooms. They agreed to meet in the main lounge at seven o'clock for pre-dinner drinks. Scott said, 'I might be late. Must get back to the office, then home to change. But if I am, don't delay on the first drink.'

Wessels said, 'We're not that crazy, Charles,' and Scott went on his way.

TWO

That night they dined on the verandah. It was cooler there than in the crowded dining-room and better suited to private discussion. From their table they looked out over the Indian Ocean where the moon had already set and sea and sky merged to mask the horizon. The pall of darkness was broken by the sweeping beams of lighthouses on Chefine and Cabo Inhaca, and the lesser lights of the fairway buoys. A cool breeze came in from the sea, and somewhere deep in the hotel there was the muted throb of beat music.

Johnson had joined them for drinks in the lounge before dinner. That, and the promise of adventure to come, had made for a cheerful meal with inconsequential chatter and frequent laughter. When they had finished Johnson insisted they sample the hotel's Napoleon to get what he called flying speed.

'Powerful stuff,' said Scott, sampling it. 'More *infuriatoro* than Napoleon to me.' He put down the glass, tidied his military moustache with a forefinger. 'We'd better discuss plans for tomorrow while we're still sober.'

'Great idea.' Johnson winked at Wessels. 'Charles is a born leader.'

'I'll pick you up here at nine tomorrow,' said Scott. 'We'll join up with the northbound convoy outside the town. It'll stop at Xai-Xai for the night, go on to Inhambane next day. The boat and fishing gear are at Maxixe, across the harbour from Inhambane. We'll spend Tuesday night at the Blue Marlin, it's the *pensão* in Maxixe. Pretty

15

run-down these days but all that's available. Federico, our African skipper, and his mate live in Maxixe. He'll have things ready for us.'

Pienaar said, 'Why do we have to join up with the convoy, man? Why not drive straight through to Maxixe? Give us an extra day's fishing.'

Scott's irritation was reflected in a frown. 'This is not the Transvaal, Pienaar. There's a bush war going on in Mozambique. The government forces – the Frelimo – are engaged in a life and death struggle with Renamo.'

'Who are *they*?' Pienaar's speech was slow, thick.

• 'You should know,' said Scott tartly. 'Pretoria backs them. Destabilisation's the name of the game.'

Wessels looked at Pienaar. 'Charles is talking about the MNR – Mozambique National Resistance. Here they call them Renamo. They're the Africans who don't like Machel's communist set-up, or their ANC pals.'

'Nor do we.' Pienaar blinked. 'Anyway, I thought the rebels did their stuff in Northern Mozambique. Not down here.'

Scott leant back, hands behind his head. 'Yes, they're fairly well established in the northern provinces ... Niassa, Zambésia and Tete, but they've carried out attacks here in the provinces of Gaza and Inhambane. Like the massacre at Homoine last year. That's near Maxixe. Well down in this direction.'

Johnson agreed. 'There's no way you can guarantee how far south Renamo come. They're guerrillas. Always on the move, living off the country. Burn and pillage African villages, kill indiscriminately, steal the cattle, rape the women as they go. But main centres like the port of Inhambane are still pretty secure. There's a fair-sized garrison there.'

Scott tasted the dubious Napoleon, held the glass away from him and squinted at it with narrowed eyes. 'Tomorrow's convoy takes supplies to Inhambane. That's why it's strongly guarded.' With a slight shrug, an indi-

16

cation perhaps that he thought the explanation unnecessary, he added, 'And that's why we're going with it and not driving through to Maxixe in a day.'

Pienaar looked put down, so Scott added, 'We could have flown in, of course. Matavia run a service there . . .'

'So do I,' interrupted Johnson, affecting an injured air.

'We'd use you, JJ,' Scott said. 'But we've got to take up fuel for the boat and other things. So it's the Land Rover. You'll be back in the act in Inhambane when you pick up Jan and Piet next Saturday. I'll bring the Land Rover down with the southbound convoy. Angelo, Federico's crew, wants to see his family. His wife and kids are here in Maputo, so he'll come with me.'

More brandies arrived and the conversation drifted on. Scott wanted to know if they'd taken anti-malarial precautions.

Wessels said they had. They were on Paludrine.

For Pienaar's benefit, Scott explained the fuel problem. Fuel was strictly rationed in Mozambique but he was able to get private supplies for the syndicate. They were brought up to Maputo in a coaster belonging to the South African shipping company he represented. The syndicate's boat, *Sunfish*, used diesel. It was twin-engined, but normally they used only one engine in order to conserve fuel.

'Where did you get the boat?' Piet accompanied the question with a hiccough. '*Ekskuus* – pardon.' He looked round the table with an embarrassed expression.

'We bought it from the people who used to run the fishing set-up at Pomene. It's old but still good. Lot more room than a ski-boat.'

'Isn't that where we're going to fish? The sea around Pomene?'

'Yes,' said Scott patiently. 'We are.' He spoke then of the old days when they used to fly into Pomene, land on the airstrip and stay in the Vila da Pesca. 'It was a tropical paradise,' he said. 'Air-conditioned bungalows with their

17

own bathrooms. A fine lounge in the main block with a view over the sea. There was the Marlin Bar and the Sundowner Terrace, and of course the dining-room. And my goodness,' he enthused, 'what food! Steaks of grilled bonito, or sunfish or marlin – whatever. Depended on what had been caught during the day. That was before the Portuguese cleared out and Samora Machel and his Frelimos took over. They'd knocked the stuffing out of the Portuguese after a long and bloody bush war.' Scott shrugged. 'The dream ended. The lush life for whites was over. The airstrip at Pomene fell into disuse and the Vila da Pesca packed up. There's nothing there now but vandalised buildings. I expect the last visitors were Renamo guerrillas – in which case God help the local Africans.' He sighed wearily as if the cares of the world were upon his shoulders. 'That's why we now have to tackle some of the best big-game fishing in the world the hard way.' He gave Pienaar a conciliatory smile. 'But it's worth it. If you get stuck into a big marlin it's still one of the great excitements left to man.'

'But not to the marlin,' said Johnson. Turning to Scott he asked in an undertone, 'Was that Andrada Gouveia going past a moment ago? Couldn't really be sure in this light.'

'It was. Sniffing around as usual.'

'Plenty to sniff for here, I guess.'

Pienaar broke in, 'Who's sniffing what?'

'Nothing,' said Johnson. 'We were talking about a friend.'

Scott and Wessels began to discuss baits and lures. Live carvalho, they agreed, were best for marlin. Scott said Federico would be sure to have netted some for the trip. The discussion on bait continued, the merits of dorab and garfish, and *repolas*, the lures made in Finland, and small plastic squid being compared. 'But give me carvalhos every time,' reiterated Scott.

'I've had some big marlin on my own lures,' claimed

Wessels. 'Red feathers and silver-foil. Marlin can go bloody crazy over them.'

While Wessels and Scott were discussing bait, Pienaar asked Johnson about his onward flight plans. 'How will you fill in the time before you pick us up on Saturday?'

'Fly to Mutare tomorrow. Take up mail and parcels.'

'Any passengers?' Pienaar hiccoughed again.

'Not yet. They may show up. My agent sometimes produces an odd one or two at the last moment. Mostly they travel that route by TTA, Matavia or the Zimbabwe air services.'

'So it's Mutare tomorrow, Monday. How about the other four?' Pienaar wiped a perspiring face with a handkerchief, looked along the verandah and yawned.

'A lot can happen in four days,' said Johnson. 'Maybe I'll bring passengers and mail down here, or perhaps a trip to Quelimane, or Zambia. Could even be to Okavango or Etosha – tourists you know. Any place, any time. Never a dull moment.'

Wessels heard the remark, butted in. 'And make plenty bread, I guess.' He winked at Pienaar. 'JJ drives a Porsche.'

'My wife's. Mine's a BMW,' said Johnson.

'You make the point.'

'You farmers don't do too badly, Jan. You're putting a lot of cash into a few days' fishing.'

'I get by. A man has to live.' Wessels leant back, patted his stomach with both hands and grinned.

19

THREE

Piet Pienaar slept well that night. Waking next morning to the screech of seagulls he went to the window, stretched, yawned and looked out across the bay. The sun had risen above the morning mist, its light reflected on streaks of cirrus cloud floating in a blue sky to promise another burning day; the long drought would continue.

The islands of Chefine and Inhaca, distant blurs along the horizon, seemed to enclose the bay but for the break which led to the open sea. Closer inshore a light wind ruffled the channel where marker-buoys gleamed white in the sunlight. There was little maritime activity but for a dredger moving sluggishly up the bay to dump its load, and fishing boats making for Inhaca, the chug-chug of their diesels beating a distant rhythm.

Pienaar took deep breaths of sea air; it was great to be alive, to be there on that day with such good companions and so much to look forward to. Determined to make the best of it he slipped on bathing trunks, took a towel from the bathroom and made for the pool which lay blue and inviting on the terrace below the hotel. Early though it was, others had got there before him. He counted them: seven men and four women, some swimming, others sun-bathing. A few were deeply suntanned and he gave them the benefit of the doubt, they could be whites, he supposed, but the majority were blacks and inwardly he bristled. Why didn't they have a pool of their own? With a forlorn sigh he remembered that even in his own beloved Republic things were changing in a big way. Blacks in the top hotels,

20

in cinemas, on the white beaches, in municipal swimming baths – blacks everywhere, even black commanders in South African Police stations. That was a madness which would destroy the white man. The *kaffer-boeties*, the white anti-apartheid activists, were responsible. They were traitors to their own kind. He knew what he would do about them if he were State President. He shrugged, gave up. The fine day, the lovely setting, drove away the bitter thoughts. He found a deckchair, left his towel and sunglasses on it, and jumped into the pool. With those people looking on he'd have liked to have used the springboard but he decided against it. An indifferent swimmer, he managed a slow breast-stroke for a couple of lengths before turning on his back to float. In that position he paddled towards the shallow end, colliding on the way with another bather. It turned out to be one of the deeply-tanned women, the one he'd noticed earlier. A fine girl with gleaming white teeth, firm well-rounded breasts, and well-shaped limbs.

'Sorry,' he said. 'Couldn't see where I was going.'

She smiled, said something in a foreign language. It might have been Portuguese, he wasn't sure. But there was no way of making progress with her so he got out of the pool, asked the African attendant to bring a coffee and set about drying himself. I should do more of this, he said to himself in the middle of vigorous towelling. Get rid of some of the fat. Not that he was really too bad. In fact he was on the lean side, but there were tell-tale indications that his stomach was beginning to bulge. 'Too much good living,' he admonished himself. In Afrikaans, the language of his thoughts, the words were stronger, more censorious.

He put on sunglasses and settled himself in the deckchair. Near him a short man with cropped hair was rubbing suntan oil on to a pallid white body. New arrival, probably from Russia, decided Pienaar, who remembered Scott's remarks about the mix of colour and nationalities in the lounge the night before. 'Cubans, Russians, East Germans,

21

Chinese, Koreans, Ethiopians and God knows what else – a polyglot bunch.' Afterwards, when they were alone, Pienaar had asked Wessels what *polyglot* meant. 'A confusion of languages,' said Wessels. 'Like the Tower of Babel.' Wessels had graduated from Stellenbosch. He knew English words like that. Words you didn't learn at a farm school in the Schweizer-Reineke district.

The African attendant came back with the coffee. Pienaar took it, signed for it. 'Sorry, my boy. Can't tip you. No cash on me.'

'I am man – not boy.' The African stared at him with sullen eyes. Pienaar, about to tell him not to be cheeky, recalled Wessels' advice. 'In Mozambique the black man's boss. Watch out how you speak to him, Piet. Remember, it's not the Republic.'

Since he had no intention of apologising, Pienaar said nothing. When the African had gone he lay back in the deckchair, soaking in the early morning sun, his thoughts on what lay ahead. After breakfast they would drive up the coast through strange country with the military convoy. He wondered if there would be an encounter with guerrillas. He hoped not, though in a dangerous way it could be exciting. But most of all he looked forward to the big-game fishing. Scott and Wessels were old hands at it. They would show him the ropes. He was fit and strong and reckoned he'd be quick to learn. He just might have beginner's luck, get stuck into a big marlin like those they'd been talking about the night before.

Some years back, Scott had said, two young farmers came down from the Lowveld by truck, arrived at Pomene in late evening and had a heavy session in the Sundowner Bar. 'They'd booked a boat for the following morning, put themselves down for a call at six. Morning came but they ignored repeated calls until nine-thirty, and it was not until ten o'clock that they got to the beach where the boat was waiting.'

At this stage Scott paused, looked at his listeners in

silence. 'And d'you know what happened? They were back by lunchtime with two blue marlin, one of 680 kilograms, the other – a record – 775 kilograms.' He'd finished the story with: 'And that's how fishing can be. You never know what the day will bring.'

Maybe the day might bring him luck like that, decided Pienaar. He was trying to imagine the feel of a great fish on the end of a rod when his attention was diverted by the girl with fine teeth and firm breasts. As she walked past, towelling her shoulders, she smiled at him, said something. He managed a friendly smile but made no reply, hoping she'd understand that he couldn't speak her language. She went on to where she'd left a beach bag, removed her bikini top and lay face down on a lilo. Moments later the African in the deckchair next to her was rubbing a suntan lotion on to her back. Pienaar turned away in disgust. How could she let a black do that? When smouldering resentment had ebbed away his thoughts returned to the immediate future.

It was a marvellous break, an assignment which combined duty with something as exciting as big-game fishing. That didn't come the way of many people. He would always be grateful to the Brigadier for the opportunity, and of course to Jan Wessels. But for him it couldn't have happened.

He thought of the briefing: the Brigadier's cold grey eyes set deep in the gaunt face, the rolled Rs of his Afrikaans revealing that he'd come from the Western Cape, probably the Malmesbury district. The Brigadier was one of the top men in BOSS, responsible for the Bureau's counter-insurgency intelligence operations in the Witwatersrand area. He was a stern, austere man, exceptionally able and much respected by those who worked with him. Like most of his staff he dressed as a civilian, notwithstanding his rank.

Captain Le Roux, his personal assistant, had been the only other person in the room during the briefing. The

Captain was a plump, pink-faced, bespectacled man with a walrus moustache and a high-pitched voice. He was said to be outstanding, to have an elephantine memory and the ability to see at once through a maze of detail to the kernel of a problem. Pienaar assumed that Le Roux's reputation was deserved, for the Brigadier was a man who demanded a high level of efficiency from those around him. Though Pienaar disliked Wilhelm Le Roux, thought he was *nat* – wet, a bit of a crawler, he had to be polite to the man. As the Brigadier's personal assistant Le Roux wielded power; it was better not to offend him.

Pienaar recalled details of the operation the Brigadier had outlined at the briefing. It had been carefully planned, little left to chance, the predictables marshalled alongside the un-predictables. He supposed Le Roux's talents were involved.

'Nothing is foolproof,' the Brigadier had said, leaning forward, his forearms on the big *kiaat* desk, his eyes on the crystal ball beside the blotter. 'But we have done our best to make it so. What you see and hear must determine what you do. Time is limited but if our assumptions are correct that should not affect your assignment. We don't know the identity of those in the command structure but we hope that you may learn something useful in that regard. Most important, of course, is the drop. We believe that is probably how operational orders are getting through. If we can catch those on the ground at the time it will be a major breakthrough.' The Brigadier had looked up from the crystal ball – his focal point, he called it – to observe with an icy smile, 'I think we know how to make them talk. So it's over to you, Pienaar.'

'Yes, sir. But there may not be a drop this time.'

The Brigadier's mouth had tightened in a hard line and he'd frowned. 'Of course there *may* not be. But we've reason to believe there *will* be. I don't have to tell you what the ANC has threatened.' The moment of irritation passed, the tone softened. 'Make a success of this, Pienaar, and – ' he spread his hands in a fulsome gesture. ' – it will be very much in the Republic's interests. Not to mention your own.'

There had been a lot more, of course, including a homily on method. 'Get friendly, chat them up, show you like them. But be casual, discreet, never seem to be too interested in your questions. Remember, if a man likes you, feels he can trust you, he'll tell you things after a few drinks.'

Well, there hadn't been much time so far though there'd certainly been a few drinks, but he had done all he could. Not that he'd heard or seen anything unusual or, for that matter, particularly useful. When Scott had talked about the guerrilla war Pienaar had feigned ignorance of Renamo and the areas in which they operated, and he'd pretended, too, to be a little drunk; but it hadn't really led to anything except Scott's sharp rejoinder about Pretoria backing Renamo, which gave the impression that he was pro-Frelimo. Was he in on the act? In the lounge before dinner he'd noticed that Johnson was on good terms with a strange lot of people. He'd exchanged greetings with them, gone across once to a table where a mixed group of Africans and whites were sitting together drinking. He'd stayed with them for a few minutes, talking animatedly and laughing. It seemed that he knew these people well. Pienaar had asked Scott who they were.

'Government officials and some of their East European friends. It's important to Charter Couriers RSA to keep in with the officials. Government contract, you know. Johnson's a good PR man. Gets on with everybody.'

Pienaar had changed the subject. After dinner when Wessels and Scott were talking about lures and bait he had in a casual way asked Johnson why he used a single-engined plane. Wasn't a twin much safer, especially for long distances over the African bush? Johnson had put down his lager, looked across the lounge and waved to a bizarrely attired man on the far side. 'Interesting guy, that,' he'd said. 'NBC newsman. What he doesn't know about the goings-on in this part of the world isn't worth knowing.'

25

Pienaar had said a disinterested 'Is that so?' before re-peating his question.

'We've got twins, of course.' Johnson had turned back to him. 'I use the Stationair – that's the Cessna single – when I have to get in and out of small airstrips like Wessel's farm at Dullstroom. The Cessna needs a much shorter run than a twin. And if the engine does cut – it hasn't yet and it's done a few thousand hours – it could be a lot easier to put down in bush country than a twin. It's a great little aeroplane.'

So, one way and another, he hadn't learnt much. But time would tell. It was early days yet.

Hunger prompted him to look at his watch. It was later than he'd thought. He got up from the deckchair, slung the towel over his shoulder and went up the terrace towards the hotel.

Since there were few people about at that hour, he made a detour to the reception desk to inquire whether the South African newspapers had arrived. Approaching the desk he saw a man looking through the hotel register. Pienaar stopped, faced the rack on the wall near him, and pretended to read the framed copy of the day's menu.

The man lifted a page, ran a finger down it, said some-thing to the African receptionist and, when he'd received an answer, turned to another page. He was still checking the page when Pienaar, barefooted and still in bathing trunks, abandoned the menu and made for the lifts. He had recognised the man at the register.

It was Andrada Gouveia.

FOUR

High in the eastern highlands of Zimbabwe, to be more exact in the Chimanimani Mountains, lies Mutare. Although not large the town, known as Umtali before Mugabe gained power, is important because it stands astride the principal road and rail links between Harare and Beira. With the advent of the guerrilla wars, first that of Zimbabwe's long fight for independence – the Nkomo-Mugabe versus Smith era – and, that settled, the present bitter struggle between the Mozambique Government and the rebel forces bent on unseating it – the MNR or Renamo – these lines of communication became of paramount importance. It is for this reason that nowhere is the power struggle in Mozambique more bitterly contested than in the Beira Corridor, the two hundred or so kilometres between Beira, the seaport so vital to Mozambique and its African neighbours, and Mutare close to the border between Zimbabwe and Mozambique. The rebels, determined to sever road and rail links, keep the Corridor under constant hit-and-run attacks. They are said to be supported by Pretoria and certain elements in Portugal, notably the *retornados*. The Mozambique and Zimbabwe forces which oppose them are equally determined to keep these vital lifelines open. They in turn receive support from Russia and her satellites, various African countries and, perhaps incongruously, from Britain.

It is this scenario which has attracted to Mutare a diverse assortment of people, among them military experts, instructors and intelligence agents from foreign powers,

27

foreign contractors involved in rebuilding and rehabilitating rail and road systems in the Corridor and, of course, arms dealers, mercenaries, soldiers of fortune, media men and others exploiting the political cauldron.

Inevitably Mutare has become a place of intrigue and rumour, and the names or pseudonyms of most of those involved have appeared at one time or another in the registers of local hotels.

The hotel was at its busiest at sundowner time and from the verandah came a lively buzz of conversation broken at times by bursts of laughter and occasional shouts, mostly of merriment and sometimes to settle an argument or summon a waiter.

Those at the tables wore the light clothes appropriate to a tropical climate. Among the men uniforms, mostly combat-camouflage, were in evidence, and they too were appropriate, because the western end of the Beira Corridor – the war zone – was no more than a score of kilometres from the verandah. And since it was a guerrilla war, a campaign of stealth and movement, it sometimes spilled over into Zimbabwe itself.

At a table in a corner a man and woman sat talking. The man, tall with crew-cut hair and a scrub beard, had just arrived. Dressed in slacks and an open-necked shirt he wore horn-rimmed glasses and an air of middle-aged authority. The woman's age and looks were masked by her sunglasses, but the firm flesh of her face and neck, her moist lips, and the glow of her hair suggested the late twenties or early thirties.

The man with the crew-cut fumbled with a cigarette packet, got it open, held it out to her.

She shook her head. 'Not for me, Greg. I don't.'

'Sorry, I forgot.' His nose twitched. 'Force of habit I guess.' He pulled out a cigarette, twiddled it for inspection, put it in his mouth and lit it.

'You were saying you had something to tell me,' she reminded him, wondering once again about the American's nervous twitch. He would sniff two or three times for no apparent reason, his nose twitching as he did so. She found the twitch tiresome. It had to be something to do with chain-smoking, she told herself.

He looked along the verandah, spoke in a low voice. 'Yep. Mauritius has confirmed they will meet here Tuesday noon.'

'Where's here?'

'Right here in this hotel, Trudi.'

She took a small diary from her shoulder-bag, opened it.

An elderly woman at a nearby table who'd been watching turned to the white-haired man with her. 'Married or lovers, d'you think? She's much younger.'

Her companion put down the whisky he was drinking, shook his head, tapped his ear. 'Switched off. Too damned noisy.'

'You always do,' she reproached him, 'when I have something interesting to say.'

'Tuesday noon,' Trudi repeated. 'Tomorrow.' She made an entry in the diary, put it back in the bag. 'D'you know who *he* is going to be?'

'Gottwald probably, otherwise Kahn.'

'It would help if I knew.'

'How? You've not met either. They couldn't be more different. An East German and a Pakistani. You have their photos, physiological data, etcetera. No problem.'

'I suppose not.' She produced a lipstick and mirror and began to work at her lips. 'Has Mauritius *any* idea who the contact is?'

The tall man shook his head. 'None at all. That's your job. First find out who he is. Second, look out for a handover. That won't be easy. Third, most important, check his subsequent movements.'

'You don't expect much, do you?' She made a face. 'Wonder what he'll be like? Dishy?'

'It's not necessarily *he*, Trudi. Maybe it's a woman. I guess you'd better keep your mind open on that. If you're looking for a man you may miss the miss.'

She wrinkled her nose, showed the tip of her tongue. 'You *are* clever, Gregory Nielsen.'

'How come?'

'The play on words. Quite brilliant.'

'Don't get it.' His nose twitched and he sniffed.

She put away the lipstick and mirror. 'Bet you do. What's Gottwald's route in?'

He blew out smoke, lifted his shoulders. 'Haven't a clue. Nairobi, Lusaka maybe. Who knows? It doesn't really matter. And don't just be keeping a lookout for Gottwald. Remember, it may be Kahn. Another thing, don't assume they'll be using those names.' He signalled a passing waiter. 'Another of those?' he asked her.

'Yes, please. Lots of ice. It's so hot.'

'You're right. Cold lager for me.'

The waiter came, noted the order on his pad, put the empty glasses on a tray and made for another table.

They were silent for a moment before she said, 'When are you leaving?'

'First thing tomorrow morning. Must make Harare before lunch.' He stubbed out the cigarette, lit another.

She took off the sunglasses, put her elbows on the table, made a steeple with her fingers, looked at him over them. 'So you're deserting me, Greg,' she said sadly.

His smile exposed flawless white teeth. 'Chance would be a fine thing.'

Wessels and Pienaar were at breakfast on the verandah outside the Polana's dining-room when Scott arrived, dapper and military as always but dressed now like the others in shorts and bushshirt. He tapped his wristwatch as he reached their table. 'Hope you've settled the account, got your gear ready. We leave in fifteen minutes. The convoy won't wait.'

Wessels, mouth full, toast in hand, said, 'We're all set, Charles. Bills have been paid, luggage is with the porter. Give us five minutes.'

Scott looked displeased. 'The Land Rover's in front,' he said tersely. 'I'll be waiting for you.'

'He's a nice guy,' said Wessels when Scott had gone. 'But Christ he fusses. Everything's got to be bang on time, done with a click and a snap. Forgotten he's left the army.'

Pienaar looked up, coffee cup in hand. 'What army's that?'

'The British Army. He left it fifteen years ago but he's still with it in spirit.' Wessels pushed back his chair, got up. 'Come on, let's go.'

Pienaar said, 'I'll be along in a moment.'

With Scott fussing round them like a hen rounding up her chickens, Wessels and Pienaar collected their luggage grips in the foyer and transferred them to the waiting Land Rover already laden with drums of diesel and other gear for the boat.

Johnson, bleary-eyed and generally looking the worse for wear, arrived at the last moment to see them off.

Scott eyed him critically. 'That Napoleon didn't do you any good, JJ.'

Johnson yawned, stretched his arms. 'Too late to bed was the real trouble.'

Scott climbed in, settled himself behind the wheel. Wessels and Pienaar got in beside him.

Johnson shut the Land Rover's door on them. 'Take care, boys. See you in Inhambane, Saturday, three o'clock sharp. Don't be late. Take-off's three-thirty at the latest. If you can't make that you've had it. Tight lines.'

'Not to worry,' said Scott. 'I'll get them there on time.'

31

Pienaar, nearest to Johnson, leant over the door. 'When d'you take off for Mutare?'

'Ten-thirty.'

'Got any passengers?'

The Land Rover began to move forward.

'Ja. A couple. Picking them up at Inhambane then on to . . .'

The end of the sentence was lost to Pienaar as Scott accelerated and the Land Rover passed through the gates and out on to the road.

They found the convoy assembling on the outskirts of the town. Scott presented his documents to the military commander and the Land Rover was assigned a place in the long line of vehicles. The start was delayed but no one seemed particularly concerned except Scott, who rattled on about 'typical bloody inefficiency' while the convoy was forming.

At last it began to move, the command vehicle – a camouflaged armoured personnel carrier with high pole aerials – preceded by a strange-looking contraption, a truck perched high on its wheels, its underbelly V-shaped. 'The Africans call it a spider,' explained Scott. 'Carries mine-disposal personnel and their equipment.' Another armoured personnel carrier occupied the centre of the column, while a third APC brought up the rear. These and a number of camouflaged military trucks made up the body of the convoy; the Land Rover and other civilian vehicles were stationed in the middle of the long snaking line. Men in combat camouflage carrying AK47s were much in evidence. Pienaar was reassured. He was sorry he hadn't an AK47 of his own. For most of his life he'd carried a firearm. A man was vulnerable without a gun.

*

The convoy travelled at a moderate pace until it passed the small town of Manhica some fifty kilometres north of Maputo. After that the character of the country began to change, became more rural and speed was reduced. Though life in most of the larger villages they passed through appeared normal, a number of the smaller ones visible from the road were deserted, the huts dilapidated, with no signs of human activity, cattle or crops. 'The people have cleared out,' explained Scott. 'Made for Maputo or the nearest refugee camp. Drought and the guerrillas have been too much for them.'

It was a burning day, the heat rising from the baked soil as if from the open door of an oven. The dust-covered leaves of trees and bushes lining the road drooped dry and listless, waiting like the brittle veld grass around them for rains which would not come.

At times a handful of Africans would appear at the roadside, their bodies bone-thin, the children pot-bellied and wide-eyed. They would wave tentatively and some-times there would be shouted exchanges with the convoy's soldiers.

North of Manhica a helicopter appeared.

'It will patrol ahead of us,' said Scott. 'The pilot keeps in radio touch with the command vehicle.'

The convoy moved more slowly now, stopping at bridges, culverts, causeways and recent indications of road repairs. The men in the mechanical spider would dismount to check for mines. That done, the all clear was given and the convoy would resume its journey.

It was late afternoon when they crossed the Limpopo at João Belo. Not long afterwards a ragged silhouette of buildings showed up in the distance, beyond it the shimmer of water.

'Xai-Xai,' said Wessels. 'And the sea.'

'About time,' grumbled Scott.

The long line of vehicles rumbled into the once popular seaside resort to be welcomed by a motley collection of civilians and soldiers. The armoured vehicles parked in a crescent on the inland side of the town, the lesser military transport parking behind them and nearer the sea. Scott stopped the Land Rover next to a camouflaged truck. Fluent in Portuguese and the local African dialect, he chatted briefly to its crew. 'They'll keep an eye on it,' he told the others as they climbed out and he locked the doors.

Carrying their luggage they walked down through a grove of casuarina trees towards the hotel. The sprinkling of seaside villas looked weather-beaten and for the most part deserted, one of many indications that Xai-Xai had seen better days. The hotel was a large, grey, barrack-like structure, its peeling paint, rusted metal and rotting timber telling of long neglect. The concrete promenade fronting it ran for some distance in either direction along the line of the beach.

The hotel manager, a tired-looking man with a haunted expression, knew Scott and Wessels and greeted them warmly; few tourists, it seemed, now came to Xai-Xai.

The new arrivals produced their passports, completed the police *fiches*, signed the register and went upstairs to their rooms. Like the hotel itself these were tired and drab and smelt of long ago. Having dumped their luggage they went down to the verandah where soldiers sat at most of the tables.

Sitting in the shade, looking out over the lagoon to the reef on which waves were breaking, Scott and his companions talked about the journey, drank their beer, and discussed the journey still to come.

A cool breeze from the sea fanned the verandah bringing with it the steady rumble of surf. Pienaar, tired and hot, decided that Xai-Xai was a good place to have reached after such a long, slow and often interrupted journey. It had been a disappointing day with none of the glamour and excitement of his expectations, the drought-scarred country drab and colourless, and the day hot beyond reason. He comforted himself with the knowledge that the real excitement, the fishing, was still to come. There was only one snag. He'd not done any fishing from a small boat far out to sea. Would he be seasick? It was a worrying thought.

FIVE

JJ arrived at the hotel in Mutare late that afternoon. He'd been delayed at the airport where he'd told McLeod, the chief mechanic, that the Cessna had developed a fault in the fuel system. Once in his room he washed away the heat and sweat of a long day under a cold shower. After changing into a clean shirt and slacks he combed the thick, unruly hair which had earned him the nickname 'Thatch' at school. A final check in the wardrobe mirror reminded him that his beard needed tidying. Long practice limited this task to a few minutes. Satisfied, he put away the scissors, locked the wardrobe and bedroom doors, put the keys in his pocket and went down to reception.

'Hullo, Sonia,' he said to the sandy-haired girl who had her back to him. 'You're looking as smashing as ever. Any mail for me? Room number – hold on – I've forgotten.' He felt in his pocket for the key tag.

She turned, half smiled. 'One-one-seven.'

'Marvellous memory you've got.'

'How could I forget your room number, Mr Johnson?' She went to the pigeon-hole rack. 'No letter, just this phone message – and your paper.' She handed him both.

He put the newspaper under his arm. Read the message. It was brief. 'Ring McLeod – airport.' He went to a phone-booth, dialled the number, waited for what seemed a long time before an unfamiliar voice said, 'Flight maintenance.'

'Johnnie Johnson for Jock McLeod,' he replied. There was another wait before a Glaswegian accent came on to the line. 'Is that you, JJ?'

'It is,' confirmed Johnson. 'What's the diagnosis?'

'Definitely fuel system but we'll have to check it through.'

'How long's that going to take?'

There was a pause. 'Depends on what we find. If all goes well the job should be finished noon tomorrow.'

'If not, Jock?'

'Ah, weel. If there's problems, say more like before noon Wednesday.'

'Bloody hell. I'm short of time. Do your best, Jock.'

'That I will, JJ. I'll let you know how things are in the morning.'

'Thanks a lot. Bye now.' He hung up the receiver, looked at his watch and made a face before going through the foyer to the verandah.

It was crowded. He was looking for somewhere to sit when two men in combat camouflage at a table near him began making ready to go.

He said, 'Okay if I take this table?'

One of them nodded. 'You're welcome. We're pushing off.'

They left and he sat down. He unfolded the newspaper, caught a waiter's eye and ordered a lager off the ice. As was his custom he combined reading the headlines with watching the comings and goings, checking the who's-who of the verandah.

He was doing this when first he saw the woman. She was sitting alone at a nearby table, but she was looking in his direction. Whether or not she was looking at him he couldn't tell because white-rimmed sunglasses masked her face. He was wondering about this when she took them off and began dabbing at her eyes with a tissue. When she looked up he saw that she was young, good to look at. He was still not sure whether she was looking at him or beyond, but then their eyes met and he smiled. After a moment's hesitation she returned the smile in a distant, impersonal way. She put on the sunglasses, replaced the tissue in her bag and concentrated on what she'd taken from it.

She was probably waiting for someone, he decided, but that did not deter him. When he saw a waiter approaching with a loaded tray, he got up and walked down the verandah. Abreast of where she sat he stood aside to let the waiter pass, nudging her table with his thigh. He turned, saw her looking up at him. 'I'm sorry,' he said. 'Stupid of me. Hope I haven't upset your drink?' Though the nudge had been contrived he managed to look concerned.

'There was nothing to upset.' She shrugged. 'You made me smudge my diary.'

He had begun to apologise when the waiter interrupted. 'Your lager, Mr Johnson.'

'Put it on my table. I left the newspaper there.'

'Your table has gone, sir. Others have taken it.'

Johnson looked back, saw two men at the table. 'You're right, Tom. My fault.' He took the lager from the tray, signed the chit. The waiter moved on.

'Sorry about the smudge.' He looked at the empty chair. 'Are you waiting for someone?'

She shook her head. 'No.'

'Mind if I join you?'

'If you want to.' The tone was cool.

'Thanks.' He sat down, put his drink on the table. 'Like a drink? Keep me company?'

She thought for a moment. 'Orange juice?'

'Dash of vodka in it?' he suggested.

'No, just plain orange juice.'

While his eyes searched the verandah for a waiter he said, 'Johnnie Johnson. They call me JJ.'

'I knew it was Johnson. I heard the waiter. I'm Trudi Braun.'

He saw a waiter, beckoned, turned to her. 'Hello Trudi.'

'Hello,' she said with a brief smile.

*

38

At first he found talking to her difficult. She made no effort to keep the conversation going, leaving it to him, and he sensed that she was thinking of other things. But he persevered and in time they got past the banalities of the guerrilla war, the drought, how crowded the verandah was and how noisy its occupants. Then, slowly, she began to thaw and he led the conversation into things more personal, learnt that she was a visitor from Johannesburg who hoped to be going back there shortly. By way of exchange he told her how he came to be in Mutare. 'I was due to fly on to Quelimane tomorrow. But it now looks as if that's not on.' He explained why. She remarked that he seemed to get about a lot and he smiled and said that was the fun of being a charter pilot. It wasn't as boring as flying scheduled air services.

'So your headquarters are Jo'burg?' She took off the sunglasses and he found the cool appraising stare of her brown eyes disconcerting.

'Charter Couriers RSA, my company, is based on Grand Central Airport. Nearer Pretoria than Jo'burg. But I live in Bryanston. Hope to be back there in a few days.'

'Lucky you,' she said.

'What's the trouble? Don't you like this place?'

'It's all right but I'd like to get back.'

'What's stopping you, Trudi?' She gave him a quick look. It was the first time he had used her name in the conversation.

She was evasive at first but he was a sympathetic and skilful questioner and gradually her story emerged. She was, she said, born in Düsseldorf. Her parents had settled in South Africa when she was a child. Her mother had died when she was still in her teens. Her father, a consulting engineer, was often away from home and, though only eighteen, she'd had to take over the household and look after a younger brother and sister who were still at school. Her father had remarried in due course but she had found that she couldn't get on with the young stepmother; there were constant rows and eventually she left home. After sampling several jobs in Johannesburg she had ended up in a travel agency where her German was useful. The work was interesting but after some years, and a long and hopeless affair with the manager, a married man, she had left to work for a firm of computer consultants.

In her second year there she had met a man from Harare, a US business machines representative. They got on well together, dined and wined on several occasions and, since he was very much what she needed at the time, she had confided in him. He had asked her what she planned to do and she'd said she was thinking of visiting Zimbabwe in the hope of seeing her brother, a mechanical engineer working in the Beira Corridor who went up to Harare periodically to report to his head office. Greg, the American, had suggested that she travel back to Zimbabwe with him. Pleased at the opportunity of getting away from Johannesburg, she had agreed and they had motored up to Harare. On arrival there they stayed at an hotel for two days. 'He paid for both of us. Like in Jo'burg, money seemed no problem.'

'Expense account?' suggested Johnson.

'I suppose so,' she agreed in a tired way. She went on with her story, explaining how later, at Greg's suggestion, she had come down with him to Mutare where he had business to do. She had agreed because Mutare was close to the Beira Corridor and she thought it might make it easier to see her brother.

The waiter arrived with another round of drinks, Johnson signed the chit, the waiter removed the empty glasses and they were left alone again.

'And so . . .' he prompted.

The cool brown eyes considered him. 'Well, I suppose you can imagine the rest?'

'No. Tell me.'

She sighed wearily. Closed her eyes. 'We got here two

days ago. We had a silly row last night after dinner and this morning he cleared out. Didn't even leave a note.'

'Perhaps he's had an accident? You say he had to go into the country on business each day. He may have gone into the Corridor. Plenty of accidents there. Like road mines and ambushes.'

'No. It wasn't an accident. We'd agreed to meet on the verandah after breakfast at eight-thirty. He hadn't turned up by nine so I went up to his room. A maid was cleaning it. I asked if she'd seen him. She said, yes. He'd taken his luggage and left at about seven o'clock. Later, I went to reception. Asked the cashier if he'd settled his account. She said he had. I must have looked a bit put out because she told me I wasn't the first woman to be hotel-dumped by a man. She said there was usually a wife and kids somewhere in the background.'

'In other words a bit of a shit,' Johnson frowned. 'So what are your plans?'

She laughed without humour. 'Plans? Don't have any really. I'm waiting to hear if Bill – that's my brother – can get up here to see me. But I'll have to make up my mind in a day or so. Can't afford to stay much longer. Greg was to pay my bill but of course he didn't.' She shrugged, made a face. 'What an idiot I've been.'

Johnson looked away, spoke quietly. 'Trusting someone you like is not being idiotic. It's just that he was no good.'

She became silent and preoccupied and the conversation dried up. A few minutes later she put her sunglasses and diary in her shoulder-bag, looked at her watch and pushed back her chair. 'It's late, I must go.'

He nodded, got up from the table. 'I suppose so. But before you do there's something I'd like to ask you.'

'What's that?' Once again the brown eyes were challenging.

'If you're not doing anything tonight, do me a favour. Have dinner with me.'

41

For a moment she seemed lost in thought. Then she said, 'Where?'

'At Costa's. The food's really good there, and it's quiet.'

'You're a kind man, JJ.' Her expression softened. 'I'd like to do that.'

They parted then, having agreed to meet in the foyer before eight that night.

SIX

The convoy's departure from Xai-Xai next morning was delayed by a mechanical defect in one of the armoured personnel carriers.

'He says it's the steering system,' was Scott's gloomy report after talking to the Frelimo major in command. 'They've been working on it through the night. Another hour or so, he thinks, before the job's finished.'

Wessels made a disapproving noise. 'An hour or so. Christ! What a bloody waste of time.'

'Show Pienaar the sights.' Scott looked despondent. 'I'll hang on here.'

The sights were limited but they went to the beach and walked up and down the length of the lagoon. Pienaar asked if bathing was safe.

'In theory yes,' said Wessels. 'The reef is supposed to keep out sharks but it doesn't always. Years ago, before the troubles, a young couple from the Transvaal were honeymooning here. They came down from the hotel for an early morning dip. He was a strong swimmer, but she wasn't so she stayed in the shallows. He'd swum well out towards the reef when she heard him scream. She was floating on her back but she turned in time to see his body lift high out of the water as if someone was pushing him. Then she saw the jaws of the shark clamped round his waist. She screamed and fainted. They pulled her to safety, then put out a boat and collected what the shark had left. It wasn't much, they say.'

Pienaar was visibly shocked. 'My God! Terrible, hey? Did they get the shark?'

'No. African fishermen said it would have gone out on the next high tide. But the story soon got round and it was a long time before anybody with a white skin swam in the lagoon again.'

The sun was well up and the heat making itself felt by the time the convoy began its noisy, rattling exit from Xai-Xai.

The journey on to Maxixe followed the pattern of the day before with intermittent halts to check for mines, while the helicopter searched the route ahead. Once again the small villages in the drought-scorched countryside were apparently deserted, with no sign of inhabitants or cattle.

During the afternoon, on the longish stretch between Quissico and Helene, the convoy stopped at a culvert for the customary search and on this occasion two mines were found. They were detonated by the spider's crew after which the long line of vehicles rolled on. The helicopter which had been searching the area around the culvert flew well ahead before turning and coming back towards the convoy. It was a hundred metres or so to the left of the road when it banked steeply, dropped a smoke-flare into thick bush and opened fire with a machine-gun. The convoy increased speed, the leading APC, the command vehicle, directing machine-gun and mortar fire in the general direction of the smoke-flare.

The APCs in the middle and rear of the convoy took no part in the action, keeping their weapons trained on a cluster of casuarina trees to the right of the road. Moments later there was an excited shout from Pienaar: '*Daar loop hulle* – there they go.' He pointed to where three men with automatic rifles were running across a clearing to the left of the smoke-flare. There was a renewed burst of fire

44

from the command vehicle and one of the running figures stumbled and fell. There was no further action, the convoy continuing at a sharp pace for about a kilometre before dropping back to its normal speed.

With eyes flashing, Pienaar challenged Scott. 'Tell me, man. Why didn't one of the APCs leave the road and chase those bastards in the bush?'

'Because the commander of the convoy isn't a bloody fool,' said Scott, his manner brusque and military. 'To get an APC off the road and into the bush where they'd prepared an ambush is exactly what those guerrillas wanted. They were probably attempting to create a diversion. If we'd stopped to deal with the decoy on the left I expect the main attack would have come from the right, from the casuarina trees. I imagine the mined culvert was part of their tactical plan. Intended to detonate while the convoy was crossing.'

Pienaar's dark, deeply-lined face broke into a smile. 'So our black major's not too bad, hey?'

'Colour doesn't decide what sort of tactician a man is,' said Scott abruptly. 'Training does. The major is probably Russian trained.'

In late afternoon, after the skirmish, the lagoon showed up ahead, its waters reflecting the pastel pinks and greys of the sky as the sun sank behind layers of cloud.

The spider's crew having checked the bridge, the convoy crossed the Inharrime river which flowed into the lagoon, passed on through the small town of Inharrime, and made for Lindela where the convoy split, the main body forking right for Inhambane, while an APC, a military truck, the Land Rover and another non-military vehicle continued on to Maxixe, arriving there well after sunset.

*

She had got to the verandah early, chosen the table carefully. From it she could watch both the steps which led to
the front entrance and, through a picture window, the
foyer. She wondered what had happened to JJ. They had
agreed to meet on the verandah for a drink at eleven-thirty.
It was already past that time but there was no sign of him.

She thought of their dinner the night before. Costa's had
been what he had promised: the food really good, the
restaurant unpretentious, and the absence of noise helpful
to conversation. JJ had been good company, considerate,
interesting and amusing, so the time had gone quickly. At
midnight, over a night-cap in the hotel lounge, they had
made the date for the morning. It was when they'd gone
up in the lift and she had unlocked her door and faced him
to say goodnight that he put the question she had expected.

'Like me to tuck you in, Trudi? Tell you a bedtime
story?'

She'd shaken her head. 'Oh dear. You're not another
Greg, are you?' Without waiting for his reply she had
added, 'The answer is no, JJ. But thank you for a super
dinner. You really are a lovely man.' She had stood on her
toes and kissed him then, and he'd smiled and said, 'Sorry,
Trudi. But it was worth trying.' With a 'See you at eleven-
thirty,' he'd gone and she was left thinking that the bedtime story could have been fun if there were not so many
ifs and buts.

Before dressing she had once again checked mentally
through Greg Nielsen's briefing, finishing with a long look
at the physiological and photo data on Gottwald and Kahn.
She did not think she would have any difficulty in identifying either.

Once again wondering what had happened to JJ, she
looked at her watch. He didn't seem to be the sort of man
who'd stand a girl up on a date – but one never knew. Her
thoughts were interrupted by the waiter who came to the
table to ask if she would like to make an order. She was
explaining that she was expecting a friend when she saw

JJ, large and cheerful, coming up the steps. He waved his newspaper at her, she waved back, and soon he was at the table. He sat down, put the newspaper and bush-hat on an empty chair. 'Sorry, Trudi.' He was out of breath. 'Held up at the airport. Tell you later. What'll you have?'

'What's been happening at the airport?' She brushed a lock of hair from her forehead.

'There was a problem in the fuel system. I take off at eleven tomorrow morning.'

'For Quelimane?'

'No. Should have done that today. Mail and parcels for Maputo tomorrow. Spend the night there, fly back to Grand Central on Thursday.' He leant back in the chair, mopped his face and neck with a handkerchief. A waiter came to the table and drinks were ordered. When he'd gone she moved her chair slightly. JJ's large body had partially blocked her view of the front steps.

'You all right?' he inquired.

'Yes. A table leg was in the way.'

'Any news of your brother?'

'No!' She shook her head. 'Phoning the Beira Corridor isn't easy. I'll try again later. The girl on the switchboard says between one and two might be better.'

'Yes. Lunch hour's best. Traffic's usually heaviest in the morning.' He looked at his watch. 'Excuse me for a moment, Trudi.' His blue eyes twinkled. 'Got to see-a-man-about-a-dog. Be back in a jiffy.' He left the newspaper and bush-hat on the table and went down the verandah.

She saw him go through the rotating doors into the foyer. Her watch showed 1155. She took off the sunglasses, picked up the paperback. Five more minutes, she said to herself – if he's punctual. He was. A clock somewhere in the town clanged the twelve strokes of noon as he came up the steps. The sunken cheeks in the narrow Asian face, the scar on the right temple, the sleek black hair, thin gaunt body – height 1.76 metres, weight 68 kilograms – yes, unmistakably, this was Abdul Kahn. Dressed in beige

47

slacks and a white, open-necked shirt, he was carrying a black briefcase. He went in through the front entrance and she got up and followed him into the foyer where she sat on a settee pretending to consult her diary.

After that things happened quickly. She saw Kahn cross the foyer, push through the swing-doors of the men's room at the far end and disappear from sight.

There was no sign of JJ and she realised he must already be in the men's room. The implications of that caused a sudden chill in her stomach. It had never occurred to her that he could be the contact. But why else had he looked at his watch and left her exactly five minutes before Kahn's noon appointment?

With her heart doing funny things she continued to watch. After a minute or so the swing-doors opened again and Kahn emerged. He crossed the foyer and went out through the main entrance; he was still carrying the black briefcase. While she was waiting for JJ to appear a strange-looking man came from the men's room. Of medium build, he wore a blue shirt and jeans with a broad, metal-studded belt. But it was the rest of him which commanded attention: the thick black hair, long and unkempt, the heavy brows over dark eyes set deep in a bony face, the broken nose and mandarin moustache. As if these were not enough, he wore gold earrings and a loosely-knotted red scarf. A pyscho, decided Trudi – inadequate, insecure, compensating by drawing attention to himself.

She watched him go over to the blackboard and easel which advertised events for the day. For minutes he stood there reading it while he scratched his tousled head. Incongruously, he was carrying a green shopping bag emblazoned with a supermarket logo.

A dark, handsome woman left the reception desk and joined him. He took her hand and they disappeared down the corridor which led to the lifts and the dining-room beyond.

It had all happened so quickly, a matter of two or three minutes, that Trudi was bemused. But of one thing she was quite certain: JJ had still not come through the swing-doors of the men's room. She waited for some time, perhaps five minutes, before returning to the table on the verandah where she continued to watch the foyer through the pict-ure-window. She was doing this when she was aware of someone stopping at the table where she sat. She turned and saw that it was JJ.

He grinned amiably. 'Sorry to have been so long, Trudi. While I was in my room McLeod phoned. He confirmed that the Cessna will be ready for take-off at eleven tomorrow morning.'

Relief showed in Trudi's smile. 'You haven't been long. I've been checking at the desk about calls to Beira. They must think I'm a nuisance.' What she couldn't tell him was the enormous sense of relief she felt. It had not occurred to her that he might go to his bedroom to relieve himself. She'd taken it for granted that he'd gone to the men's room. He must have come down from his room and on to the verandah by way of the dining-room. That explained why she had not seen him in the foyer.

So he wasn't the contact. But who was? Apart from the psycho, several other men had come through the swing-doors while she watched; one of them, an elderly bearded African, had been carrying a briefcase. He might have been the contact though reason suggested that it was more likely to be the psycho whose way-out appearance could have been a means of identifying himself to Kahn. The more she thought about this the more likely it seemed that it was to the psycho that Kahn had made the handover. Hence the green shopping bag.

JJ's voice broke into her thoughts. 'You haven't touched your drink, Trudi.'

'They're both untouched. I've been waiting for you.'

She held up her glass of orange juice. 'Happy landings, JJ.' He could not know with what sincerity she had said that. She liked him and was immensely relieved that her fears had not been justified.

'Same to you, Trudi ' he said. They touched glasses.

During the discussion which followed he wanted to know what her plans were once she'd made contact with her brother.

'It depends. If he can get up here to see me in a day or so I'll hang on. If he can't I'll have to get back to Harare and beg, borrow or steal enough to pay my fare to Jo'burg.'

He was silent, momentarily preoccupied. 'I'll probably be able to give you a lift back tomorrow if it's any good to you,' he said. 'I've no passenger bookings so far. If there are vacant seats you're welcome to one.'

She explained that she had barely enough money to pay her hotel bill and the train fare back to Harare. She made a face. 'I couldn't possibly afford an air fare to Johannesburg.'

His smile was full of sympathy. 'Not to worry. You'll be my guest.' Frowning, he added, 'Have you a visa for Mozambique?'

'Yes. I got it before I left Harare so that I could go down to Beira to see Bill if he couldn't get up here.'

'Not easy to get quickly. How did you work that one in a few days?'

'A good friend of Bill's has pull in Harare. He's a senior civil servant.' She gazed at him in her direct, disconcerting way. 'Do you really mean it?' she asked. 'The lift to Johannesburg?'

'Of course I do. I wouldn't have suggested it if I hadn't.'

She put out a hand, touched his arm. 'You really are a kind man. Don't think I'm ungrateful when I say I must make contact with Bill before deciding. You understand that, don't you?'

'Yes, I do. As long as you can let me know by, say, ten tomorrow morning, there's no problem.'

'You may not have a spare seat.'

'Highly unlikely, Trudi. There are five passenger seats. I rarely carry more than two or three on trips between

Zimbabwe and Mozambique. Our contract doesn't allow competition with local air services.'

'What will your company say if you carry me for nothing?'

'It's *my* company, Trudi. And if I ask myself that question I'll have to be honest and say it's because I like you.' He grinned cheerfully. 'I'll be seeing my agents after lunch. I'll tell them I've got a passenger.'

Before they parted it was agreed they would again have dinner together. She had stalled at first, fearing that he might feel she was imposing on his kindness, but he persisted and in the end she gave in. 'Of course I'd love to, JJ. But I hope to goodness you don't think I'm . . .' she shrugged.

'You're what?'

'Sponging?' She looked at him uncertainly.

'Have no fear.' He shook his head. 'No way would I think that about you.'

It was not the first time Johnson had given that sort of assurance. He liked women, he had money and he enjoyed spending it.

SEVEN

As in Xai-Xai, the *pensão* at Maxixe – the Blue Marlin –
and the weatherbeaten, run-down buildings around it bore
the scars of recent years. And so, too, did the inhabitants
for apart from the ravages of drought the war had moved
closer with the massacre at Homoine, twenty-five kilometres to the west; notwithstanding the garrison across
the water at Inhambane, fears of a guerrilla incursion into
Maxixe ran high. Set among palm trees, the little town
looked over a narrow inlet of mud, sand, mangroves and
blue water to the Port of Inhambane. The latter, with its
harbour facilities, airfield, radio station and rail link with
Inharrime, was an important centre on Mozambique's long
eastern seaboard.

Federico was waiting at the *pensão* when they arrived. He
greeted Scott warmly. Visits by the syndicate's members
meant an interesting and lucrative break for him and his
assistant, Angelo, both of whom earned a precarious living
as local fishermen. Federico liked and respected Scott, a
white man who not only understood big-game fishing but
spoke the African dialect. Although a strict disciplinarian
Scott was appreciative of work well done and generous
to those who served him. Unlike some members of the
syndicate he did not permit the drinking of alcohol while at
sea. This, especially, commended him to Federico. Having
paid his respects and assured Scott that the boat and the
fishing gear were in order, Federico left the *pensão* in

company with Angelo who had been waiting outside. It had been agreed that *Sunfish* would proceed to sea at six-thirty next morning.

The fishing party was called at five-thirty, at much the same time as the sun began to show above the eastern horizon, painting the clouds and sky above it a fiery red, holding out hope of a break in the drought which had for so long plagued Mozambique. But red sunrises, unlike the rain, had come and gone and for the Africans watching it was no more than a hope, and in the minds of many a forlorn one.

After a nominal breakfast of coffee, toast and jam, the fishing party drove down to the pier where *Sunfish* was lying. To Pienaar the white boat with its tall outriggers and glass-windowed canopy over the wheelhouse was smaller and lighter than he'd expected. How would it cope with bad weather, with high winds and rough seas? He confided his misgivings to Wessels who smiled knowledgeably. '*Moenie bekommer nie, man* – Don't worry, man. I've had rough weather in her. She's a fine little seaboat. Anyway, you're dead lucky. The weather's real good today. No sign of wind.'

A period of considerable activity followed: *Sunfish*'s fuel tanks were replenished from the drums of diesel in the Land Rover, the lunch hamper and a jericho of fresh water were loaded and, finally, the fishermen went aboard where a bucket of bait, dorab and carvalhos, caught by Federico and Angelo, was already in the sternsheets. Wessels looked through the fishing gear with Angelo, while Scott checked charts, fuel tanks and oil levels with Federico. These tasks done, he spoke by radio to the Port Captain's office in Inhambane. After repeated attempts he got through to a sleepy official to whom he explained the purpose and duration of *Sunfish*'s journey, and from whom he received permission to proceed, the Port official signing off with, '*Boa pesca*, Senhor Scott – good fishing.'

After a number of attempts to get the diesel engine started it coughed and thumped into life, Federico's expression during the process changing from patient resignation to bright-eyed triumph. These emotions were evidently shared by his youngest wife who had come down to the pier to see him off, for when the engine at last started she had executed a little dance of joy, holding her baby in the air as if it were a sporting trophy.

'Fifteen minutes late,' complained Scott as *Sunfish* chugged away from her berth. 'Typical bloody inefficiency. That fellow in the Port Captain's office must have been asleep on watch.'

The crimson sky of morning was reflected in the waters of the inlet where seabirds and Africans stalked the mudflats in search of food, paying little attention to *Sunfish* as she headed up the buoyed channel between reefs, sandbanks and mangrove swamps towards the open sea.

With the red cliffs at Ponta Chicuque to port and the palm-covered islets of Dos Ratos and Dos Porcas to starboard, *Sunfish* went on past the flat, thickly-wooded peninsula which guarded the entrance to the Rio Inhambane. Eventually the buoy marking the end of the channel was reached and course was set for Ponta da Barra Falsa, some three hours to the north.

Angelo had already begun preparing the fishing gear, setting rods in the port and starboard gunwale-holders, running lines up through the outriggers, making ready the fighting-chair, selecting hooks and lures, placing gaffs and mallets and securing the buckets of bait.

A few miles south of Barra Falsa rod lines were streamed. Wessels had told Pienaar to look on until he had seen a big fish caught. Pleased that *Sunfish's* motion in the south-westerly swell did not make him seasick, Pienaar hadn't demurred.

The first worthwhile catch came soon, Scott bringing alongside a fifty kilo bonito after a brief struggle. Pienaar watched, fascinated, as Angelo gaffed, killed and boated the big fish. Wessels said, 'Remember, Piet – if the line begins to race from the reel, the important thing is not to strike too soon. Count twenty slowly, light a cigarette, put it in your mouth, *then* grab the rod and strike, and strike hard, man.'

So Pienaar waited, keyed up, tense, his eyes on the outriggers. He had already learnt that their constant flexing and whipping was due to the movement of the bait through the water, but when Scott's bonito took the bait the line had screamed off the reel and he'd seen that there was no mistaking. Pienaar's thoughts were interrupted by Wessel's yell, 'Yours, Piet,' as once again the high-pitched whine of the reel spinning-off line sounded an alarm to which the response was instant. Angelo took the rod from its holder and passed it to Pienaar who began to play what felt to him like a very big fish. But despite advice and exhortation from Scott and Wessels he lost the long silvery barracuda when it broke free with a great leap from the water. Pienaar hated losing it, but the thrill of a big fish on for the first time remained.

'How big?' was his eager question to Scott.

'Twenty-five to thirty kilos, I'd say. Good first catch – *if* you'd got it in.'

Shortly after eleven o'clock the lighthouse at Ponta Barra Falsa was abeam, about three miles distant. In the heat haze of forenoon it was no more than a slender finger pointing skywards above the headland behind which lay Pomene. In the run up to Barra Falsa several sunfish and barracuda had been caught but no marlin.

Wessels, a quiet, unemotional man, complained, 'Where

are they? Everything seems right but...' He shrugged. 'Where are the marlin?'

Scott's stare, the twitch of his mustachioed upper lip, conveyed disapproval. 'For God's sake, man. We're not halfway through the day yet. Federico knows these waters like the back of his right hand.' He looked to the wheelhouse where the African sat at the controls. 'If we can't find marlin you can take it from me they're not here.' He paused, relented. 'At least, not at the moment.'

Federico called out something in Portuguese, laughed, pointed to dark banks of cloud massing in the south-west.

'He thinks those clouds will bring rain,' explained Scott. 'He's excited because the people in the hinterland are starving.'

'I hope it does bring rain,' said Wessels. 'My God, the country needs it. The Lowveld also.'

Greg Nielsen tilted back the swing-chair in his Harare office, took a cigarette from the packet of Camels lying on the desk and examined it with care before lighting it. The young man opposite him looked up from the file he had been studying and frowned. Nielsen, typically, had chosen to light the cigarette immediately after announcing, 'Sure do have news, son. Plenty happening in Mutare yesterday.'

Nielsen's technique of heightening interest by delaying the punchline irritated Titus Luena, who was understudying the American prior to taking over the newly-established unit. The fact that he disapproved of smoking did nothing to diminish this irritation, but it did cause him to make a mental note to prohibit smoking in the office once he was in charge. This resolve was, however, almost immediately cancelled. The Minister would not be pleased. Tobacco was among Zimbabwe's prime exports.

Nielsen's voice interrupted Luena's thoughts. 'Trudi came through to me on Goschen's scrambler round three o'clock in the afternoon. Told me it was Kahn not

Gottwald who showed up. She wasn't one hundred per cent certain about the contact but she reckons it's a guy who was in the men's washroom at the same time as Kahn. A weirdo with a mandarin moustache, gold earrings and a red handkerchief round his neck. She says Kahn went in with a black briefcase and came out with it. She'd not seen the weirdo go in, but he'd come out with a shopping bag. A woman joined him in the foyer and they went along the passageway to the lifts.'

'Or to the dining-room?' said Luena. 'It leads to both.'

Nielsen puffed at his cigarette, stared at the younger man with quizzical eyes. 'You know that, son?'

Luena nodded. 'I know the hotel.'

'That's right.' Nielsen sniffed and his nose twitched. 'Never take anything for granted.'

'And so . . .?'

'I told her she was doing a great job. Asked her to report again at seven o'clock last night. She asked why. I said on account I'd know more by then. She told me she was having dinner with Johnnie Johnson, the Charter Couriers pilot. I said in that case to ring me at eleven o'clock. She agreed and I hung up. Half an hour later Jake Motlani comes through on the scrambler, and boy, is he excited. Tells me he's identified the contact . . .' Nielsen stubbed out the cigarette, picked up the packet of Camels once again and went through the slow, deliberate business of selecting, checking and lighting another.

Luena curbed his impatience, waiting until the cigarette was alight, before asking, 'So, who is the contact?' He put the question in an offhand way, determined not to contribute anything to Nielsen's dramatic style.

But the American liked the game played his way so he spun things out with a blow-by-blow account of what Jake Motlani reckoned he'd seen from his car parked outside the hotel.

'When Trudi called me at eleven I told her Jake's story. She didn't like it at first. Asked what must she do? I told her.

57

Before we finished she said she'd learnt who the weirdo was. He and his girlfriend had come up to their table at dinner that night. It was obvious from the way he and Johnson talked that they'd met before – in Maputo it seems. Johnson introduces the guy, names him Mavro Costeliades, explains he's an NBC journalist covering the guerrilla war. Trudi says this Mavro guy hands Johnson an envelope and says, "Here's the address you wanted." Johnson gives him a queer look, takes it, says, "Okay," and Mavro and his girl go over to a table further down the room. Johnson puts the envelope in his pocket, doesn't look at it. We checked out Mavro Costeliades with our people here and with Andrada Gouveia in Maputo. And sure he's an accredited NBC journalist.' Nielsen drummed on the desk with his fingers and puffed away at the Camel. 'When she phones this morning and I tell her Jake's news and that Mavro's in the clear, Trudi goes dead quiet, like she's upset. Can't rightly figure why. Maybe because her hunch blows up in her face. Tells me she still reckons the odds are that Mavro's the contact, that being an NBC man doesn't clear him.'

Luena rubbed his nose. 'Who is Mavro's girl?'

'Felicia Santos – from Maputo. Well known there. High-class lay, according to Andrada.' Nielsen wiped his face with a linen handkerchief.

Luena stretched, yawned. 'If what Motlani saw means what he thinks – yes, it is a surprise. But the Scirocco belongs to Addison Travel. Maybe some guy there is the contact.'

'I've thought about that, son. It's possible but not probable. Why do they have to wait until they've lent Johnson the car? They could have parked it any place in town for that sort of handover – *and* not run the risk of Johnson looking in the boot. It just doesn't fit.'

'So what do we do?'

Nielsen ran a hand over his crew-cut. 'We follow Jake's hunch.'

'What's the scenario for that?'

'Trudi will do what she can. Things have worked out well for that. Johnson swallowed her hard-luck story. He's giving her a free ride. Fancies her, I guess. She's a clever girl, is Trudi. And what she may see is important, to us and to Groenewald.' Nielsen blew smoke at the ceiling. 'Jo'burg's his territory and Jo'burg's the end of the line. That's where the action is.'

Luena shut the file. 'When does she get there?'

'Thursday. They take off from Mutare at eleven this morning. Overnight in Maputo, on to Jo'burg tomorrow.'

Luena moved to the window, looked down into the street, muttered something.

'What's that?' challenged Nielsen.

'Nothing. I said shit, that's all.'

'How come. What's the problem?'

'Nothing. Just wish I had Trudi's assignment. Doing something out there in the front line. Not just sitting on my arse in a Harare office. Why can't I get a field assignment like hers?'

'For a number of reasons, Titus. Like your Honours Degree, your political background, your family connection.' Nielsen paused, sniffed like a bloodhound, nose twitching. 'Like the Minister in his wisdom decided you should head the new unit.'

'Okay, okay.' Luena raised his hands as if fending off an attack. 'But why doesn't my training include some action up front? Why do the Trudis of this set-up have to get the plum assignments while I hang around this office shuffling paper?'

'Because it's your job, son. When I go Stateside this desk is yours. You'll be the boss then. And in our line of business, bosses don't take on field assignments. They've more important responsibilities.'

'Like shuffling paper,' said Luena bitterly. 'That's a hell of an exciting job.'

'You're certainly a persistent guy, Titus.' Nielsen scratched his well-cropped head. 'So – you ask, why hasn't your training involved an assignment like Trudi's? Right? I'll tell you for why. First, you don't have her shape, looks, charisma or sex. Repeat SEX. Ladies can go places, get into situations, play roles, that men cannot. That's why no worthwhile intelligence service operates without them. Got that, son?'

Luena looked away, shrugged.

'On top of which,' continued Nielsen, wagging an admonitory finger, 'you're not a South African, you're not white, you don't speak Afrikaans and, as I've said, you're no lady. For what Trudi's doing right now you need to be all those things. Got it?'

Luena's face clouded and his fists clenched, but he said nothing. Shaking his head he went out into the passage, put a coin in the dispenser and got himself a Coke. He drank it quickly, crushed the empty cup and dropped it in the bin. When he got back to the office the wall-clock was showing 10.30 and Nielsen was lighting another Camel.

In Mutare the morning had broken fine and clear, wisps of white cloud floating overhead heightening the blue of the tropical sky.

'Great day for it,' said Johnson as they came out on to the verandah. As always for flying he wore a khaki safari suit, the bush-hat with the leopardskin band, and dark sunglasses. Trudi in pink slacks and a white shirt looked cool and slim against the big, bearded man.

They went down the steps of the hotel to the car, a porter following with their luggage. He put it in the Scirocco's boot, then opened a door for Trudi before going round to the offside where Johnson tipped him. 'Thanks, George. Take care.'

The porter looked at the bank note, grinned. 'Thank *you*, sir. Have a good flight.'

'We ought to.' Johnson glanced at the sky. 'It looks good.'

He put the pilotcase on the back seat, got into the car, started the engine, pulled away from the kerb and filtered into the traffic. They drove in silence for the first few blocks until he said, 'Too bad you couldn't get through to your brother, Trudi. But it's not surprising. There's a war going on down there.'

There was a pause as if she were thinking about what he'd said before she answered in a subdued voice, 'Well, I tried to.' He looked at her sideways, puzzled at the sudden change of mood. At breakfast she'd been exuberant, excited at the prospect of the flight, at the thought of getting back to Johannesburg. But now she was quiet, staring ahead. Upset, he supposed, at the way things had worked out for her in Zimbabwe. Respecting her mood, he made no further effort at conversation. In due course the last traffic light showed up ahead, turning green as they approached. Once past it, he swung the car on to the road for the airport.

An African clerk from Addison Travel – agents to Charter Couriers RSA Ltd – was waiting for them. He handed Johnson manifests for the mail and parcels to be carried, confirmed that they had been loaded, took over the Scirocco, wished them a good journey and drove off.

With their luggage on an airport trolley they went on into the concourse. Leaving Trudi with the luggage Johnson went to the flight offices, filed his flight plan, checked the weather and other data, including military activity along the proposed route, and completed the documentation for his passenger. He rejoined her in the concourse after which they went through immigration and security with the minimum of formality for he was well known to the officials. Then, followed by an African with their luggage, they went out across the tarmac to the Cessna.

Johnson talked to one of the ground staff. Yes, the fuel system had been checked through, cleaned and pressure tested, and all was well. Yes, the tanks had been checked, cleaned and refuelled. Would he please sign the relevant invoices for forwarding to Addison Travel.

Johnson went round the Cessna, methodically checking flaps, elevators, rudder, undercarriage, fuel caps and other externals. Satisfied, he signed the invoices, put a copy of the certificate of airworthiness in his pocket and they climbed aboard. He sat on the left in the pilot's seat, she in the seat to his right. He busied himself with switches, checked the controls and instrument settings, and started the engine. A few minutes later he waved to the ground staff and the wheel-chocks were removed. He called the control tower, received their instructions and taxied out on to the runway.

A number of traffic movements were taking place but before long he got clearance from the control tower. 'Here we go, Trudi,' he said, as he opened the throttle. The Cessna raced down the runway and was airborne after a comparatively short run. At two thousand feet he levelled off and set course for the east.

'We'll hit the coast south of Beira,' he explained. 'Be across the border into Mozambique shortly. That's when we go down to deck level. We'll be flying over guerrilla war country. Both sides have ground-to-air missiles and both are trigger-happy. If we keep down on the deck we're safe. Anything above five hundred feet and we could be a target. You'll find it bumpy on a hot day like this. Can't be helped.' He grinned cheerfully. 'Better bumps than bullets.'

Not long afterwards he put the Cessna's nose down and began to lose height. At three hundred and fifty feet he levelled off, but to Trudi they seemed much lower, the bush country racing past beneath them in the way it did in travel films.

The thought that Renamo guerrillas could be concealed somewhere in the bush, that their missiles might come streaking towards the Cessna at any moment, frightened her; but fear soon gave way to exhilaration. She touched his arm. 'Oh, isn't this marvellous.'

He turned, saw that her eyes were bright. 'Wait till we fly down the coast, Trudi. That's really something.'

Her mood has changed, he told himself.

EIGHT

Once past Barra Falsa, Federico steered *Sunfish* in towards the bay at Pomene, the red roofs and white gables of Vila da Pesca and its cluster of bungalows taking shape as the land came closer.

About a mile offshore he swung the boat round to seaward again, this time on an easterly heading. After a while he called to Angelo who then took the sea temperature. He handed the thermometer to Scott. The Englishman was pleased, it showed 79° Fahrenheit and the sea was getting bluer, just about the colour of Reckitts. Speed was reduced so that *Sunfish*'s rods were doing a slow troll, the outriggers flexing and whipping, the baited hooks skittering along the surface astern. Federico turned in the wheelhouse seat, called to Scott in Portuguese.

'He says conditions are dead right,' announced Scott. 'Reckons something'll happen soon.'

But whatever that something might have been it was slow in coming and while they waited the south-westerly breeze freshened into a wind, ruffling the tops of the big indigo swells and bringing closer the dark banks of cumulus.

Wessels frowned at them. 'The weather doesn't look too good, Charles. Think we ought to be turning.'

Scott glanced to the south-west, shook his head. 'Those clouds are still a long way off. We can always run into the lee of Barra Falsa if the weather really worsens. But let's try for a big one before we do that.'

During the next half-hour there were alarms, barracuda

chopping the carvalhos baits so that Angelo switched to dorab and garfish and the men waited, thinking and watching the splashing baits astern and the outriggers jigging in disjointed harmony, and nothing happening except for the weather which was deteriorating, the black clouds shutting out the sun, darkening the white-streaked sea, the wind hissing louder in the outriggers and *Sunfish*'s movements increasingly boisterous.

Pienaar held on as long as he could before vomiting over the side after which, white-faced, red-eyed, and miserable, he huddled in a corner of the wheelhouse.

Scott was about to tell Federico to make for Barra Falsa when a reel sounded its shrill alarm. Shouting, 'Mine', Wessels scrambled into the fighting-chair and grabbed the rod from Angelo in one quick movement. The line was racing off the reel and he was remembering his advice to Pienaar and saying to himself, take it easy man. He did, and when he reckoned enough time had passed, and sufficient of the four hundred metres of line was out for the metal of the reel to show through, he leant forward, braced his shoulders and struck. Once, twice thrice, powerful blows, and he knew the hook was in. A moment of pause followed, the suggestion of an agonising shock deep under water, then the line was once again screaming off the reel.

Federico brought the boat round in a wide circle so that Wessels recovered some of the lost line, a task made difficult by the plunging and yawing of the boat. The fish began to sound and Wessels yelled, 'Could be a bloody great shark!' but while he was praying that it might be a blue marlin the line went suddenly taut, vibrating, throwing off a fine mist. He was about to give more line, not that there was much more to give, when Angelo shouted as a dark shape rocketed from the water a couple of hundred metres from *Sunfish* and fell back into the sea with a splash

65

like a shell-burst. Scott, seeing the long beak, shouted, 'Marlin.' It was a big fish, the biggest blue marlin he'd ever seen, and knowing that Wessels was in for a long fight he began to worry about the weather. Barra Falsa was a faint smudge on the horizon. Scott's instincts told him that now was the time to make for it, to get in behind the headland before the worst of the storm hit them. But with a marlin like that on? Hell, no, how could they? A blue marlin that big had to be a one-in-a-lifetime chance.

So he ignored his instincts and instead watched, fascinated, as the great fish fought with all its wild strength and anguish, surfacing, grey-hounding, tail walking and sounding, and all the time Federico was working the boat so that a long bight of line lay in the water to increase the marlin's death load.

Twenty more minutes went by and Scott's worries grew because a marlin like that could fight for two or three hours and if killed would be too big and heavy to bring inboard. It would have to be chained alongside, something scarcely possible in that weather, and even then the sharks might take the best of it. His thoughts were interrupted by a low moan from the wheelhouse. 'For Christ's sake,' Pienaar groaned. 'Forget the bloody fish. I can't take . . .' Before he could finish the sentence vomit exploded from his mouth and splashed down over his shirt.

Hearing this, Wessels shouted, 'No way, Charles. Not until I've killed this giant.'

The struggle continued, the marlin's fight involving *Sunfish* in a long haul round to port until the boat, once again closing the coast, was running before the storm with the south-westerly wind and sea on her port quarter. Changing its tactics the marlin turned suddenly and began a run towards them, making Wessels work feverishly at the reel to pick up slack line. To help him, Federico swung the boat sharply to starboard at the precise moment that the marlin changed direction again; the line quivered, tautened to breaking point, as a wave smashed on to

66

Sunfish's starboard side forcing the port gunwale under. The starboard side lifted high, another wave struck it and the boat capsized, hurling Scott and Angelo into the sea.

Now under water with the hull above them, the three men left in the boat began to struggle for their lives.

The Cessna reached the sea, turned south and followed the coastline, flying at about three hundred feet, a mile or so to seaward.

To Trudi the never-ending line of surf looked as though a great piece of chalk had been used to delineate the East African coast, to separate the greens and browns of the land from the intense blues of the Indian Ocean. Flying over the sea under a cloudless sky the bumps and jolts experienced over the land had gone and she was entranced. Above the roar of the Cessna's engine she listened, fascinated, to JJ's running commentary.

'That's wild country over there.' He pointed inland. 'Mostly bush, plenty of marshland when the rains fall. The Africans know how to live off it when things are normal, but now it's ravaged by drought and marauding guerrillas. They've killed a lot of the game, stolen the cattle, and the people are starving, poor devils.'

There was distress in his voice. Complex man, she thought; if only I knew what was going on in that mind. She looked at him but saw no more than the familiar sunburnt face, the grey-tinged hair and beard, the eyes inscrutable behind sunglasses. She thought of something she'd have preferred to have forgotten: Greg Nielsen's account of what Jake Motlani said he'd seen. It worried her even though she regarded Jake's report as flawed. To see Kahn coming from behind a car parked in a city street didn't necessarily mean what Jake had decided it did. Kahn might simply have walked between parked cars when crossing the road. She believed that Motlani and Nielsen had jumped to a conclusion which fitted most neatly

67

into their assumptions. They'd cleared Mavro Costeliades because he was an NBC man, but for her that didn't mean he couldn't be involved. All sorts of people got involved. Greg didn't agree, but he'd promised to keep tabs on Costeliades. For her, based on what she'd seen, the NBC man was still the prime suspect.

JJ's voice disturbed her thoughts. 'That's the Save River down there,' he was pointing to the right. 'Reaches the sea at Mambone.'

'What's the small town at its mouth?'

'That *is* Mambone.'

'When do we get to Maputo?'

He laughed. 'You bored?'

'Of course not,' she said indignantly. 'I just wondered.'

He looked at the instrument panel. 'We've a head-wind. Say another three hours. That'll be about 1600. Okay?'

'Yes. Great. It'll give me time to look around. Where are you going to stay, JJ?'

'At the Polana.' He glanced at her. 'So are you.'

She shook her head. 'No. I'm going to find something not so lush.'

'You're *not*, Trudi. You're my guest.'

She protested, said he was already doing more than enough for her. But he wouldn't accept that. Said he'd offered her a lift to Jo'burg and, like it or not, that included the Maputo stopover and that was the way it was going to be. So she gave in and he changed the subject. 'Lot of cloud ahead. Cumulonimbus, storm clouds. Could mean rain for those poor sods down there, but probably doesn't. That's a characteristic of African drought. The clouds come and the clouds go, but the rain stays away. Makes you wonder if there is a God. Killing all those people. All those kids.'

She looked ahead, saw the vast banks of cloud. 'Let's hope this lot's an exception,' she said.

*

68

The Cessna was flying over a channel of blue water, the coast on one side and a string of islands on the other. 'The big one's Bazaruto,' he said. 'The little one between it and the coast is Santa Carolina. Years ago fishermen and honeymoon couples named it Paradise Island. Bloody great marlin and swordfish, barracuda and bonito there. You name them – they're there. That's what the fishermen went for. The honeymooners – well, you guess. Only a few tourists risk it these days. They fly into Inhassoro or Vilanculos, then take a boat. But the hotels and the ski-boats are pretty clapped out, and the war's too close.'

'Sad,' she said. 'Must have been a gorgeous place to honeymoon.'

'That's gorgeous anywhere,' he said.

While she was talking he was thinking, worrying about having to drop her off at Dullstroom. He'd not yet told her that. Next morning in Maputo, over breakfast, he'd tell her there was a snag about the flight to Jo'burg – that Charter Couriers had phoned him during the night to report a Government assignment which had just come up, to be completed before he collected the fishing party in Inhambane on Saturday: a party of Water Affairs Department officials to be picked up in Lydenburg and flown down to Lesotho that day, then returned to Pretoria on the Friday. So he'd have to drop her off on Jan Wessels' farm at Dullstroom – private airstrip so no landing charges, he'd explain – and she could get the train to Johannesburg. It wasn't much of a journey and Tina Wessels would run her to the station. He would insist on being reponsible for the train fare. The changed plans would mean she wouldn't make Jo'burg till late the next afternoon. But she'd understand, and time couldn't be all that important to her at the moment.

No sooner had he sorted out the problem in his mind than Vilanculos was showing up on the right, and she was looking at it and asking why the light had suddenly faded and he'd pointed to the dense clouds above them. 'The

69

rain clouds we saw ahead. We're under them now.' He told her that in a few minutes he'd show her something really interesting.

She looked at him with a curious half smile. 'What's that?'

'The Chichocane Inlet. It's a tidal inlet. About fifteen miles long. Sea water at first, then mud and mangrove swamps. Fantastic breeding ground for birds. Bit late in the season now, but we'll go down and take a look.'

He pushed the stick forward, the Cessna's nose went down and just as Trudi thought they were going to hit the sea he levelled off, and soon a mosaic of water, sand, mangroves and mudflats was flashing past beneath them.

At first there was little to be seen but then, quite suddenly, there was bird life in abundance: colonies of egrets, storks, herons, waterfowl, stilts and waders bringing life and movement to the marshy swamps below. At the far end of the inlet he pulled back the stick and the Cessna climbed steeply.

He turned to Trudi. 'What d'you think of it?'

'Fabulous, JJ. Absolutely marvellous.'

'It's drought now. You should see it when there's rain. Unbelievable, I reckon . . .' He left the sentence unfinished as the Cessna's engine coughed, spluttered, coughed again several times and died. But for the swish of wind there was an ominous silence.

With a muttered 'Christ' he pushed the stick forward with one hand while turning the fuel tank switches to *all on* with the other. But there was no response, the engine was dead. He settled the aircraft in a shallow dive. 'I've got to put her down, Trudi. Right *now*,' he said, looking straight ahead. 'Sit well back, take off those sunglasses and cross your arms over your forehead.' She saw that he had already got rid of his.

The steadiness of his voice, the absence of any sort of panic, to some extent reassured her and she obeyed his instructions. Feeling anything but calm, her heart doing funny things, she pushed herself back in the seat and waited, peering ahead apprehensively through the small gap between her crossed arms.

As the glide continued JJ was busy shutting down and switching off fuel and electrical services, while at the same time searching desperately for somewhere to put the Cessna down. The terrain ahead was not promising, the only thing on offer a small clearing immediately beyond a range of sandhills, its far side lined with trees. The sandhills made a conventional approach impossible, but having cleared them by inches he lowered the flaps and steered for a gap between the trees. At the last moment, realising that the clearing was too small for a safe landing, he pulled the stick back in a deliberate stall. The Cessna hit the ground hard, bounced, hit the ground again and slewed to the left. Knowing that he had lost control, and acutely aware of the trunks of palm trees racing towards him, he slammed on the brakes, let got the stick, ducked and clasped his arms over his forehead. The last thing of which he was conscious was the appalling noise of the impact.

High in the anonymous grey building in Johannesburg's business centre the Brigadier paced his office, hands clasped behind his back. Tall and erect, he moved his head forward in rhythmic jerks as he walked, as if keeping time with his feet.

Captain Le Roux sat silent at the small table beneath the photograph of the President, waiting for the Brigadier's comments on the telex messages he had just handed him.

The tall figure stopped at a window, looked down into the street below before turning to his assistant. 'So, Le Roux, it is noon on Wednesday and already events are moving faster than we expected. The fishing has begun and the Cessna has left Mutare. I don't know what Pienaar will catch but I do know what *we* hope to catch.' The Brigadier managed a tight-lipped smile. 'And what is more, we now don't have to wait until Saturday for that.'

Le Roux smiled dutifully. '*Ja*, Brigadier.' Poking with a finger at his spectacles, settling them more firmly on the bridge of his nose, he said, 'The situation is complicated by the change of day, but the report from Kirst suggests that the conditions necessary to set the operation in motion now exist.'

The Captain's sentences, delivered in a stereotyped officialese as pompous as his manner, tended to irritate the Brigadier who frowned before resuming his pacing. 'The characteristics are the same,' he said. 'On both occasions the aircraft was described as a single-engined, high wing monoplane, silver and brown in colour. Why single-engined?' He fixed Le Roux with a grey-eyed stare but the Captain, knowing the question to be rhetorical, said nothing.

'Because,' continued the Brigadier, 'the stalling speed is lower than a twin's. That makes for an accurate drop. There were no passengers on the two flights concerned. This was confirmed at Grand Central where the aircraft landed at times consistent with the estimated flight times between the dropping points and the airport. Both incidents took place in deserted areas – the first some fifty-five Ks north-west of Johannesburg, the second about sixty Ks south-east. Both drops were close to physical features easily identified from the air – one a bend in a *spruit*, the other beside a clump of blue gums at the foot of a granite *koppie*. In both cases not far from seldom-used farm roads or cattle tracks. Now for the eyewitness reports.' The Brigadier interrupted his pacing to take another look down into the street.

Le Roux suspected that the purpose of this pause was to enable the Brigadier to refresh his memory. Le Roux also believed that the Brigadier's habit of running through the details of a mental dossier arose from a desire to ensure that his assistant would correct him if necessary.

'The first report,' continued the Brigadier, 'mentioned two cars parked together in the immediate vicinity – one black, the other grey. Unfortunately the farmer who saw them did not note the registration numbers or makes. Since there was a model aeroplane lying on the roof of one car, and another lying on the ground nearby, he assumed the three men to be model aeroplane enthusiasts – that what he'd seen was connected with their hobby – so he didn't stop. The African who witnessed the second incident was cycling down a farm road. He saw just one car and two white men. That car also had a model aeroplane lying on the roof, and there was another in the air close by. He, too, assumed they were model aeroplane enthusiasts, and did not stop. He said the car was black, but of course he did not take its number.'

The Brigadier made another window stop. 'It is unfortunate that the reports were not made directly to us at the time. It was a week or so before we got news of either and then only because the witnesses had mentioned the incidents to others in casual conversation. By the time the news reached us it was secondhand, third hand, God knows what hand.' The Brigadier's glare and shrugged shoulders told of his exasperation. 'But this time we are prepared. A lot of hard work has gone into this and . . .'

At that point Le Roux could not resist a '*Ja*, Brigadier' for most of it had fallen to him and Lategan at Grand Central. It had involved complex and highly detailed investigations, all of which had had to be conducted in the most circumspect fashion in order not to arouse suspicion.

With a slight frown at his assistant's interruption the Brigadier continued. 'The exact time of take-off tomorrow will be communicated to us as it occurs, the aircraft will be continuously tracked by radar, SAAF helicopters will be responsible for close surveillance and for directing the patrol cars.' He stopped pacing, and faced his assistant. 'Have I omitted anything, Le Roux?'

'Two points only, sir.' The Captain's expression was a mixture of pleasure and dread.

'And what are they?' The Brigadier's cold-eyed stare fed Le Roux's apprehension.

'Nothing important, sir. You will remember that if the dropping area appears to be inaccessible to patrol cars, the helicopters will land and make the arrests. Secondly, the suspects are to be taken alive, even if they attempt to escape or otherwise resist arrest. These instructions are included in the operational orders.'

The Brigadier nodded approval. 'Dead men can't be interrogated. Once those on the ground are in our hands it won't be long before they talk. With their help we'll flush out the rest of their ANC comrades.'

'I've also indicated in the orders that a model aeroplane *on a car roof* is almost certainly the method used to assist identification from the air.'

'Good,' said the Brigadier. 'Now lose no time in putting all concerned on standby for tomorrow morning.' He went to his desk, ran a hand across his forehead and sat down. 'And let them know that failure anywhere along the line will be severely dealt with.'

With a hasty, '*Ja*, Brigadier,' Le Roux left the office.

NINE

Wessels had let go his rod as *Sunfish* went over, but there'd been no time in which to release the canvas straps holding him in the fighting-chair. Upside-down and under-water, the hull above him shutting out daylight, there was little he could see as he fought unsuccessfully to release the buckles. The seconds ticked away until he remembered the sheath-knife at the back of his belt. Forcing himself forward in the chair, the pain in his lungs increasing, he got his fingers round the handle, pulled the knife clear and slashed at the straps until he was free. He clawed his way out of the chair, but the buoyancy of the life-jacket held him against the upturned hull and a new struggle began until, with the energy of desperation, he hauled himself clear of the sternsheets and shot to the surface. Exhausted, he hung on to the slotted bilge-keel to recover his strength, while the hull, beam on to the sea, rose and fell with the passing of each wave, their crests washing over him.

There was no sign of any of the others and he was accepting that he was the sole survivor when he heard chilling screams. As the next wave lifted the hull he looked in the direction from which the sound had come and saw with anguish the cause of the screams; black fins surrounded by a maelstrom of foaming red water. The wave rolled on, the hull slid back into a trough and there was a new sound; a muffled thumping in the wheelhouse beneath him. He was baffled until he realised that someone must be down there, caught in an air-pocket.

Holding on to the bilge-keel with one hand, he pulled

off his life-jacket with the other and tied its tapes to a slot in the keel. Taking a deep breath, he forced himself under the hull and struggled into the wheelhouse. In the dim light from the submerged window he could see Pienaar on the starboard side. To port the dead body of Federico was wedged under water between the wheel and the helmsman's seat. Wessels made for Pienaar, broke surface in the pocket of trapped air when he reached him, and was able to breathe again. Pienaar turned, saw his rescuer, and some of the horror drained from his face. Working fast Wessels helped him remove his life-jacket – Pienaar protested at first – after which Wessels urged, 'Take a deep breath, Piet, and follow me. Keep close.' Plunging back beneath the water he led the way out of the wheelhouse and up to the surface, Pienaar close behind him. Once above water Wessels moved along the hull to where he'd tied the life-jacket to the bilge-keel. Pienaar was a poor swimmer so he gave him the life-jacket and helped him put it on.

Driven by the instinct to survive the two men clung to the bilge-keel, the hull wallowing in short steep seas kicked up by the offshore wind which showed no signs of abating.

Rough though it was the sea was warm and this, Wessels realised, would enhance their chances of survival; but when after a time Pienaar, older and weakened by seasickness, gasped that he couldn't hang on much longer Wessels realised that something had to be done quickly if his companion were to survive. He was acutely aware, too, that it would not be long before sharks, still busy with the corpses of Scott and Angelo, turned their attention to the drifting hull.

'Hang on for a few more minutes,' he urged Pienaar. 'There's a rope trailing from the stern on the windward side. We can lash ourselves to the hull with it. I'll go for it.'

Without waiting for a reply he clawed his way up on to the hull using the bilge-keel as a step and the low centre-keel as a handhold. Slowly he worked his way along it to the stern, using the projecting sternshafts as hand and kneeholds until he reached the inverted rudder and wedged himself between it and the twin propellers. At times the tops of seas broke over him but he managed to haul in the rope hand over hand, laying the bights over the rudder until he'd recovered about twenty metres. Securing one end to the rudder post he crawled forward along the hull, legs and arms astride the centre-keel, until he was over the wheelhouse, the point at which the hull was highest out of the water.

There he passed the rope end through gaps in the bilge-keels, port and starboard, centred the bight, knotted it and hauled the rope taut. Satisfied with the lifeline now rigged along the length of the hull, he coiled the rope left over and secured it to the forward end of the lifeline. With his remaining strength he helped Pienaar on to the top of the hull and lashed him to the lifeline with the spare rope. That done he tied himself to the lifeline.

Exhausted, he looked at his wristwatch. It showed 1605. So much had happened that he found it difficult to believe *Sunfish* had capsized less than an hour before.

The south-westerly wind came from the land and because they were only a few miles offshore the seas were short and steep; seen from the hull to which they clung, constantly swept by spray and the broken tops of waves, the dim line of the coast was barely visible. Wessels knew that they were on the edge of two currents, the southward drift of the Mozambique current and, closer inshore, the northward drift of the counter current. Until dark when the flashing light at Barra Falsa would be visible there was no means of knowing whether they were drifting north or south. Their chances of survival depended very much on this and he offered a silent prayer to the Almighty that the set might be southerly for that held out most hope.

*

77

For Trudi, sitting rigidly in her seat, arms crossed over her forehead, there had been one terrifying instant when she was aware of a violent impact, the Cessna had seemed to disintegrate, and she had fainted.

She came to soon afterwards. Puzzled and semi-conscious she tried to make out what had happened. Still dazed, she unfastened her seatbelt with bleeding hands and saw on her lap the shattered remains of the sunglasses. JJ, she thought. Where's JJ? She looked at the seat beside her and then, as if she'd made a discovery, she saw that he was still strapped into it, bearded chin on chest and trickles of blood oozing from hs nose and mouth. Pieces of broken cockpit and a loose seat were festooned about him, the bush-hat with the leopardskin band somehow wedged into the smashed windscreen.

She tried to free him, working frantically because of her fear of fire, a fear fanned by the smell of petrol and the heat of the engine which seemed overpowering in the damaged cockpit. But Johnson was large and heavy and she was getting nowhere with her task when he suddenly came to; though groggy he was able to move but his speech was thick and he rambled, apparently unaware of what had happened. It seemed a long time before they disentangled themselves from the wreckage, but she realised from her watch that it had been no more than five minutes at most.

Johnson's first action was to check the radio. He'd had no time to put out a Mayday and it was soon apparent that there wasn't going to be a Mayday. The transmitter and receiver were both smashed and unserviceable. Next he began to search what was left of the Cessna's cabin for various bits and pieces he had stowed away in the lockers. His first concern was the pilotcase. It was undamaged, as were a number of other things. The package of emergency rations: *biltong* – dried game meat – biscuits, raisins and vitamin tablets. The plastic water-container, with its precious load. The Mauser automatic in its holster, and the emergency hatchet in the ceiling rack. Most precious of all, the flying map. 'Thank God I've found it,' he said. Like hers, his sunglasses had not survived the crash.

Pushing aside the wreckage which blocked the starboard exit door – the port door had been crushed against a palm trunk – they climbed out on to the ground, Trudi aware that her right ankle was extremely painful. They found their bags intact in the luggage-locker but he was more interested, even excited, about the .22 high-velocity rifle which he took from it and fondled like a child.

'It's okay,' he mumbled with evident relief. 'Absolutely okay.' For a moment he stared at her as if she were a stranger. 'I always have it with me. That and the revolver. Just for something like this.' His laugh was humourless. 'Not that I thought *this* would ever happen.'

He looked at the sky. 'Clouding over. Perhaps it'll rain. That could be useful.' Shrugging, he added, 'If it comes.'

Then he swayed, wobbled for a moment, before ending up on his knees. 'Sorry. Feel funny. Head aches like hell.' He dropped the rifle and fingered his mouth. 'Christ! Some of my teeth are broken.'

'There's blood at the back of your head,' said Trudi severely. 'Let me look.' She took his head in her hands. 'You've had a nasty bang there, JJ. It's all cut and swollen. Isn't there a first aid kit somewhere?'

'Yes. But it's under the crushed side of the instrument panel. We'll never get it out.'

'Let me try.' She asked him exactly where it was, and she went back into the cabin with the hatchet and hacked away at the damaged panel until she'd got it out. With cotton wool soaked in water from the plastic dispenser, she washed JJ's head wound before applying antiseptic dressings and bandaging it. After attending to his other damage as best she could, mostly lacerations on his knees, arms and hands, she made him lie in the shade where he soon fell asleep. She knelt beside him, felt his heart and listened to his breathing. He's in deep sleep, she decided.

The heartbeat had seemed all right but the breathing was irregular. Severe concussion, she decided. Next she did what she could about her own injuries, most were body bruises, but she also had a swollen ankle and scratches on her face which were wet with blood. She almost wept when she saw these in a vanity mirror before she'd wiped away the blood with cotton wool soaked in water and disinfectant.

The heat was intense and she rested for some time in the shade of the palms. Later she got up and examined the wreckage more closely. The wings had sheared off as the Cessna crashed through the palm trees. The front of the fuselage, including the engine housing, had suffered most damage. The four rear seats of the cabin, and the fuselage around them, including the luggage locker, had escaped serious damage though access to the cabin was difficult.

She sat down next to Johnson, her thoughts a worrying jumble. Would help come? How and where from, and when? Was he going to recover? Would wild animals and African guerrillas attack them?

Distressed and exhausted she lay down in the shade once more and had soon fallen asleep.

For the men on the upturned hull time stood still, the events of each minute no different to those before in the continuing struggle to survive the lash of wind and water, the lurching, the constant drenching, the tug of seas forcing flesh against rope lashings, and the harsh noises of the storm.

The black clouds brought darkness early, and with it the first glimmer of hope: a light winking in the south-west.

'Barra Falsa,' shouted Wessels hoarsely.

From the huddled shape next to him came the sound of vomiting.

'Flashing light at regular intervals,' continued Wessels.

'We've drifted north of Barra Falsa. Must be in the counter current.'

'What d'you say?' croaked Pienaar.

'Drifting south would have been better but – ' The rest of Wessel's sentence was drowned by a sudden scream of wind. After that he gave up any attempt at conversation. It was important to conserve energy, to concentrate on immediate things like the need to take up slack on the lashing, and to avoid swallowing sea water. Talking to a half-drowned man was a waste of time. His thoughts went instead to the problem that was likely to confront them if they did drift ashore on what was probably a hostile coast.

It was past midnight when the wind dropped as suddenly as it had come, and though seas continued to wash over the waterlogged hull they were smaller, less violent. By daylight the storm was over, the sun rising early into a cloudless sky.

There was no sign of land but Wessels knew that in those conditions – crouching low on an unstable, water-logged hull – visibility could be little more than a mile at most. He realised, too, that there was always a chance that the counter current might take them to a shore which was, perhaps, closer than they thought.

With the improvement in the weather the violent motion had gone and he eased his lifeline lashing enough to enjoy limited movement. After he'd stretched numb and aching limbs he spoke to Pienaar. 'Better let me slacken your lashings, Piet.' He began to do this but Pienaar protested.

'No, leave it, man. I'm weak. I can fall off.'

'Better for your circulation if the lashing is slack, Piet.'

'No, man. I'm okay. Just leave it, for Christ's sake.'

Wessels shook his head, said nothing. The condition of

the bedraggled shape lashed down on its side was anything but okay: the unshaven face seemed to have fallen in, there was a bloody gash across the left cheek, the inflamed eyes stared fearfully and the voice was a harsh croak. It was difficult to accept that this was the strong, confident, sometimes aggressive Pienaar of earlier days.

Wessels had been brought up in the belief of his Voortrekker ancestors that man could survive in the wilderness with the aid of a bible and a rifle. Well, this was no wilderness, a rifle wouldn't help and he had no bible – but there was always God. He was a religious man and so he prayed, ashamed as he did so because a part of his mind doubted the ability of his God to help in such hopeless circumstances.

Sometime later dark clouds gathered overhead and for a short time it rained. Since water was vital to survival Wessels believed that God had heard his prayer. But though it refreshed their bodies, little of the rain reached their mouths in spite of their attempts to catch it in cupped hands.

By midday the sea was comparatively calm and Pienaar at last gave in to Wessel's insistence that his lifeline lashings should be slackened. But for Pienaar's orange life-jacket they wore nothing but soaked and torn shirts, and shorts held up by belts with sheath-knives. Both had lost their sun-hats and shed their shoes; it was easier to cling to the hull with bare feet. But they were exhausted, their arms and legs cut and bleeding, and Pienaar's face made ugly by the gashed cheek.

Though surrounded by water they were plagued by thirst. When the rain stopped they tried wringing rainwater from their sodden garments, only to find that sea water had contaminated it. Then they licked their arms and each other's legs but with much the same result, these efforts doing no more than increasing their thirst.

For most of the time they were silent, each busy with his thoughts. At one stage Pienaar's had gone back to his briefing in the Brigadier's office: 'You have nothing to worry about, Pienaar. Carry out your instructions to the best of your ability and all will be well. Everything that can be anticipated has been dealt with, no detail overlooked. Le Roux has done a first-class planning job for this operation. Our agents in Maputo and Mutare have been alerted and briefed. Now it's over to you. Remember, it is on the return flight that you will play the key role.'

Nothing to worry about. That had to be the worst joke he'd heard. All right for the Brigadier and Le Roux in their comfortable offices with nice homes waiting for them at the end of the day. Not like what had happened to him. He cursed his luck. Why had he ever agreed to come on the goddam assignment? Looking across to where Wessels crouched he felt once again an immense bitterness. But for Wessels they would have been fishing again after sheltering from the storm in Pomene Bay. And on Saturday they'd have been picked up by Johnson in Inhambane, and been back home that night.

Why did Wessels have to hang on to that marlin, shouting to Scott not to make for shelter while he was fighting it? It was only a bloody fish. Now they faced almost certain death. Wessels, no one else, was to blame. They should have run in behind Barra Falsa when the weather turned bad. They were going to die because of Wessels' selfishness. Three men had already died; three lives lost because Wessels wanted to show what a great guy he was: 'Look at this photo of the blue marlin I caught off the Mozambique coast; 750 kilos, plus. Helluva fight. No, Piet had no luck. But he's a beginner. It takes a lot of experience to bring in one of these giants.'

Well, Wessels also was going to die. That's what his giant had done for him.

*

Not long after he had prayed, Wessels' belief in God was further reinforced by a light breeze from the east blowing towards the land.

And they were no longer alone. Nearby, seabirds swooped on a shoal of fish, and a school of dolphins closed in to inspect the drifting hull, leaping and diving in graceful harmony, so close that their spray drifted across the survivors.

Though he did not mention it Wessels had seen something else; two dark fins showing at times close astern; silent, purposeful and ominous.

Pienaar saw them too, and shivered.

TEN

Towards evening it rained and that was good for not only did it bring Johnson out of his torpor but it provided drinking water.

He was in a deep sleep when it began to fall and Trudi, anxious not to disturb him but certain that something should be done, improvised a catchment by spreading her windcheater under the Cessna's tailplane where rain was running off in a silvery cascade. The windcheater was waterproof and half an hour later when the rain stopped a sizeable pool filled it. Pleased with what she'd done she limped across to where Johnson sat in the shade with his back against a palm trunk; evidently refreshed by the rain, he was now awake and able to manage a lopsided smile.

'Got news for you, JJ,' she said.

He nodded. 'Good news?'

She told him of the rainwater in the windcheater. 'Enough for a few days,' she said. 'We must drink from the emergency container, top it up each time from the windcheater. There may be enough now to wipe our hands and faces.'

He smiled again. 'Clever girl. But we're not here for that long, Trudi.' The damaged mouth had thickened his speech, altered the sound of his voice so that it was as if someone else was talking. 'We'll be sighted from the air before long. They'll be out looking for us,' he said.

He was still muzzy and she didn't tell him what she feared: that there was nothing to be seen from the air. The

Cessna was buried deep in the bush in the shadows of palm trees. They could not in their weakened state possibly muster enough strength to pull a severed wing or other large piece of wreckage from the undergrowth and drag it into the clearing.

'Talking of water has made me thirsty, Trudi. Think I could have a drink?'

'Of course. I'll get the container.' When she came back she held it to his damaged mouth as carefully and gently as she could. Complaining that she was treating him like a child he pushed her hands away and held it himself, drinking in gulps, the water spilling from the sides of his mouth washing away the trickles of blood which had already stained his beard. She worried about that. Was it internal bleeding or just blood from the gashed mouth? She said nothing of her fears.

'Would you like a biscuit or some chocolate, JJ?'

'No thanks.' He shook his head, pointed to his mouth. 'Not yet, later perhaps.'

The rain that had fallen and the water that he'd drunk marked some sort of turning point for he got to his feet and soon afterwards announced through swollen lips that he felt better.

'That's great,' she said, wishing her ankle didn't hurt quite so much. 'But take it easy. It'll be dark soon. A good night's rest should make all the difference.'

'That's right,' he said. 'It's just what I need.'

She was thinking that it was odd that he had showed no interest in her condition when he said, 'You okay? I've noticed you limping.'

'My ankle got twisted. That's the worst damage. The rest is cuts and bruises.'

'Your face is not too good,' he said. 'Or your arms.'

She held out her arms, examined them carefully. 'Cuts and scratches,' she said. 'Same with my face. Nothing serious.' She didn't tell him that his face looked pretty ghastly with its damaged mouth and blood-stained beard;

instead she remarked that the crash could have been a lot worse.

'Yes. It certainly could. No fire, thank God.' He took her hand, held it firmly, his eyes worried. 'Sorry it turned out like this, Trudi.'

'Not your fault, JJ.' She was about to ask him what had caused the engine failure when it occurred to her that it wasn't a fair question to put to a man in that condition.

He complained about the sandflies and mosquitoes. 'God knows where they come from. The place is drought-stricken.'

'You're immune to malaria, aren't you, JJ?'

'Yes. Years on Paludrine – and whisky. And you?'

'Yes. I'm on Paludrine, thank goodness.'

Captain Le Roux all but burst into the Brigadier's office, omitting the customary ceremony of knocking and waiting for the peremptory 'Come'; his unusually cheerful expression indicated that the telex message he handed the Brigadier contained good news. It was from Mutare and it reported the Cessna's departure for Maputo with mail that morning. Thereafter, on the following morning, reported the telex, it would proceed to Grand Central Airport via Dullstroom. The aircraft had left Mutare with only one passenger, a Miss T. Braun, booked through to Johannesburg. She had been staying in the same hotel as Johnson and appeared to be on 'close terms' with him. Reservations had been made for them at the Polana Hotel for the overnight stop in Maputo.

It was, however, the final sentence which electrified the Brigadier: *Jack's recovery now assured.* Johnson's code-name was *Jack*, recovery was the code-name for *handover*, assured that for *confirmed.* So Kirst had confirmed a handover involving Johnson.

The Brigadier slapped his thigh, his grey eyes glittering

through the steel-rimmed lenses. 'That's splendid news, Wilhelm. It's what I've been waiting for. Kirst's work, no doubt. I'll not forget that.' The Brigadier rarely used Le Roux's first name; when he did so it signified particular pleasure.

'But he has a passenger, Brigadier. On the other occasions he had no passengers.'

'So?' said the Brigadier. 'No problem. The telex says they were on close terms, whatever that means. I'd say she's either an accomplice or, more likely, a girlfriend and he'll land her at Dullstroom before making the drop.' The Brigadier got up from his chair and began pacing, an indication that action was imminent. 'Carvalho is to report the Cessna's take-off from Maputo as it takes place. You will now alert SAAF headquarters: helicopters to be on standby at Nelspruit, radar tracking to commence as soon after the Cessna's take-off as possible. Patrol cars to take up station tonight. You drafted the operational plan for *Doodslaan*, Le Roux. Now get busy.'

The Captain hurried from the office in response to the dismissive flourish of the Brigadier's hand.

That night they slept in the back of the Cessna's cabin, the hatchet having been used to cut branches from thornbushes for a *boma* across the smashed doorway. 'To keep out prowlers,' Johnson said.

Earlier, he had strapped her ankle with a bandage from the first aid box, and she had swabbed out his mouth with cotton wool and disinfectant. Neither of them had felt hungry, but the hot tropical night made for thirst and there was frequent recourse to the water container.

Despite the discomfort of sleeping in seats, and the unfamiliar noises of the night, the cries of jackals, the howling of hyenas, the barking of baboons and the sound of movement in the bush, they slept well, shocked and exhausted by the happenings of the day. At times Trudi was wakened by muttered ramblings from JJ who was in deep sleep. But her periods of wakefulness were brief, and for most of the night she slept.

'*The Citizen* gives the most detailed report, sir. In the others it's no more than a paragraph.' Le Roux looked up from the table where he sat, the newspapers spread out in front of him. 'Would you like me to read it, sir?'

The Brigadier stopped writing, lifted his head as if he had just become aware of the Captain's presence. He put down his pen. 'No. I'm busy. Summarise it for me.'

Le Roux set his spectacles more firmly on the bridge of his nose, looked once more at the Brigadier, and cleared his throat. 'According to *The Citizen* a motor fishing boat which set out from Inhambane early yesterday morning with three South Africans and an African crew failed to return last night. The boat – '

'Three South Africans could be anybody,' interrupted the Brigadier.

Le Roux smiled politely. 'No, sir. It's quite clear who they were.' He quoted from the newspaper: 'Two of the missing men were from the Dullstroom district, one a farmer, the other an agricultural machinery salesman. The third was resident in Maputo where he represented a South African shipping company.' The Captain's eyes gleamed triumphantly through thick lenses. It was not often he was able to correct his master.

'Get on with it,' said the Brigadier, with an impatient wave of his hand.

'The report indicates that the boat might have put into the coast to shelter – it seems there was a sudden tropical storm in the area yesterday afternoon – or it might have had engine trouble. The boat, the *Sunfish*, is known to have two-way radio on board, but no messages were received.' Le Roux looked up from the newspaper. 'That is, substantially, what the report says.'

The Brigadier was optimistic and explained briskly why: Scott, Wessels and the African crew knew the coast well. If, as seemed likely, they'd put in somewhere for shelter they wouldn't use their radio; the coast north of Inhambane was known to be frequented by guerrillas. Scott would not want to advertise the boat's whereabouts.

'A fishing boat is a fine prize, Le Roux. With it you can get fish. Renamo guerrillas are short of food. Same with Frelimo units in the bush. They often take matters into their own hands where whites are concerned. No, Scott would not make that mistake.'

'But if they've had engine trouble and they're just drifting? It's already Thursday, sir. Johnson has to pick them up in Inhambane on Saturday.'

Elbows on desk, the Brigadier stared at Le Roux over clasped hands. 'If they had engine trouble and were drifting they would have used the radio. The fact that they didn't seems to me to confirm that they took shelter while the storm lasted. They're probably already on their way back to Inhambane. You worry too much, Le Roux. Remember what Ludendorff said: "The greatest threat to the Prussian Army is the industrious but . . .",' the Brigadier hesitated before coming out with it, ' ". . . stupid staff officer." In your case for *stupid* I would read *apprehensive*.'

Le Roux blinked, flushed, and as if to reassure himself tugged at the ends of his moustache. But he remained silent. The Brigadier wasn't the sort of man you contradicted, whatever your thoughts about him might be, so he said dutifully, 'Is that all, sir?'

The Brigadier picked up his pen. 'Yes. Keep me informed.'

Le Roux tucked the newspapers under his arm and left the office, closing the door discreetly behind him.

Throughout that day the drift continued, the sky blue, the sun merciless, a giant radiator poised high above the survivors on the drifting hull. They could now manage

90

limited movement in the few feet of space available. No longer did they keep themselves lashed tightly to the lifeline, so it was possible to turn from one side to the other, to kneel and to sit. Because of the intense heat Pienaar had taken off the life-jacket and wedged it under the lifeline. In vain they had looked for ships, and once their hopes had soared when they heard an aeroplane, the sound coming from inland. Though they strained their eyes they could not see it. Soon there was silence again and fear and misery returned, heightened by the dashing of false hopes. Though it was less than twenty-four hours since the capsize, the lack of water, and to a lesser extent of food, was beginning to tell; their lips were blistering, their eyes bloodshot and sunken in drawn, stubble-bearded faces.

In mid-afternoon Wessels thought he could see land, a thin blur shimmering in the heat haze to the west. At first he had thought it was a mirage, but when it was still there almost an hour later he shouted a hoarse, 'Land. I can see land, man.' Pienaar could not see it at first and was doubtful but in time he too agreed that it must be land and their spirits rose. Later the distant blur faded and they were left wondering if it had ever been there.

Towards sunset, Pienaar, deeply pessimistic, pointed out that it had been Wessels' determination to catch the blue marlin that had caused the disaster. In a plaintive croak he stated his complaint. 'Charles Scott wanted to run for shelter but you said no. You had to catch that bloody fish. Why, man? Tell me why.'

At that Wessels lost his temper. He reminded Pienaar that he had saved his life after the capsize, given him his life-jacket and lashed him to the hull. He ended the rebuke with, 'For God's sake, stop whining and shut up.'

Since Wessels was the bigger, stronger and younger man, Pienaar fell into a sullen silence. But it was a turning point in their relationship. Things were never to be quite the same after that.

The day had passed with infinite slowness and when night ultimately came Pienaar felt that hope had gone, that death was close. His faith in God undiminished, Wessels refused to accept that there was no hope; but at times, perversely, he wondered how much longer they could survive to enable God to do what had to be done.

ELEVEN

When the sun began to show, Johnson and Trudi removed the *boma* and climbed out of the Cessna's cabin, stretched their bruised limbs, blinked their eyes and confronted the day. Sleep had done them good, but Johnson's thick voice and his tendency to ramble worried her. In spite of his protests she once again examined his injuries, put a fresh dressing on the head wound, and with cotton wool soaked in rainwater and Dettol she washed his damaged mouth and other cuts and abrasions. When she'd done that she treated her own injuries as best she could, finding that the lacerations on her face and arms caused nothing like the pain and discomfort of the twisted ankle and the general bruising of her body.

In a large tree near the Cessna a troop of monkeys leaping in the branches screeched and shrilled as if terrified. 'What's worrying them?' She pointed to the tree.

He looked at it, shielding his eyes from the sun. 'Nothing,' he said. 'Just family squabbles over breakfast. Let's help ourselves.' He began collecting the yellow, plum-like fruits which lay on the ground beneath the tree.

'Can we eat these?' Trudi asked anxiously.

'Anything monkeys and baboons eat is OK. But we mustn't have too many. It's a marula tree. The ripe fruits ferment quickly once they've dropped. It's – ' he stopped, frowned, shook his head as if he'd lost the thread of what

93

he was saying. 'They can make a man drunk. Monkeys and elephants too. Try one.' He passed it to her.

She looked doubtful, removed the skin and tasted the white fibrous flesh around the kernel. 'It's delicious,' she said. 'Sort of sweet-acid taste.'

They ate a number of the little marulas, washing them down with water from the container. She asked him if he'd like any of the emergency rations and he said no, they shouldn't be used as long as they could find bush food. 'It may be scarce in places where the guerrillas have been,' he said, 'though it doesn't look like they've been around here lately.' He glanced at Trudi with a worried expression. 'I thought of something . . . a moment ago . . . something important. Can't remember what it was.' For a minute or so he stood there looking lost. 'Oh yes, it was the map. I'll fetch it.'

She watched him walk over to the Cessna's cabin and decided he was not as wobbly as he had been on the previous afternoon. He's getting over it, she said to herself, that's marvellous.

He came back with the map and they sat on the ground in the shade looking at it. 'We're here,' he pointed to a blank space on the map, about seven or eight kilometres south of the Chichocane Inlet. 'An African village, Cheline, is over there, see? On the main road about twenty-five Ks to the west. Pomene is about fifty-five Ks to the south, but . . .' He stopped, looked puzzled, seemed again to have lost the trend of what he was saying.

'So?' She watched him uncertainly. 'What's the plan?'

He looked up, frowned. 'The plan?'

'Yes. What are we going to do?'

'What are we going to do?' The silence which followed was broken only by the noise of his breathing. It sounded as if there were bubbles in his throat. She hoped it was no more than concussion, but the trickle of blood from the side of his mouth worried her. Was it from the injuries to his mouth? She hoped fervently that it was.

94

At last he said, 'Yes. I'm going to make for Cheline. Check what's going on there. Hide in the bush and watch. If it looks okay I'll go in and get help.'

'And if it doesn't?'

'Then I'll move a few kilometres south. Stay in the bush alongside the road. Sooner or later there'll be a military vehicle. I'll explain that we're South Africans – show them my passport, tell them I'm on contract to the Mozambique Government to carry mail.' He looked towards the wrecked Cessna. 'There's two bags of it in the luggage locker. I'll produce the consignment notes.'

She looked at him anxiously, doubt in her eyes. 'Can you speak the language, JJ?'

'Lot of them have worked on the mines along the Rand. They understand Fanagalo, and some English and Afrikaans. I speak those.'

'What about me?'

'You stay here, Trudi. The Cessna's cabin is the safest place for you, especially at night. The smell of petrol masks human scent. Keeps predators away.' Quite suddenly he put his hands to his head and winced. 'I'll leave you the automatic and the hatchet.'

'Are you all right, JJ?'

'Not too bad. Just this goddam headache.'

'D'you really think you can do a long walk through the bush, in this heat?'

'No problem. But for the headache I'm okay. Lot better on my feet than yesterday afternoon.'

'So I stay here?' The question was put like a plea for remission of sentence.

'Yes. It's safer and it gives two chances of rescue – Cheline and here.'

'How's that?'

'We'll lay out wreckage, mailbags, anything moveable. Put them in the clearing. An aircraft searching for us may see them.' He stood up, swayed a little. 'Let's do that right now.'

But it was oppressively hot, they were both weak, and there was little they could move apart from the mailbags, the luggage-grips and a few small pieces of wreckage. Trudi did not say so but she felt that even if seen from the air the display would look like a jumble of rocks.

For most of that morning they pottered about exploring the sandy, grass-tufted clearing, checking to see what lay beyond the trees and undergrowth around it but never moving far from the Cessna. All that they saw confirmed that the crash had happened in a remote, lonely place. Often during the morning Johnson had looked into the sky, shading his eyes, turning slowly on his heel. But apart from an occasional bird and soaring vultures they saw nothing in the sky. 'They should be searching for us now,' he said. 'But it'll be difficult for them.'

'Why?' she asked him.

'The flight plan I filed gave our route as over the sea. It didn't include a look at the Chichocane Inlet.' He shrugged. 'Can't be helped. Anyway, there's always Cheline.'

At noon they ate more marulas, drank more water, and lay down in the shade. It was not until close to two o'clock that he sat up, yawned loudly and said, 'It's time for me to go.' He got to his feet, put a hand to his bandaged head. 'If I take it easy I'll make Cheline by midnight,' he said. 'Good time to arrive.'

'How's the headache?' she asked.

'Not too bad. Comes in spasms.'

They went across to the Cessna and he began making preparations for the journey. First he gave her the Mauser and a spare ammunition clip, and showed her how to load and fire the pistol. Next, he shared out the small store of emergency rations before putting aside the few things he would take: the rifle, a spare ammunition clip, his share of the rations, the flying map and the pilotcase.

96

She said, 'Water, JJ. You can take the container. There's enough for me in the windcheater.'

He shook his head. 'No, it's too big. Awkward shape, extra weight. There's still rainwater on the leaves in the undergrowth. That'll do me.'

He was putting the iron rations and other things in the pilotcase when she asked him why he was taking it.

'Why not?' His abrupt reply suggested that her question was unnecessary.

'It's just extra weight. Couldn't you put those things in the pockets of your safari jacket?'

'No, I must take it. My pilot's licence, passport, aircraft registration documents, flight papers, mail receipts and delivery notes, the lot, are in it. Everything that says who I am and what I'm doing in Mozambique. Plus the emergency rations and spare ammunition for the rifle.' His tone softened and he grinned. 'And a teddy bear.'

'A teddy bear?' Her eyebrows arched in surprise. 'What on earth for?'

'For Clara.'

'Who's she?'

'My daughter.'

'Must you take it?'

'Yes.' He grinned again. 'Unlucky to leave it. No trouble. Just something I saw.' She shrugged, shook her head, pulled the belt from her slacks. 'Here, take this. Put it through the handle of the pilotcase. Use it as a shoulder-strap. It'll be easier to carry that way.'

He frowned as he considered her suggestion. 'Good idea.' He took the belt. 'Yes, I'll do that.'

Their parting was perfunctory. He told her to take care, smiled, looked once more at the sky, gave her a thumbs-up sign, and set off on his journey, the rifle over one shoulder, the pilotcase slung by the pink belt over the other.

His walk was normal though slow and she assumed he was pacing himself because of the heat. Her last view of him was at the far end of the clearing when he turned and waved, the bush-hat with its leopardskin band perched awkwardly on his bandaged head. Soon afterwards he disappeared into the bush.

It was not long that Thursday morning before there was more serious news for the Brigadier. It came in the shape of a telephone call from Grand Central; from Lategan, the Department's eyes and ears at the airport. 'Charter Couriers have just had a call from Maputo, sir. From Carvalho. The Cessna flown by Johnson is down somewhere between Mutare and Maputo. It was due there yesterday afternoon but failed to arrive. There's been no news of it. No Mayday, nothing. Mutare airport says it went off their radar screens when it crossed the border into Mozambique soon after take-off. It was then heading for the coast. In accordance with his flight plan Johnson would by then have gone down to a few hundred feet.'

The Brigadier swore into the phone. Collecting his thoughts he said, 'Why has the news taken so long to reach Charter Couriers?'

'You know what Maputo's like, sir: *môre 's nog 'n dag* – tomorrow's another day. Nothing is urgent to the lot down there.'

'That doesn't excuse Carvalho.' The Brigadier's eyes glinted like twin daggers. 'Have Charter Couriers any idea where the Cessna's likely to be down? In the bush or over the sea?'

'No, sir. Nothing more than I've told you. If there's any news I'll pass it to you at once.'

'Do that,' said the Brigadier. Not that it'll help, he thought as he put the phone down. He rang for Le Roux, the Captain arrived and the Brigadier told him of Lategan's report. 'Cancel *Doodslaan* right away, Le Roux. Inform SAAF and all others concerned.'

'Including Maputo, sir?'

'Carvalho already knows the Cessna's down. What I want to know is why he failed to advise us yesterday. Why do we have to wait for Lategan to give us the news at least eighteen hours after the event? Tell Carvalho that I'm bloody angry. I want his reasons in writing. What the hell does he think we pay him for?'

When Le Roux had gone the Brigadier sat head in hands, staring grimly at the green blotter in front of him. *Doodslaan*, death blow, carefully laid, meticulously planned, was in ruins. First the *Sunfish* problem and now the Cessna. Whether the aeroplane was down in the bush or in the sea made little difference. There'd been a hand-over in Mutare. What was handed over was in the Cessna. The documents would probably have burned in the crash if it had been on land, or they would be at the bottom of the sea if the Cessna had come down off the coast. Had it been shot down by a ground-to-air missile? That was the most likely cause since there had been no Mayday. In that case the aircraft would certainly have burned. The Brigadier drew a noisy breath of frustration. He had set his heart on the successful outcome of the operation. The Department's minister was much involved. The Brigadier recalled his words. 'It's not enough to suspect that the man acts as a courier for the ANC, Brigadier. In any case, your present evidence is flimsy. Wouldn't stand up in court. No, you've got to catch him in the act of making this drop you talk of. Seize the evidence and the people on the ground then and there.'

The Brigadier knew that he'd soon have to report failure. It was a task he feared. It would be known that it was in no way his fault but the Minister had a Cabinet to report to and he'd be thinking of the political mileage lost by failure. No ANC operational orders to underground commanders in the Transvaal to show to the Prime Minister, to be studied and made good use of for security and propaganda purposes. Most important of all, no arrests of those on the ground, which meant no opportunity for interrogations which could in turn have led to important arrests in the cellular command structure, and the communication links. That was what the Minister would be thinking about, and he would be anything but pleased.

TWELVE

At the end of the clearing he turned and waved to Trudi before going down a game-path into the bush. He was not sure he had done the right thing in leaving her at the crash site, but then he wasn't really sure of anything at the moment. Nothing seemed real other than the stabbing headache and a feeling of being out of touch, his head somehow detached from his body. It was as if all that had happened over the last twenty-four hours had been something he'd been watching on a wide but hazy screen.

His thoughts went back to her. With the *boma* across the front of the Cessna's cabin, animals couldn't get at her. If Africans came along . . . well, it depended on who or what they were, and she had the hatchet and the automatic. So perhaps . . . he gave up. Thinking was too much of an effort. If she'd come with him she might have been in greater danger. He knew the bush and the Africans and how to handle them, but she was a city girl, a German at that . . . and if they ran into armed gangs, Frelimo, Renamo, whatever? He'd be able to cope, but she was a woman, an attractive one. No, it was better the way it was. Anyway, there was no point in worrying about that now. The important thing was to get to Cheline. Through the bush, following game-paths like he was, he reckoned it would take all of ten hours. He ought to make the main road about ten o'clock. It would be dark then and that was good. Under cover of darkness he could get close in, hide, and with daylight watch to see who was there, what was going on. The moon wouldn't set till well after midnight. That was good too.

Something was coming through the bush on his left, making a helluva noise. Had to be a buck being chased. The sound came closer. Moments later an impala leapt across the game-path ahead of where he'd stepped aside behind a *withaak* thornbush to watch. Nothing followed the impala. He wondered what had caused the commotion. Lion, leopard, cheetah? Or just a bigger ram?

This sun certainly blazes down, he thought. The heat comes up from the ground and down from the sky. A man gets it both ways. Why had the Cessna's engine packed up? He'd had to wait two days in Mutare while they checked through the fuel system, cleaned everything including the tanks, and fitted new filters. McLeod was a reliable guy, but who'd actually done the work, carried out the final checks? Maybe it wasn't the fuel system. Electrics perhaps? Not that knowing what it was could help now.

Christ, it's hot . . . the rifle and pilotcase are a bloody nuisance . . . heavy too . . . and these damned sandflies. He swished them away, looked at his watch. Only an hour since he'd left Trudi. It felt a lot more than that. Well, he'd have to push on. The sooner he got to Cheline the sooner he'd get help, get back to her. She's a good one, that girl, plenty of guts, knows how to look after herself.

Maybe he'd be in luck and see an army truck on the road before Cheline. But, no good, that wouldn't work. It'd be dark. No way to tell friendly headlights from hostile ones in the dark. His thoughts trailed away. He felt he was going to faint or be sick or his head would burst or something bloody awful like that was going to happen. He needed a rest but it would have to be a short one. He left the game-path, went deeper into the bush. Not far from the path he sat down in the shade, his back against the shining white trunk of a fever tree, rifle and pilotcase beside him. He pulled the safari hat over his eyes, felt drowsy, lost consciousness.

A burning sensation in his mouth woke him. It seemed to have come alive, a hot crawling plasma moving about in there and in his nose. He rubbed his mouth and nose, then looked at his hands. Ants . . . ants . . . ants. Hundreds of ants. Around his eyes, too. He got on to his knees, faced the trunk of the fever tree, pulled himself to his feet. With wild motions he tore the ants from his face, scratching and scraping with his fingers, then from his arms and knees. He saw that his fingers were bloody.

He took off his shirt and shorts and Y-fronts, shook them vigorously. The ants were all over his body . . . red, spiky little ants. It took time to get rid of them. Some stuck to his skin, crushed by his fingers. With trembling hands he fumbled through the pockets of the safari jacket, found the packet and the lighter, took out a cigarette and lit it. Because of his mouth, the first since the crash. He wasn't going to sit down again. Or fall asleep. God, what heat. He puffed furiously at the cigarette, blowing the smoke at the column of ants climbing the white tree trunk. It didn't seem to worry them. His mouth and nose hurt inside. He ran a finger over his teeth. Three missing, three jagged stumps in the centre of his mouth. How bloody awful. He hated the idea of false teeth. He'd always had good strong teeth and looked after them. But the ants! God, those ants in his mouth and nose. It must have been the blood they were after. He felt his beard. It was wet with blood. He staggered away from the big tree, fell down, a dark screen moved across his eyes, he felt himself losing consciousness – the floorboards were creaking, Kath was coming into the room. What was that she was saying? Oh no, not that again, not the same old record: I scarcely see you these days, JJ. Why do you do so much flying yourself?

103

What's the good of being the boss if you have so little time for your home? For me and for Clara? I know you give me everything – the Porsche, the diamonds, fabulous clothes, holidays in Mauritius, the Seychelles, wherever. I know you're clever, successful, make lots of money. I know that takes time and hard work. I know all that. But I want you, JJ . . . and you've gone . . . you aren't there any more. I want my kind old JJ. Yes, I know you're still kind, but you're different now . . . you've changed. You're not mixed up in something funny, are you? Oh God, I hope you're not getting involved with those Commie blacks in Zimbabwe and Mozambique. You're always down there these days. And, and – for God's sake, she never stops. No wonder my head aches.

Jesus! What's that? Looks like a man with a rifle . . . on the game-path . . . coming this way . . . Frelimo? Renamo? No, for Christ's sake, it's a teddy bear . . . a teddy bear with a rifle . . . crazy! No, looks more like Kahn now. Dark, hollow sort of face. Kahn, Abdul Kahn. What's the guy really like? Strange sod. We see each other, never speak, never show recognition . . . only met once . . . in Mauritius . . . for a few minutes, at the beginning. Gottwald says, 'You better know how you guys look to each other. Purposes of identification only.' Gottwald with the flat, immobile face and wide-apart blue eyes. 'Baby Face.' Jesus, some baby! But he's a clever bastard. The cell? Him, Kahn and me. But we haven't a clue who his linkman is. Only Gottwald knows that. My linkman, Transvaal end? Haven't a bloody clue, have I? Just a little aeroplane on a roof. Come to that, maybe Gottwald doesn't know his Mauritian linkman. Could be a post office box with two keys. Yah. Very clever is friend Gottwald.

What's happening? Why am I here? The crash? What crash? Ah, the Cessna. Twelve thousand hours in my logbook, SAAF and civil. Not a damaged wing tip . . . now a bloody write-off. Fuel lines blocked? *Both* fuel lines? Balls! More likely sabotage.

104

'Christ, this pain I can't . . .' The hoarse cry trailed away into a long fit of coughing, bloodied phlegm oozing from his mouth. Once again the dark screen was shutting out the light and he felt himself drifting into unconsciousness.

For two days the upturned hull of *Sunfish* drifted north along the Mozambique coast with its human load clinging to it. The wind, still from the east, was now no more than a fitful breeze ruffling the surface of the indigo swells which rolled in towards the land. Wessels believed *Sunfish* was for most of the time between two and three miles from the shore: but seen from the waterline the distant coast, shrouded by day in the heat haze, was scarcely visible. The flashing light at Barra Falsa no longer showed at night, nor had the only other light he knew of appeared, that at Ponta Chambure, about fifty nautical miles north of Pomene.

By day the blurred coastline seemed featureless so that he had no means of judging the rate of drift. Moreover, without a chart, he had no idea of the character of the land they could so faintly see. Explaining these difficulties to Pienaar he said, 'It's bush country. Only thing we might see would be African camp-fires. This is a deserted stretch of coast. As far as I can remember when we were off it last year, Charles said there were a couple of villages on the main road thirty to forty Ks inland. Very likely Renamo country now.'

Pienaar's only reply was a long groan.

Both men were in a bad way. Sea water and intense sunburn had aggravated their cuts and abrasions and blistered scorched bodies which were steadily dehydrating due to lack of drinking water.

Both suffered from partial blindness, particularly when the sun was high. Wessels regarded Pienaar's verbal ramblings, now more frequent, as signs of approaching madness. Lack of food did not worry them as much as that of water. They had tried splashing sea water over their bodies, but though it acted as a temporary coolant it made worse the ravages of sunburn. So they gave that up and crouched this way and that in their efforts to escape the relentless heat of the sun and the agonies of cramp.

Pienaar tried to protect his blistered body with the life-jacket but it was an unsatisfactory compromise and to add to his problems he was suffering from diarrhoea, a complaint which Wessels had not helped by remarking, 'At least the shit's chased the sharks away!' This lack of sympathy had been too much for Pienaar who had ended an angry outburst with a fit of sobbing. Wessels had tried to comfort him but their relationship had reached a stage where antipathy was more powerful than sympathy, and he soon gave up.

In physical terms they found night kinder than day. But mentally, psychologically, the nights were worse for there was the constant fear of another storm, of somehow falling off the hull, of being passed by a ship unseen, or hidden by darkness from help from the shore. Worrying, too, was the thought that daylight might reveal that they had drifted out of sight of land.

It was in the early hours of morning, well before dawn, that Wessels' wild shout sounded in the darkness. 'Hey, Piet! Listen, man.' Pienaar woke from uneasy sleep. 'What? What is it?' he croaked.

'Surf, man. Waves breaking. We must be close to the shore.' There was something close to hysteria in Wessels' voice.

Pienaar's reaction was to complain that he could hear nothing, and he accused Wessels of a cruel joke. But he interrupted himself to yell, 'Jesus, man! You're right. I can hear it. I can hear it. It's not far.'

'Not so close either,' corrected Wessels. 'But get ready to move quickly if necessary. Loosen the lashing a bit and check that your life-jacket is properly fastened.'

While they waited in the darkness they said little, conserving their strength for the struggle to come. The predominant sound now was the distant rumble of surf, closer to hand the splash and gurgle of water against the hull. The moon had set but the southern sky was bright with stars.

The first shades of dawn revealed the line of broken surf towards which they were drifting. It was, perhaps, a few hundred metres away. Ahead of them the coastline reached out gently across the direction in which they had been heading.

Wessels said, 'It's not that we've drifted closer. It's because the coastline has turned in an easterly direction.'

Pienaar said, 'So the luck is with us, hey?'

Wessels shook his head. 'Not luck, Piet. God is with us.' Prompted by the thought he was about to say a prayer of thanks when it occurred to him that it would be wiser to delay it until they had got safely ashore. It was possible that the most dangerous time was still to come.

After that they waited in a state of high excitement, exclaiming, shouting, watching the broken surf come closer, until a throaty yell came from Wessels. 'It's a coral reef. We're going to run ashore on it.'

'Christ! We'll never make it, man.' Pienaar's melancholy cry was lost in the roar of the surf where the easterly swells approaching the land became wave crests, foaming and frothing, until they broke on the reef where the air was misty with blown spray; beyond it lay a lagoon into which the remnants of each spent breaker swirled on towards the beach.

'Okay, if we keep our heads,' shouted Wessels. 'There's calm water on the far side. Once over the reef it's only a short swim to the beach.' With a humourless smile he added, 'And you've got your life-jacket.'

As time went on the reef came steadily closer, the hull lifting on the slopes of forming waves, lurching forward

107

as they passed, sinking into their troughs until lifted again by following waves, the thunder of the surf masking all other sounds.

'Now,' shouted Wessels. 'Hold on tight – get ready to jump.' The curving wave lifted the hull high, hurled it forward and down into the maelstrom, the waves breaking around them in a roaring mass of foam. Clinging to the lifeline they held on grimly as the hull crashed on to the reef, the inverted superstructure absorbing the shock as it splintered, the forces released by the broken wave tugging at them. Well before the next wave reached them Wessels shouted, 'Jump, man!'

With the remains of *Sunfish* stranded on the reef they let go of the lifeline, jumped into the lagoon and began swimming through lace-like patterns of foam towards the beach. Though weakened by exposure, Wessels swam steadily ahead until he turned to see how the other man was getting on. Pienaar, an indifferent swimmer and encumbered by the bulky life-jacket, was making poor progress so Wessels went back and helped the gasping, struggling man. With Pienaar ashore at last, Wessels struggled to his feet and stood for the first time since the capsize, flexing his legs before walking uncertainly up the beach to lie down in the shade of palm trees.

For several minutes Pienaar remained on his hands and knees at the water's edge; to Wessels, the crouching man was an incongruous sight, the orange life-jacket suggesting a saddled horse waiting for its rider.

When Pienaar at last joined him Wessels said, 'We must thank God, Piet. He heard our prayers.'

'*Ja*, that's true, I guess.' Pienaar's husky croak had in it a note of penitence. Breathing heavily, he took off the life-jacket and stretched out on the sand near Wessels. But he made no effort to join him in prayer.

THIRTEEN

For several hours they lay on the beach resting in the shade and it was not until the sun had passed its meridian that Wessels said, 'Come on. Piet. We must look around this place.'

'You go,' groaned Pienaar. 'I'm clapped out. Must have water.'

'*Ja*. Me too.' Wessels stood up. 'But we won't find it on the beach. Come on, man, there's no future in lying here.'

Pienaar got to his feet, groaning and complaining, and they made their way over the white sand-dunes which fronted the beach and began to explore the land on the far side.

As far as they could see the country appeared to consist of rolling sandhills covered with veld grass, thornbushes and mopani trees, their leaves tired shades of green, yellow and brown. Barefooted, they had to tread carefully to avoid the thorny litter which abounded – the droppings of countless seasons. In places the unpromising landscape was relieved by oases of palms and larger trees, their leaves green in spite of the drought. But the oases, fed by underground streams from the marshlands of the interior, were without the surface water so much needed by the two men.

To Wessels, brought up in the Transvaal Lowveld, much was familiar and before long he had found a wild fig and near it a bird-plum tree. They ate greedily of the fruit they could reach and, where it had not rotted, that on the ground.

Used to such creatures, the two South Africans ignored a troop of baboons in a nearby tree despite barks and screeches of anger and alarm. For the survivors the fruit was not only food but desperately needed liquid, from which baboons were certainly not going to keep them.

'Don't eat a lot, or too fast, Piet,' cautioned Wessels, a wild plum in his fingers. 'Not good on an empty stomach.'

Pienaar's bloodshot eyes fixed on the younger man in an aggressive stare. 'Look, I'm not a kid,' he growled. 'You don't have to tell me how to eat.' An argument developed, became acrimonious and led to a sullen silence, broken only by the buzz of sandflies which constantly attacked them.

Their thirsts and appetites partially satisfied, but their physical resources still depleted, they walked back slowly the way they'd come. Crossing the sand-dunes once again they reached the beach and made for the shade of the palms where they slept until the sun was low. Waking refreshed, they took stock of their situation. The tide was out and looking across the lagoon to where the hull had struck they saw that the upturned boat had moved across the reef; its back now broken, one half drooped into the lagoon, the other slewed round to face the beach. While they watched a sea broke over it and when the foam and spray had subsided they saw that what was left of *Sunfish* had moved once again.

Some distance along the beach a buttress of rocks ran down from the sand-dunes towards the sea; in it, well above high-water mark, they found a small, sandy-bottomed cleft. 'This,' said Wessels, 'is where we sleep tonight. But first we make a *boma*.'

Pienaar complained that he was exhausted but Wessels insisted so they went back over the dunes and, with hands and sheath-knives, gathered the branches to make a thornbush *boma* across the entrance to the rock cleft. Its purpose was to keep out wild animals, though they'd seen nothing more than the baboons, some warthogs, monkeys and a *klip-springer* – a small antelope – during their explorations.

Before attempting to sleep that night they sat on a rock and discussed plans for the following day. Wessels suggested going south along the beach. 'We must be some-where between Pomene and the light at Ponta Chambure,' he said. 'We never got in sight of that light, so I reckon we're at least fifteen kilometres south of it. No good going there. It's automatic, not manned.'

Pienaar yawned wearily. 'How far south to Pomene?'

'At a guess – about fifty to sixty Ks.'

Pienaar didn't know the coast and couldn't argue. The decision as to which way to go was, however, clinched when Wessels stressed that north was more likely to be guerrilla country than south, and that the nearest town of any sort in the north was Vilanculos, a trek of more than a hundred kilometres. On one point there was no choice: their lack of shoes meant that they would have to keep to the beach on the trek to the south.

'We'll have a rest tonight, eat more fruit tomorrow,' said Wessels. 'We'll feel okay by then.'

'Pity we haven't got matches,' said Pienaar. 'Good to have a fire.'

'What for?'

'Keep lion and leopard away.'

'And attract guerrillas.' Wessels shook his head. 'Not a good idea.'

'You say that about anything I suggest, don't you?'

Wessels ignored the complaint. 'Lion and leopard won't come down close to the sea. The big herds of game are further inland. That's where they'll be.'

Captain Le Roux, conscientious as ever, was working late in the Johannesburg office when a telex came in from Maputo via the Department of Foreign Affairs in Pretoria. Before he'd finished deciphering it he decided he'd have to

111

inform the Brigadier. Since the Brigadier disliked being bothered at home with matters which could wait for the morning Le Roux often found it difficult to decide what could wait and what couldn't. His expression of concentrated anxiety reflected the recurring dilemma as he keyed the ex-directory number and switched on the scrambler.

The Brigadier's cold, 'Yes, Le Roux, what is it?' set the younger man's nerves jangling.

'Telex, sir. From Foreign Affairs, Pretoria, reporting Embassy message from Maputo. Begins – *Have conveyed to the Mozambique Government offer of South African Air Force assistance in search for Charter Couriers missing Cessna. The Mozambique Defence Minister has expressed his Government's thanks but states that such assistance is not regarded as necessary. Two of their military aircraft have during the last thirty-six hours carried out an intensive search along the Cessna's route but with negative results. He says that the pilot's flight plan filed at Mutare airport before departure suggests the strong probability that the Cessna came down in the sea.* Message ends.'

There was silence at the other end of the line.

'You there, sir?' enquired Le Roux anxiously.

'Yes.'

Le Roux bore the silence for some time longer before asking, 'Is there anything else, sir?'

The incisive, 'No,' was followed by a mechanical click as the Brigadier rang off.

Trudi's first night alone in the Cessna was a troubled one, a confusing mixture of dreams, realities, fantasies and disturbing thoughts. She had put off getting into the cabin as long as she could, but as always in the Tropics darkness came soon after sunset, and knowing she could no longer delay she climbed in, pulling the big branch of thornbush – the *boma*'s door – into the gap through which she had come. The heat was humid, stifling, but there was little she could do about it other than take off her shoes and loosen her shirt and slacks. Fortunately the broken front of the cabin ensured fresh air, and when she'd fully reclined the padded seats at the back they made a reasonably comfortable bed. Apart from her sore ankle and the incessant buzzing and biting of mosquitoes her troubles were more mental than physical.

Mostly she worried about JJ. Would he be strong enough to get through to Cheline, or even the main road? Should she have let him go in that condition? In a sense the question answered itself, no. But when she'd raised it he had made it clear that he was determined to go. She couldn't have stopped him had she tried. He was a strong-willed, determined man in spite of his geniality and kindness. She thought of the teddy bear for Clara – *Just something I saw*. That, she thought, was typical of the man.

More than ever she was convinced that Nielsen's suspicions about JJ were groundless. That she had deceived JJ, abused his kindness, she found deeply worrying until professionalism reminded her that judgement had to be objective, unencumbered by personal considerations. Subject to that, however, she hoped and believed that events would prove her to be right.

And of course she worried very much about herself. Would JJ succeed in reaching Cheline and in bringing back rescuers, or would something awful happen to him like a chance encounter with trigger-happy Africans? His mission was an especially dangerous one, wandering through the night in that war-torn part of Mozambique where men were more fearsome predators than animals.

If he didn't get back with help what would happen to her? She'd have to leave the Cessna and make down the coast. If so, for her, travelling alone in strange, wild country, the chances of survival couldn't amount to much.

And so the night wore on with strange noises in the

bush, the cries of jackals, the howls of hyenas and, to compound her fears, the frightening death screams of a baboon somewhere deep in the bush. Sometimes she would sit up, tense, rigid, feeling in the darkness for the Mauser and the hatchet, and the torch she dare not use because each unexplained sound conjured in her mind pictures of murderous black faces moving towards the Cessna with knives and Kalashnikovs at the ready.

Then common sense would tell her that the noise was probably a warthog or an impala or something equally harmless, and she would remember JJ's remark that the smell of petrol would mask human scent and she'd be safe in the Cessna. That recollection, however, triggered another fear: would not the smell of petrol attract prowling guerrillas?

It was a dreadful night, her emotions in turmoil, and she was thankful when the first glimmer of light showed on the eastern side of the clearing. Before long she was able to step down from the cabin, Mauser in hand, and satisfy the needs of nature. To her surprise the twisted ankle was less painful.

As daylight took over and shafts of sunlight played on the clearing her spirits rose, courage returned and with the Mauser tucked in the waistband of her slacks she confronted the day. Nothing at that moment seemed more imperative than the need to wash, to clean herself. In the absence of soap she did what she could with a handkerchief soaked in water, followed by cleansing cream and perfume from her shoulder-bag. She felt better after that though the sight of her scratched and bruised face in the vanity mirror made her want to cry. There was a change of clothing in the travel bag in the luggage-locker, but she decided against using it then. Her morning toilet was completed by restrapping the ankle with the old bandage; the swelling was less than it had been and for that she was thankful.

114

Like her meal the evening before, breakfast consisted of fruit from the marula tree, and water. Remembering JJ's advice she had resisted the temptation to break into the iron rations.

FOURTEEN

Nielsen came into the office, slumped into a chair, tilted his safari hat on to the back of his head, delved in his pockets and came out with the crumpled packet. Not until the American had lit the Camel and blown smoke at the ceiling did Luena look up from his desk. 'Any news of the Cessna?' he asked.

Nielsen shook his head. 'Nope. None. Andrada says their aircraft searched the route all day Thursday and Friday. According to Johnson's flight plan the chances are that he came down in the sea. In that case . . .' Nielsen spread his hands in a gesture of hopelessness.

Luena left the desk, went to the window. 'Poor Trudi,' he said.

'You wanted that assignment, son. Guess you're right glad you didn't get it.'

Luena turned, faced Nielsen. 'That's a rotten thing to say! She's probably dead and you're asking me to say I'm glad it's her and not me.'

'Okay, okay, son.' Nielsen raised a hand in a defensive gesture. 'Not what I meant. I'm as cut up about that as you are. She had, she has, the makings of a first class agent. On top of that she's a real nice girl. But grief's not our business. Unless the Cessna's found we've lost the evidence. Know what that means?'

'I've a fair idea.' Luena, looking bored, shrugged. 'With Johnson gone how do we sus out the Johannesburg end?'

'That's right. It's back to square one. Mauritius, with Gottwald and Kahn. They'll be faced with setting up the

116

chain again. That's going to take time, son, plenty time. Finding a replacement for Johnson won't be easy. A guy who's willing to play ball, to take the risks, who owns a courier company *and* flies his own aircraft. Where do they find that again? Yeh, it's a goddam disaster, all right. For them and for us. For us it's a double one. The evidence and the linkman gone.'

'Oh, stuff the evidence. There'll be plenty more in time.' Luena pushed his chair aside, stood up, stared accusingly at Nielsen. 'But nothing will bring Trudi back. She'd be here now if you hadn't accepted Jake Motlani's bullshit as proof of Johnson's guilt. I'm inclined to support her belief that he's not involved.'

With slow, unhurried motions Nielsen took another Camel from the crumpled packet. 'I guess you're upset, son, so I won't react the way I should. But if you reckon to do any good in this job you have to be objective. That means not letting your emotions influence your judgement.'

Luena snorted. 'You're a fine one to be saying that.' He made for the door.

Nielsen said, 'Where are you going?'

'Into God's fresh air. We could do with some around here.' The young African stalked out of the office, slamming the door behind him.

I guess he fancies her, thought Nielsen. Can't blame him.

Friday afternoon found Trudi facing a difficult decision. The Cessna had crashed on Wednesday and JJ had set out for Cheline the next day. If he were not back by Saturday morning he would have been gone for over thirty-six hours. In that event there was little to be said for waiting any longer at the crash site, particularly now that finding water was necessary for survival. That morning she had found no more than a small puddle in the windcheater. She supposed excessive heat and evaporation were responsible.

117

Unless it rained the chance of replenishing supplies was nil; the stark truth was that she would have to reach the river soon or die of thirst.

Her plan was to make for the coast and, once there, travel south along the beach. JJ had said the sea was about fifteen kilometres due east. When they were discussing the fresh water problem he had pointed to a small river on the flying map; it was, he said, about twenty kilometres south-south-east of the crash site.

She had considered following him to Cheline, but decided that was too dangerous. She doubted her ability to find her way across country through the arid bush and woodland, and if he had encountered problems in Cheline she certainly would. So really, she told herself, there was no practical option but to make for the coast. Once she had reached it she would walk south along the beach until she came to the river mouth. After a night there she would continue down the beach to Pomene where there'd be Africans, food and water; she prayed that they would be friendly Africans. JJ had said there was less likelihood of running into guerrilla gangs in the south than in the north. In any event there was nowhere else she could go that offered a better prospect for rescue. She would, she resolved, begin her journey at ten o'clock the next morning.

She was adjusting to the strange noises of the bush, and the second night, alone in the Cessna, had not been as nerve-racking as the first. In fact she had fallen into a deep sleep in the early hours of that morning to be awakened hours later by shafts of sunlight streaming into the cabin.

Saturday morning came and Trudi, still stiff from her bruises, moved aside the thornbush in the *boma* and stepped down on to the ground. At the windcheater where she'd gone to wet a handkerchief she found there was little more than half a tumbler of water left. The emergency container still had about a tumbler of water in it; she resolved to conserve that and to satisfy her immediate thirst with marula plums. When she reached the big tree, however, there was nothing but rotted fruit on the ground. She supposed the monkeys had cleared the tree of ripe fruit.

The cloudless sky promised another scorching day. It was evident that to survive she would have to get to the river soon. The earlier she went the better her chances of reaching it before dark, so she decided not to wait until ten o'clock. The decision made, she began preparations for the journey, putting together the few things she would take: the Mauser, the hatchet, the iron rations and, from her suitcase, a spare shirt and knickers. These she put into her shoulder-bag, together with her passport and other things. The hatchet was a problem but she took the belt from her spare slacks, put it on, and tucked the hatchet handle into it.

She wrote a brief note on a page of her diary: *Water finished. Left today, Saturday, for the coast. Intend to walk south along the beach to rivermouth then on towards Pomene.* When she'd signed and dated it she put it on a back seat in the Cessna. She was worried, apprehensive, even sad about going because it meant leaving the familiar for the unknown; but she had to go.

Before leaving the crash site she used the last of the bottle of lotion to clean her face; afterwards she rinsed the plastic bottle and filled it from the emergency container then swallowed what was left in the container.

The coast was due east. The sun which she had for three days seen rising over the bush told her roughly where that was, so shortly after seven-thirty that morning she set off on her journey, hoping to make the coast somewhere north of the river. She had left the clearing and gone down a game-path when she heard the faint sound of an aircraft somewhere to the west. She hurried back into the clearing and anxiously searched the western sky where she could see nothing other than vultures circling high over distant undulations of bush and woodland.

The sound of aircraft engines soon faded. Sad and dispirited, she went back to the game-path and recommenced her journey.

Because she was tall she wore flat heels and for that she was thankful. High heels would have made the going difficult and bare feet would soon have become casualties to thorns and sharp stones. The ankle which she had strapped again that morning felt better and she was able to make her way through the bush at a fair pace, following game-paths where they led in the right direction and leaving them when they didn't to undertake what JJ had called bush-whacking. At times there were sudden, frightening alarms, mostly caused by game she had disturbed. Once she was about to cross a clearing when she saw a lion and lioness on the far side lying under a tree with their cubs; though she was downwind from them she made a wide detour. Later, she came upon a herd of wildebeest motionless in the shade; there were zebra among them, their dazzling hides marvellous camouflage against the background of dry thorn and scrub. Several times she saw elephant droppings among broken mopani trees but the droppings were old and she realised the elephants must have been there many weeks before.

Quite soon after leaving the Cessna she had taken the hatchet from her belt and carried it in her right hand. Once or twice she had used it to hack a way through undergrowth which overhung game-paths but mostly she held it for the sense of security it gave her. How she proposed to use it if attacked by a wild animal was something she had not worked out.

Her mind during this long trek was a miscellany of thoughts. What lay ahead? How and where would she spend the night? What had happened to JJ? What would he think if he got back to the Cessna and found her gone? She thought, too, about Nielsen and Jake Motlani and Titus Luena – the latter the new boy and future boss. She wondered if she'd ever get back to Harare and what her next assignment might be if she did. She loved her work. It was exciting and unusual; certainly unusual, she thought, if the last few days meant anything.

The heat hung over the bush like a fiery pall, tangible and suffocating, the sea breeze from the east, warmed by its short passage overland, giving little if any relief. The character of the country was changing as she drew nearer the coast, the hard earth inland giving way to sandy hillocks covered with veldgrass and thornbush, the few trees leaner, more twisted than before. Swept by winds and plagued by drought, the coastal strip was even more arid than the interior.

At times she stopped to rest but fearful that she might not reach the river before dark she pushed on, face, body and clothing wet with sweat. Remembering childhood experiences she sucked a pebble to fend off thirst during the long intervals between sipping water from the plastic bottle which, because it tasted of cleansing lotion, she fought against using too often.

In mid-afternoon, beyond the sandhills, a stretch of blue water glinting in the sunlight showed up in the distance. She leant against the trunk of a palm tree, and tears of relief rolled down her cheeks. So the sea was there, it wasn't a mirage, it really was there. Deep blue sea. She began to hum an improvised tune, its lyric a jubilant repetition: 'So Trudi's found the sea, the deep blue sea.' When at last she got to the beach she bathed her face and feet in a rockpool and felt marvellously refreshed. After a short rest she set off down the beach carrying her shoes, keeping to the wet sand close to the sea. The going under-foot was wonderfully cool and smooth.

Towards sunset she came to the river. It was larger than she had expected with a sandbar across its mouth and a rocky headland reaching into the sea on its far side. A short distance upstream from the sandbar there was a small island, the river flowing past its southern side; the northern side, where she stood, was bounded by a broad strip of wet sand which reflected the coppery shades of the western sky. The high-water mark beneath the bank showed that the tide was out and she realised that when it came in the wet sand would be under water, and the island truly an island, its long dimension conforming to the line of the river. Covered in bush and tall trees, the vegetation lush from river moisture, the little island domi-nated the estuary.

With no doubt in her mind that this was the place to spend the night, she made for a gap in the mangroves which lined the bank and set off across the sandstrip at its narrowest point. Once on the island she put on her shoes and made for the up-river end where the cover was thick-est. The sun had almost set.

FIFTEEN

The two men walked up the corridor together, the tall, fair one making the other look shorter and plumper than usual.

'His mood's not too good,' warned Le Roux as they reached the unnumbered door. '*Stadig oor die klippe* – slowly over the stones,' he said, quoting an old Voortrekker adage. He held a finger to his lips and knocked on the door.

On hearing the Brigadier's '*Kom*,' Le Roux opened the door and they went in. Both men wore plain clothes.

'Captain Kirst, sir,' announced Le Roux.

The Brigadier looked up from his desk. 'Take a seat, Kirst.' He gestured Le Roux to a chair.

Leaning forward, his elbows on the desk, clasped hands under his chin, he stared at Kirst in silence for a few moments. 'I asked Pretoria to send for you because I wanted to hear your report first hand. Now tell me what happened.'

The fair man met the challenge of the cold grey eyes with a neutral smile. He was not in the Brigadier's area of jurisdiction, the Witwatersrand, but he was well aware of his reputation.

'We put a tail on Kahn as soon as he arrived at the airport. That – '

'Who was the tail?' interrupted the Brigadier.

'Silas Bulage.'

'Still operating as a taxi driver?'

Kirst nodded. 'It's great cover.'

'Yes. And so?'

'Bulage tailed Kahn's taxi to where it stopped, half a

123

block short of the hotel. He parked near it, saw Kahn get out, say something to the driver, then walk on towards the hotel. He did not pay the driver so Bulage assumed he had told him to wait.'

The Brigadier rose from his chair, began pacing, his head bent forward. 'What then?' he demanded.

'Sonia reported that at noon Kahn came through the main entrance into the foyer. He walked across to the far end and disappeared through the doors into the men's room. He was carrying a black briefcase. Three minutes later he came out of the men's room, still carrying the briefcase, crossed the foyer once more and went out through the main entrance.'

The Brigadier's eyes glistened through steel-rimmed spectacles. 'So the handover took place in the men's room?'

Kirst shook his head. 'No, sir. Sonia had seen Johnson go upstairs some minutes before noon. She'd put a phone call through to him in his room while Kahn was in the men's room. That call continued until after Kahn had left the hotel.'

The Brigadier stopped by a window, turned abruptly. 'Who was talking to Johnson on the phone?'

'McLeod, chief mechanic at the airport. They had been working on the Cessna's fuel system.'

'Your telex said the handover was confirmed. So when *did* Kahn pass the documents to Johnson?'

'At no stage. It was a drop.'

The Brigadier, silent, began pacing again.

'May I continue, sir?' Kirst smiled, calm and genial as ever.

Le Roux, watching anxiously, envied Kirst; he was evidently a man not easily ruffled.

'Yes, of course. Go on.' The Brigadier smoothed his shining grey hair with a brush-like stroke of the hand.

'Bulage saw Kahn leave the hotel and go down the street towards the waiting taxi,' continued Kirst. 'Before Kahn reached it he went in between two parked cars, opened

124

the boot of one, took something from the briefcase and placed it in the boot. Bulage could not be certain what it was. He was on the other side of the street. He saw Kahn close and lock the boot before walking to the taxi. He was still carrying the black briefcase.'

'So he had a key,' said the Brigadier.

Kirst nodded. 'Correct. He had a key.'

'And the car? Tell me about that.'

'A VW Scirocco. Registered in the name of Addison Travel Consultants. Johnson's agents.'

'Are they involved?'

'There is no evidence to suggest that.'

'Yes. And so?' Once again the Brigadier sounded impatient.

Unperturbed, Kirst went on with his story. 'Kahn got into the taxi and it moved off. Bulage tailed it to the airport where Kahn checked in for the one-thirty flight to Lusaka.'

'The handover, drop, whatever you like to call it. You still haven't clarified that.' The Brigadier's mouth shut in a tight line.

Kirst said, 'My apologies, sir. I thought I'd made it clear.'

Le Roux shivered involuntarily. Was Kirst implying in a roundabout way that what had happened should have been obvious to the Brigadier?

'You certainly did not,' said the Brigadier sharply. 'Please do so now.'

'Yes, of course.' Kirst managed an apologetic smile, cleared his throat. 'Bulage saw Kahn put the parcel, envelope, whatever – '

'The documents,' corrected the Brigadier stiffly. 'Operational orders from ANC Headquarters, Lusaka, for the ANC command structure on the Witwatersrand.'

'As you say, sir.' Kirst paused, looked thoughtful. 'When Bulage had finished tailing Kahn he phoned Sonia at the hotel, asked her if Johnson had anything to do with the Scirocco. She said, yes, he had. Addison Travel sometimes lent him the car when he was in Mutare. She added that he had just left the hotel in the Scirocco on his way to the airport to see McLeod. She said he had taken his pilotcase with him. Some time on that journey he could have parked the Scirocco and transferred the documents from the boot to the pilotcase.'

The Brigadier ran the tip of a little finger along his lips. 'So Kahn used the boot for the drop. I get that. But why does he have to go into the men's room at the hotel before making it?'

Kirst smiled. 'It was presumably a pre-arranged signal. Johnson's room overlooked the hotel entrance. He goes up to the room shortly before noon, stations himself at the window. Kahn, coming up the steps to the main entrance at noon, sees him there. Johnson's presence at the window indicates that the drop can go ahead. Kahn then goes into the hotel, visits the Men's room and leaves a few minutes later. That is his signal to Johnson that he is about to go ahead with the drop.'

The Brigadier considered the point before saying, 'Yes, that makes sense. If there's a snag on Johnson's side he doesn't show himself at the window at noon, if it's on Kahn's side he doesn't go into the hotel. No visible contact between the two men. Variation on an old theme. Simple but effective.'

The Brigadier sat down at his desk, leant back in the swing chair, clasped his hands behind his head, and directed a penetrating stare at the man opposite. 'Tell me about the woman.'

Kirst told him she was from Johannesburg originally, the daughter of a German immigrant family. She had apparently come to Zimbabwe in the hope of seeing her brother, a contract engineer working in the Beira Corridor. In Johannesburg, where she was working for a firm of computer consultants, she had met an American, Greg Nielsen, a US business machines representative. It turned out to be an opportune meeting because she had at about that time decided to go up to Harare to see her brother.

'Nielsen gave her a lift there,' said Kirst. 'Harare was his base. He was involved in establishing some sort of new unit for the Department of Agriculture. Nobody seems to know what its function is. Anyway, she got a temporary job in it thanks to his pull. Some time later she told him she wanted a few days' leave to go down to Mutare to see her brother.' Kirst paused. 'Nielsen offered her a lift, said he was due to go down there on business. According to Sonia they spent a couple of nights together in the hotel – separate rooms.' Kirst's eyebrows lifted and he smiled briefly. 'But you know how it is. They had a row and Nielsen cleared out at the crack of dawn a couple of mornings later. She told Sonia that he'd reneged on his promise to pay her bill. That apparently took more or less the last of her cash. Next day Johnson flew in from Maputo and they met in the hotel. She must have told him she was broke and had to get back to Johannesburg. He took her out to dinner at Costa's that night and the next. Sonia says it was obvious that they fancied each other. At Mutare airport Johnson presented a ticket for her issued by Addison Travel, the fare debited to Charter Couriers RSA in Johannesburg – his own company. She had told Sonia that it was a free ride.'

One of the three telephones on the Brigadier's desk rang discreetly. A red light pulsed on the centre unit. He picked it up. 'Yes,' he snapped, frowning as he listened, his eyes on the men opposite. With a curt 'No' he put the phone down.

'Still no news of the *Sunfish*,' he said. 'Now, Kirst, tell me, d'you think the woman was in any way involved in Johnson's activities?' The Brigadier watched the fair man closely.

Kirst shook his head. 'There is no evidence to suggest this. Sonia says Braun was a quiet, rather dignified young woman, a bit simple about the ways of men. Sonia is satisfied that she had never met Johnson before. It was a chance encounter. According to Sonia, it was not the first time he had given a lift to a lady in trouble. He's very partial to a pretty face.'

The Brigadier shrugged. 'Who isn't?'

A faint smile crossed Kirst's face.

Watching, listening intently, Le Roux felt that men as handsome as Kirst, and armed with his smile, probably knew a good deal more about women than the Brigadier, who at that moment, and quite suddenly, rose to his feet. 'Well, that'll do, Captain. You've been very helpful. Le Roux will give you lunch and I've no doubt ask more questions.'

They shook hands, Kirst saying, 'I'm sorry you had to cancel *Doodslaan*, sir. It's too bad the way the unpredictables can foul up the best intelligence work.'

'Quite so. But we'll get these people in the end, Kirst. This time the luck was on their side. Next time it can be on ours. We may have lost this round but we'll win the fight.' The Brigadier's mouth set in its customary tight line. Kirst and Le Roux were moving towards the door when he said, 'Convey my congratulations to Sonia and Bulage. They did a first class job. Not their fault that things went wrong.'

'I'll do that, sir,' replied Kirst.

Trudi worked fast to prepare for her first night on what she already thought of as River Island.

A brief inspection of the upstream end had revealed a small, reed-free clearing on the bank of the river. There she knelt to scoop up handfuls of water. It looked clear and tasted much like the rainwater she had been drinking. She swallowed several handfuls, splashed her face with it and bathed her feet.

Next came the problem of a *boma*. She cut branches from thornbushes and dragged them across to a site near a large tree which she felt could be climbed as a last resort to escape from unspecified dangers. She was very tired and

128

it took time and energy to make the *boma*, a circular hedge almost as tall as she was enclosing a space wide enough to lie down in, its strong white thorns a formidable barrier against prowling animals.

When it was really dark she went into the *boma*, pulled the 'gate' of thornbushes into the gap behind her, put the Mauser, the hatchet and torch on one side, the shoulder-bag on the other, took off her shoes and lay down on a bed of soft leaves. It wasn't as comfortable as the Cessna's cabin but she felt it was probably safer.

Worn out by her long trek, her physical and emotional resources depleted, she indulged in the luxury of a weep. For some time after that she lay watching the star-filled southern sky, listening to the noises of the bush, among them now the croaking of frogs, and thinking of many things: Would she ever reach Pomene? What would she find there? How long should she stay on the island? For how long could she exist on a fruit diet? Was Greg Nielsen organising a search for the Cessna and would it be found? And of course she thought about JJ and what he would do when and if he found her note.

Despite the humid, stifling night it was not long before she had fallen into deep sleep.

High-pitched shrieks woke her at sunrise. Alarmed, she looked over the top of the *boma* to see that they came from a big tree near the river's edge where monkeys were leaping, swinging and screeching. She could not be sure, but she imagined the tree had fruit and that was what the quarrelling was about.

She got to her feet, stretched her limbs, put on shoes, stuck the Mauser in her belt and left the *boma*, hatchet in hand. Down at the river she found that it was no longer flowing and the water when she tasted it was salty. She panicked until it occurred to her that the tide must have turned. Though the water was no longer drinkable, she washed her face and cleaned her teeth with it, finishing the elementary toilet with an inspection of her face in the vanity mirror. She was still horrified by what she saw: cuts and bruises, mosquito bites, deep sunburn and unkempt, knotted hair which she set about with a comb but without much success. Deciding that her appearance was low in the order of priorities she gave up and made for the tree where the monkeys continued their noisy quarrels. She shouted and waved at them and when they had scurried away, jumping from branch to branch and, with great leaps, on to neighbouring trees, she sampled some of the less rotted fruit which lay on the ground. The tree was big and gracefully shaped, but her recently acquired knowledge told her it was not a marula. The fruit was small and rather flat, with a hard kernel covered in a dark fleshy substance. She tasted it and found the flavour to be bitter sweet but refreshing. Remembering JJ's advice that anything monkeys fed on was safe for humans, she ate some of the fruit.

On the way back to the *boma* she became aware of the acrid odour of her body, the product of days spent in the same sweat-soaked clothing. She was tempted to change into her spare shirt and knickers but decided she would do that later in the day after she had had a really thorough body wash, something she promised herself once she had explored the island. That, she felt, was really the top priority.

By noon she had covered the island from end to end, found monkeys eating in other trees, including a marula, and a creeper which from its flowers and fruit she took to be a wild granadilla. Apart from the monkeys, a porcupine, a jackal and many birds, some like the bee-eaters and king-fishers brilliantly coloured, there seemed to be no other life on the island. On one occasion, startled by its haunting cry, she had looked up to see a fish eagle perched high in the branches of a dead tree, its black and white plumage glistening in the sunlight. On the northern bank, beyond the reeds, she caught glimpses of warthogs moving through the long grass, their antenna-like tails erect; but otherwise that part of the bush seemed curiously empty notwithstanding the alarming sounds which came from it at night.

At midday the river was once again flowing to seaward and she knew that high water must have occurred some time during the morning; she tried to work out when but it was too complicated and she gave up. More importantly for her, the river water was once more drinkable and she was able to satisfy her thirst. To guard against future emergencies she refilled the plastic bottle.

She had learnt from her explorations that the island was less than a kilometre long and rather more than two hundred metres wide; it was a tongue of land lying in the mouth of the estuary, the shallow valley through which the river flowed stretching far inland until it was lost in the heat haze.

Later that day she made an exciting discovery; exploring the river mouth at low tide she saw little crabs scuttling about on the sandbar, and mussels on the exposed rocks. She hacked them off with the hatchet, broke them open, tasted the flesh and found it good. Then she sampled the crabs and found them acceptable though they were difficult to catch.

In the afternoon she took off her clothes and bathed in the shallows at the island's upstream end, relishing the luxury of cooling and cleaning her body. At one stage noise and movement in the reeds on the opposite bank startled her and she retreated with her clothes to the shade of a large tree some distance from the water. But though the reeds had shaken violently for a few moments nothing appeared and she thought it was probably the warthogs.

Like most white South Africans she had been to the

Kruger Park and knew many of the animal sounds; elephant, lion, jackal and hyena among them. But in the dense bush around the island the noises seemed closer and louder than in the Kruger Park where she had had the security of watching game from a car, and sleeping at night in palisaded rest-camps. That she was alone and without any of those protective things magnified her fears, as did the possibility that armed Africans might appear at any moment.

These disquieting thoughts, on top of the frights she had just had, set off a wild train of thought, an appalling picture building in her mind of the fate which probably awaited her. She was close to tears when she decided she must pull herself together. Pomene was about thirty kilometres away: being emotional was not going to get her there any quicker. After this stiffening of resolve she rinsed the clothes she had been wearing for days and spread them over a thornbush to dry. Changed into clean clothes she felt a lot better. Before bathing that afternoon she had taken the strapping from her ankle. It now seemed back to normal.

SIXTEEN

After a supper of shellfish and fruit collected during the afternoon, she went to the *boma*, rearranged the bed of leaves and generally prepared for the night. For some time she lay thinking about JJ, wondering as always where he was and how he was. She'd not known him for long but that seemed to make little difference to her feelings about him. He was a really nice man, kind and brave, and she prayed that he was safe and that they would meet again. Not that there could be anything more than friendship between them – or could there? She remembered the offer to 'tuck her in' after the first night at Costa's. It had been repeated the next night but again she had said no and he had accepted the decision with good grace and they'd changed the subject.

She knew very little about him other than that he was tough, a man's man, direct and unaffected. In the course of conversation he had said he was married, with three children – two teenage boys and a much younger daughter. He had scarcely mentioned his wife, Kathleen, other than to say that she worried a lot.

'About what?' she had asked him.

'Everything, the kids, apartheid, the future of Southern Africa, her parents, the state of the world.' With a laugh he had added, 'And me.'

'You. Why?' As she asked the question she thought she knew the answer – other women. He was an attractive man and apparently well-heeled.

He had shrugged. 'She can't understand why I fly the

company's aeroplanes when I own the company. Leave it to your pilots, she says, it's not necessary for you to do it. She worries that I don't spend more time at home with her and the children.'

'Well, there's nothing wrong with that, surely?'

'It's no way as simple as that.' He had frowned. 'I see a fair amount of her and the kids and of course they mean a lot to me. But what she can't understand is that I love flying, it's my life. Apart from which it's important that I'm in regular personal touch with officials in Maputo and Zimbabwe – important for my contracts with their governments. D'you see?'

Not only did she see, but she felt once again that he was a good man; misunderstood, perhaps, by his wife, but certainly by Greg Nielsen, who had made up his mind about him without even knowing him and upon the flimsiest of circumstantial evidence provided by Jake Motlani.

She thought about the men in her own life and acknowledged that they were not a very inspiring lot: a number of teenage attachments and then the long, slowly winding-down affair with Francis, ending with her admission of defeat after years of his constantly repeated, *But Trudi, I just can't leave her and the children.*

There had since been a few relationships of little importance; Greg had been attentive and she liked him, but he had a wife and children waiting for him in the States; it seemed that all the worthwhile men had wives and children, and she was not looking for another second-fiddle relationship. No, it wasn't really much of a love life to look back on. So, what of the future?

Yes, what of it? Like tomorrow and the next day and the day after that. These were the things she had to concern herself with now, not recollections of past relationships with men.

Thinking about the days ahead, she wondered when to resume her journey south. There was no point in staying

134

on the island any longer than necessary, secure though it might be. After some thought she decided to spend two more days there; she was feeling stronger than at any other time since the crash but still suffering from bruises and still worried that her ankle might go again. With two more days of food and rest she felt she would be in good shape for the long walk to Pomene. Since it was unlikely that she could cover the distance in one day in that heat and under those conditions, a night would have to be spent somewhere along the beach; but that was a problem to be dealt with when it arose.

She tried to remember what day it was and came to the conclusion it must be Sunday. So she would set off down the coast again on Wednesday, a week since she and JJ had left Mutare. And what a week it had been. Expectations of rescue had slowly given way to despair, for it was apparent that they had crashed in a remote part of Mozambique, one from which drought and war had driven away the local people.

Her last thought before falling asleep was the recurring one about rescue. Surely there should be planes looking for the Cessna? Yet in all the time since the crash she had seen only one, and that far away and flying high. On several occasions she had heard the distant sound of aircraft but they had always remained out of sight.

Despite their intention that one should stay awake while the other slept, both Wessels and Pienaar had drifted into a sleep which lasted until after sunrise, notwithstanding sandflies and mosquitoes. Since real sleep had not been possible during the sixty or so hours they had clung to *Sunfish's* waterlogged hull, this was not surprising.

With little more than grunts of recognition on waking, they left the *boma* and made for the water's edge for a soapless wash. It was followed by a meal of wild fruit. While this helped to some extent, fresh water was still badly needed for their dehydrated bodies and blistered, ulcerated mouths.

During the night seas had washed the remains of the hull off the reef, and at low tide that morning Wessels swam out to examine the wreckage scattered on the sandy bottom inside the reef. Near Federico's body, entombed in the broken wheelhouse, he found a canvas fishing bag with handlines, hooks and lures. The rods and reels and other big-game tackle were nowhere to be seen.

'Must have fallen into the sea with the rest of the gear when we capsized,' he told Pienaar, adding that the bag and fishing gear would be useful for their journey.

Wessels' knowledge of the coast and their lack of shoes had determined that they head south, keeping to the beach where bare feet were not a handicap. Before leaving they had collected more wild fruit and put it in the fishing bag. When Pienaar complained that too much fruit would be bad for his diarrhoea Wessels shook his head. 'Not so, Piet. The Shangaans in the Lowveld eat marula fruit to cure diarrhoea. You've got the right medicine.'

Shaking his head Pienaar had glared unbelievingly at the younger man but he said nothing.

At about nine o'clock that morning they began their journey. Walking on firm wet sand, close to the lapping surf, made for easy going but at times there were rock outcrops and clusters of boulders to block their way along the beach; then, bare-footed, they would climb the rocks or tread gingerly round their landward flanks to regain the beach. In many places the high-water mark was rimed with fuel oil, dark and sticky, and sometimes difficult to avoid. 'Tankers outward bound for the Gulf cleaning their tanks the cheap way. Polluting the sea and the beaches. The ugly face of capitalism,' said Wessels censoriously.

The day grew older and the sun beat down with unremitting ferocity as they trudged grimly southwards, their tattered shirts and shorts saturated with sweat, their bearded faces gaunt, their skin where it showed deeply burned and in places, like Pienaar's bald head, blistered.

Checking with his wristwatch, finding progress disappointingly slow, Wessels estimated that the journey would take the best part of three days allowing for overnight stops. That was if all went well, he stressed to Pienaar who replied almost savagely, 'You talk a lot about Pomene. What the hell d'you expect to find there?'

Wessels said he hoped there would be shelter, drinking water and friendly Africans from the nearby village. That could mean food, he explained, though with the drought and the war most villagers were themselves starving.

Pienaar groaned, 'That's bad, man. We can't just live on wild fruit.'

'We don't have to.' Wessels trudged on, looking straight ahead, avoiding the eyes of the man he was beginning to regard with contempt.

'So what d'you mean?'

'On this journey we can find mussels and other food on the rocks. Also we can fish with bait from the rocks.'

'What about guerrillas?'

'We do our best. No man can do more.'

'Our best – like what?' Pienaar's question was plaintive, highpitched.

'For God's sake, man, how do I know what the circumstances will be?'

'Well, they're armed. So what do we do?'

'Okay. They're armed. So we have to *pas op* – be careful. If they say they're Renamo we tell them we are South Africans. They should know we're on their side. If they're Frelimo we say we're South African tourists. Mozambique badly needs tourists. In both cases we tell them about the fishing trip and what happened. Mention that Charles Scott was boss of our outfit. If they have radio they can check with Maputo.'

'If they don't have radio?'

'Read them a lecture on the Komati Accord,' said Wessels. 'Or the Sermon on the Mount.'

'Being funny, are you?' snarled Pienaar. 'Don't suppose they even heard of that bullshit. They'll be more interested in your wristwatch.'

Ignoring the remark Wessels plodded on in silence, the fishing bag slung over a shoulder, his head bent forward as if dragging an unwilling body.

'I don't want to come across *any* black buggers with guns,' persisted Pienaar. 'I don't trust kaffirs, whatever side they're supposed to be on.'

'Maybe we will, maybe we won't. I don't know. But I reckon Pomene's our best chance. There's a dirt road from there down to Rio das Pedras. When last I heard, Pedras was in Government hands.' Wessels shrugged. 'Anyway, there's no reasonable alternative to what we're doing. Better save your breath for the trek. You'll need it.'

Later that day at low tide they found mussels and husks of redbait in a rockpool. With their knives they prised the mussels from the rocks, cut open the husks of redbait and took out the juicy fibrous flesh, eating it with the urgency of starving men.

'No wonder the fish like redbait.' Pienaar looked up, his stubbled chin dripping with juice.

'It's good,' confirmed Wessels. 'Plenty of liquid.'

They agreed that wild fruit and shellfish would see them through to Pomene. If no food was available there, they would use the fishing tackle.

'Maybe we can make a fire to cook if the kitchen in the old fishing camp has been smashed up,' said Wessels hopefully.

'Lighting it with what?' Pienaar's expression recorded a polemic victory.

Ignoring the question, Wessels put a chunk of redbait into his mouth, chewed at it vigorously.

Progress that first day had been slow, Wessels estimating the distance covered to be barely twenty kilometres. Walking in stifling heat in their debilitated condition was not easy; yet, tired as they were by evening, Wessels insisted on building another *boma*; this time against a sandbank bordering the beach. Following an undisturbed night they started off at dawn next morning. Still weak, but refreshed by food and rest, they managed a more useful pace than the day before and progress was steady.

Towards the end of that afternoon they saw ahead of them a rocky headland reaching out into the sea; a dark, forbidding barrier shutting out the view to the south. As they drew nearer reflections of the sun, low on the western horizon, showed fiery and bright on a strip of water beneath the headland.

Breaking into a shuffle, muttering excitedly, they hurried on until they came to an estuary separated from the sea by a sandbar through a wide rift in which water flowed to the sea. At the estuary's upstream end lay a narrow island, thick with bush and woodland. Its nearside was bounded by a channel of wet sand, the far side by a river, small and shallow as rivers go but the banks showed that it had been considerably larger.

'Thank God,' said Wessels devoutly. 'I didn't know there was a river here. With this drought it has to come from the marshes inland.'

'It's small,' croaked Pienaar. 'But Christ, man, it's water. Real water.'

'*Ja*. You're dead right, Piet. Fresh water,' confirmed Wessels. 'And when the tide comes in that island will be surrounded by water. Come on. Let's go.'

With the eagerness of schoolboys on a field day they made for a break in the reeds and mangroves lining the bank, crossed the stretch of wet sand and clambered up the far bank on to the island.

Before darkness set in they had found a camping place in a clearing at the seaward end of the island. There, having first tasted the river water and found it drinkable, they built a *boma*, ate the last of the shellfish and fruit, and settled down for the night.

Waking early they made for the bank where they had discovered fresh water the night before, only to find that the stream had ceased to flow towards the sea. No longer fresh, the water tasted brackish.

'No good to drink. The tide's coming in.' Wessels pointed to seaward where the spent remnants of breakers foamed in to the estuary. 'The seas are breaking on the sandbar,' he said. 'The tide has covered it.'

'You mean no fresh water?' Pienaar scowled.

'Not until the tide's turned. Then the river flows out to sea again.'

'Oh Christ!' Pienaar shook his head in disgust. 'One bloody problem after another. We spend the nights battling with mosquitoes and dreaming of fresh water. Why the hell did I come on this goddam trip?'

'Because you pestered me to organise it. Said there was nothing you wanted more than to get into big-game fishing.' Wessels glared at Pienaar. 'That's why you're here. You should have stuck to flogging your agricultural machinery, and nice little trips to the Kruger Park.'

'Bullshit! I'll tell you why I'm here.' The livid gash on Pienaar's stubbled cheek, the angry eyes, lent him the aspect of a stage villain. 'We're here because you wouldn't let Charles Scott run for it. You had to be the macho guy who caught the bloody great marlin. That's why we're here. No other reason.' Pienaar's voice trembled as he faced Wessels with clenched fists.

The big man shrugged. 'Calm down, Piet. No point in

losing your temper. You don't impress me. Only making a bloody fool of yourself.'

For a moment it seemed as if Pienaar would strike the younger man, but he must have thought better of it for he turned, stalked across the clearing to a wild fig tree and began kicking aimlessly at the rotten fruit which lay on the ground.

Wessels joined him after a few minutes and a sullen silence ensued. It was not until some time later that a measure of peace was restored and they began to explore the island.

By mid-morning they had covered most of it, only the thickly-wooded upstream end remaining. By then the sun was high, the heat intense, the sandflies active and the tide had turned, the stream once again flowing towards the sea.

They were well into exploring the remaining portion of the island when Pienaar said he wanted a drink and made for a break in the mangroves along the bank. Wessels, close behind, was dealing with a thorn in his foot when he heard Pienaar's warning hiss. '*Kom kyk, Jan.* Come and look, Jan.'

Wessels joined him and saw with astonishment the fresh footprints on the sandy bank. 'Two people,' whispered Pienaar. 'One barefoot, the other wearing shoes.'

Wessels examined them closely. 'Yes. They're fresh all right. No leaves on them. Couldn't have been there long.' He spoke in a low voice. In the brief, scarcely audible discussion which followed they agreed that those responsible for the footprints might still be on the island, though Pienaar thought that if they were, there would have been other indications of their presence, like the sound of voices or smoke from a fire. On one point, however, he and Wessels were wholly agreed; they must follow the spoor.

Wessels, experienced in tracking lost cattle in the

bushveld, stressed the importance of silence, adding a special warning against treading on brittle deadwood. With him leading, they set off in single file. They had gone no more than a few metres when he turned, a finger to his lips. He was grinning. 'We're not too bright, Piet. It's only one guy,' he whispered. 'On the bank he kicks off his shoes. Here, where the grass is crushed, he sits on his arse and puts them on again. Then it's only shoeprints we see.'

Pienaar checked, looked up. 'You're right, man. That's it. Just one of them. Not a very big guy, hey. So now?'

'We track him,' said Wessels.

Slowly, silently, they followed the footprints along a tortuous route, twisting and turning through scrub and bush until Wessels stopped suddenly. Crouching low behind a thicket of thornbush and mopani he held up a warning hand. Pienaar went down on his haunches beside him, peered in the direction in which he was pointing.

Not far beyond the thicket which screened them a woman, tall, white and naked, was washing herself in the shallows.

Pienaar hissed, 'Jesus – a white woman,' but Wessels raced like a man possessed through a gap in the thicket, shouting as he went, 'Hey, lady, look out – crocodile – in the reeds opposite.'

Seeing the reeds shaking, Pienaar yelled, 'Quick! Out of the water. *Hardloop, mevrou* – run fast, madam.'

SEVENTEEN

Among the many people in the lounge of the Polana Hotel that night the couple making their way across it were as conspicuous as peacocks in a fowl-run; Mavro Costeliades, darkly hirsute, broken-nosed, his theatrical appearance lacking only a parrot on his shoulder – and his companion, Felicia Santos, tall, slim and beautiful in white silk, black hair piled high on her head, carmine lips in an olive face framing milk white teeth. It was not surprising, therefore, that many eyes followed the new arrivals to the table where they joined an elderly man who had waved to them as they came in. Grey and balding, his face masked by dark glasses, he wore a white seersucker suit.

They reached his table, the tall beauty leant towards him with an engaging smile. 'Andrada! How nice to see you. May we join you?'

'Of course, my dear Felicia. Why do you think I waved? Forgive me for not standing. My leg, you know.'

'Oh, your leg is fine, Andrada Gouveia,' Felicia scolded. 'It's just that you are lazy.'

The old man looked at Costeliades. 'Hullo, Mavro. And how are you?' Without waiting for the American's reply he turned back to Felicia, took her hand and kissed it. She sank on to the settee beside him.

The American's indulgent expression as he watched these gallantries offset the villainy of his broken nose. It amused him that Felicia and Gouveia always spoke English in his presence, falling back on their own language only when they wished to exchange confidences.

143

Mavro said, 'You dining here tonight, Andrada?'

'Of course. And you and the lovely Felicia?'

'Sure. That's what we've come for.'

In response to Gouveia's signal a waiter came to the table and drinks were ordered.

Mavro asked, 'Any news of JJ?'

'None at all.' Andrada contemplated the glowing tip of his cheroot. 'Have you heard anything? You media men are usually first with the news.'

'Nothing that you don't know, I guess. Carvalho tells me Pretoria's offer of South African Air Force assistance was refused.'

Gouveia nodded. 'I understand our air force had already completed a thorough search.'

'I guess he must have ditched somewhere off the coast.'

'That is the theory.' Gouveia spoke guardedly.

The waiter arrived, set out the drinks. Gouveia signed the *conta*.

'His passenger, Trudi Braun?' Mavro asked in an offhand way. 'Know anything about her?'

Gouveia looked across the room. 'Not much. He apparently picked her up in Mutare. She was stranded there, they say. Short of money. I believe he was giving her a lift back to Johannesburg.'

Felicia Santos broke in to say that she and Mavro had actually seen JJ and Trudi dining at Costa's in Mutare on the previous Tuesday. Indeed, they had spoken to them briefly. Having said that, she asked to be excused for a moment. 'Won't be long.' She smiled. 'Must powder my nose.'

In the conversation which followed her departure Gouveia became increasingly aware that the NBC man was probing for information: had the Cessna really gone missing? Was the flight with just one passenger what it seemed? Or was it cloak and dagger, perhaps? Something to do with Renamo? Johnson was a South African, and in

144

his day he had served in the South African Air Force. Had Frelimo, perhaps, shot down the plane? And Trudi Braun – what was her role? Innocent passenger or co-conspirator?

'And finally the sixty-four thousand dollar question.' Mavro leant towards Gouveia, lowered his voice. 'Why is Pretoria so interested in the loss of a little Cessna with only two people on board? So interested that they offer the services of their air force?'

Gouveia stubbed out his cheroot. 'No idea, Mavro. Have you?'

Costeliades dodged the challenge.

Andrada Gouveia knew a lot more about Johnnie Johnson and the Cessna, and about Mavro Costeliades and Felicia Santos, than that gentleman credited, but the older man was not going to help the American newsman with gratuitous information. Gouveia was a gatherer of information, not a disseminator. So he counter-attacked, changed the subject to Felicia Santos. Where had Mavro met her? Where did she fit into his scenario? What was she doing with Mavro in Mutare? And so on and so forth. The questions were put with affected innocence and with the necessary degree of casual interest. That Andrada already knew the answers to most of them was of little consequence. On the other hand, if they did nothing else, the American's answers informed Gouveia of the extent to which the NBC man was truthful. That in itself was important.

'I'm very fond of Felicia,' Andrada declared, taking another cheroot from a shining leather case. 'A most charming lady. But,' he hesitated, half smiled. 'I imagine you are aware of her reputation?'

Mavro looked away as if searching some distant point of the lounge for an answer. 'If you mean what I think you mean, yeah. Sure I know. But I guess that's the way it is when a lady's unusually beautiful.'

Andrada lit the cheroot, blew a gentle puff of blue smoke

145

towards the ceiling. 'I was not being critical. My question was a friendly warning. I've been here a long time, you know. This is my domain. I thought I might, well, help you.'

Mavro set up one of his more charming smiles. 'Sure, sure, Andrada. But I'm far from home. Felicia is a lovely companion, intelligent and beautiful. She knows a lot of VIPs in this neck of the woods. What they know can be important to NBC.' His smile was, if anything, condescending. 'Pillow-talk encourages confidences. For me, Felicia has everything. Wonderful to look at, marvellous for relaxation, and brilliant for news. Know what I mean?'

Andrada nodded. 'I think I do. Believe me I am one of Felicia's staunchest admirers. But at close on seventy, lame and burdened with an unwilling heart, I am not in the running for pillow-talk. As you say, she is excellent company. A quite remarkable lady.' He dropped his voice. 'And here indeed she is.'

Frightened out of her wits by the sound of men shouting, and terrified by their message, Trudi dashed from the shallows towards them. It was not only terror that drove her in that direction but a compelling instinct to hide her naked body from strangers, particularly from strange men: in this sense her action appeared contradictory, but her clothes lay on a bush close to where Wessels and Pienaar stood and she simply had to get them.

Mumbling in a mildly hysterical way she snatched up her knickers and pulled them on over wet thighs, then her bra. Seeing the Mauser lying on her slacks which were still on the ground, Wessels grabbed it. Saying, 'Excuse me, lady,' he fired two shots at the crocodile in rapid succession. It backed into the reeds on the far bank, slowly, as if to make clear that it had no intention of being hurried.

Wessels handed the Mauser back to Trudi who was

struggling with her shirt. 'Hope you've got some spare ammunition?' he said.

'My God, you people gave me a fright.' She was breathless with agitation. Tucking the Mauser into her waistband, she added, 'Well – you *and* the crocodile.'

'Sorry, but we had to shout – and run towards you.' Wessels looked cheerfully embarrassed.

Trying to calm her voice she said, 'Of course. D'you think you killed it?'

'No, lady. A Mauser pistol can't kill a crocodile at that range. It was just enough to tickle him up and keep him away. They're timid creatures.'

'You could fool me.' She laughed nervously.

Pienaar said, 'You're got some nasty bruises, miss. And cuts on your face. What's happened? Why are you here?'

'Air crash.' She tightened the belt of her slacks. 'Last Wednesday. In the bush about thirty Ks north-west.'

'Any other survivors?' asked Wessels.

'Yes. The pilot. He went to Cheline for help. That's about thirty-five Ks from the crash. Left me at the crash.' She stopped to put on a shoe.

Wessels said, 'Were the others all killed?'

'There were no others. Just me and the pilot. After nearly three days he had not come back. I had no water, so I made for the coast.'

Wessels looked at her with admiration. 'You've been on your own all this time?' He shook his head. 'That takes some doing, lady.'

'No option, had I?'

'What sort of aircraft was it?'

'Cessna Stationair.'

Pienaar's eyes narrowed. 'And the pilot. Who was he?'

The way in which he said it made her feel that something strange lay behind the question.

'Johnnie Johnson,' she said, adding loyally, 'he was a super chap.' She picked up her shoulder-bag, took from it

147

a comb and got to work on her hair. 'I hope and pray he's all right.'

Wessels and Pienaar looked at each other in astonishment.

'JJ – my God,' said Pienaar. 'He flew us down to Maputo. Should have picked us up in Inhambane last Saturday.'

She sighed with relief. So these men knew JJ, had flown with him. It was an incredible coincidence but it was reassuring, a sort of character reference. From their accents she knew they were Afrikaners. She frowned at Wessels. 'But how on earth did you two get here? You look as though you've had an awful time.'

'It's been tough,' agreed Wessels.

That, she felt, had to be an understatement. Their appearance told its own story. Wessels, stubble-bearded, deeply sunburnt, dark pouches under his eyes; Pienaar, with days of stubble growth rent by a livid gash on one cheek, his sunken eyes inflamed; the arms and legs of both men scratched and bruised, their shirts and shorts stained and torn, their bodies gaunt. It was evident that their struggle to survive had been a lot grimmer than hers.

'You dry yet?' Pienaar's eyes appeared to be feasting on her body.

'Dry enough. The sun soon does the job.' She put her comb back in the shoulder-bag. 'Let's go into the shade. I must hear your story. Never dreamt there were other human beings anywhere near here. That's why I got such a fright.' With the assurance of a hostess showing strangers over her garden, she led them to a great spreading tree, its branches thick with shining leaves. 'Don't know what it's called but it's my best tree,' she said proudly.

Wessels grinned. 'It's a *jakkalsbessie*, lady. An ebony tree.'

'For goodness sake call me Trudi,' she said. 'Trudi Braun. What do I call you two?'

Pienaar and Wessels introduced themselves and the trio sat down in the shade.

They were there for a long time, the men taking it in turns to tell their story and answer her questions. And they, too, asked her many questions: about the crash, about Johnnie Johnson, about how she came to be his passenger, and what she was doing in Zimbabwe. It was during this part of their discussion that she realised that a number of Pienaar's questions were, directly or otherwise, concerned with the luggage JJ had had with him in the Cessna. She was puzzled. JJ had flown the two men down from Dullstroom to Maputo and was to have picked them up in Inhambane for the return flight. She wondered if there was not more to the fishing trip than she had been told. She had already decided that she disliked Pienaar. His gaping mouth and wandering eyes had shown little regard for her modesty at the nude encounter, and in the discussions afterwards he'd been guilty of clumsy sexual innuendoes which had offended her. Wessels, by contrast, had behaved with consideration and understanding. She liked the man.

In the interests of security it was agreed that he and Pienaar would, before dark, shift camp to the upstream end of the island to join her. During the afternoon they built a *boma* near hers, the two thorny enclosures no more than a dozen strides apart.

At dusk they sat in the clearing and ate the shellfish and fruit they had collected that day. The meal finished, they discussed plans for the immediate future. She told them that she had intended to set off for Pomene the next day. While they agreed that Pomene held out the best hope of rescue, Wessels said that he and Pienaar needed another couple of days' rest before resuming the trek.

'We're in poor shape,' he confessed apologetically. 'And this is a good place to rest. An island most of the time – with food and water laid on. A man couldn't ask for more.'

'It *is* a good place.' Trudi gave them a shy smile. 'River

149

Island, I call it. I've been afraid at nights. Lots of scary noises. But with you two here it's different. Thank the Lord you found me.'

'You were lucky,' said Wessels. 'That crocodile would have taken you sooner or later.'

She shuddered. 'I bathed in those shallows yesterday. Cleared out when I heard dreadful noises and saw the reeds thrashing about. Earlier there had been warthogs moving beyond the reeds. I thought it must be them.'

'Sounds like the croc was taking a warthog,' said Wessels. 'If you'd stayed there you'd have seen him go into the water with it.'

'Oh God, what for?'

'To drown it, then push it under the bank. They like their kill to rot before they eat it.'

'That's how you would have ended,' said Pienaar with a garish grin.

'Oh, don't.' She held up a hand. 'I can't bear the thought.'

The men laughed but, hot though it was, Trudi shivered.

Plans were still being discussed when the moon climbed above the trees; it was a full moon, round, luminous and enormous, and it bathed the clearing in silver light.

Wessels looked at his watch. 'It's getting late.'

Pienaar yawned, Trudi followed in sympathy. 'I'm exhausted. What a day.'

Wessels said, 'We'll have another *indaba* tomorrow. There are problems.'

'What d'you mean, problems?' Pienaar watched him with narrow, uncertain eyes.

'The headland blocks the way south along the beach. We'll have to cross the river by the sandbar at low tide. Where it meets the headland on the far side, the rock face rises steeply from the reeds. It's quite a climb. But we'll have to do it to continue the trek to Pomene. We've no shoes. We must follow the beach.'

'We could cross higher up-river,' suggested Pienaar.

'That would mean wading.' Wessels' expression sig-

150

nalled disagreement. 'Where there's one crocodile there's bound to be others.' He stood up, stretched and yawned. '*Môre's nog 'n dag* – tomorrow's another day,' he said. 'Let's sleep now, make plans tomorrow.'

EIGHTEEN

After an early meal next morning the survivors went down to the seaward end of the island to refresh their minds on the physical problem of crossing the river. It was a good time to do so for the tide was low and the sandbar well exposed.

Leaving the others on the island, Wessels crossed the sandy gully and made his way along the bank to a point where he could climb down onto the sandbar: once on it he walked across towards the river, countless numbers of little sandcrabs scurrying into their holes as he approached. Wading knee deep across the depression through which the river flowed, he crossed to the far side and continued on to where the sandbar ended in a thicket of reeds at the foot of the headland. He spent some time there examining the rock face which led up precipitously from the reeds. Satisfied that there were enough foot and hand holds, he retraced his steps along the sandbar, recrossed the gully and joined Pienaar and Trudi.

'What d'you think, man?' Pienaar looked anxiously at the headland.

'Not too bad. Plenty of ledges and clefts. Not such a difficult climb, I reckon.'

Pienaar said, 'Depends who has to do it, doesn't it? Okay for you, perhaps. You're younger than I am – and fitter.'

Suspecting what was in the other's mind Wessels said, 'In a couple of days we'll both be fit enough to tackle the climb. Even Trudi.'

'How d'you mean, *even* Trudi?' she protested. 'What a chauvinistic remark.'

'Sorry, I didn't mean that. We've all got to do the climb when we start trekking south. There's no other way for us. But to check what's on the other side of the headland – to make the first recce – it's better that a man does that. It's a man's job. We can't sit here on our backsides and leave it to you.'

Pienaar agreed, the subject was dropped, and they set about collecting shellfish and fruit. While doing this Wessels told Trudi the names of the different fruits she'd been eating, and assured her that all were perfectly safe. To this Pienaar added a touch of realism by saying that the diarrhoea from which he'd been suffering while they were drifting at sea had soon been cured by marula fruits.

The rest of the day passed uneventfully. Two crocodiles were seen lying on a sandbank, this time well up-river; Wessels explained their habits, their movements with the tides to avoid salt water. 'They can be dangerous,' he warned. 'Keep a sharp lookout if you're near the water, especially if there are reeds to give them cover.'

That evening while Trudi was talking to Wessels about Johnnie Johnson and the Cessna, trying to answer his questions about why the engine had failed, Pienaar was wondering what her relationship with Johnson had been. Was it what she said it was, a chance meeting in the hotel and her acceptance of his offer to help, or was she an accomplice in the operation in which the Brigadier suspected Johnson was involved?

If her story was true Johnson would not have been able to make a drop with her on board – unless he somehow got rid of her before they had reached Johannesburg. It was an important *unless*. Pienaar recalled the Brigadier's briefing: 'On the day you and Wessels return from Inhambane – that's the Saturday – we'll arrange for a messenger with a telegram to be waiting for you on the airstrip at Dullstroom. It will be from your company requesting your immediate return to Johannesburg on an important business matter. You will show it to Johnson, explain that you must continue with him to Johannesburg. His reaction will, for the reasons I've explained, tell us a lot. If he says he can't take you because of other commitments, you must accept that decision.'

The Brigadier had paused, focusing his eyes on the crystal ball. 'In that case,' he continued, 'the messenger – Van der Walt, he's Security Branch – will drive you into Dullstroom immediately after the Cessna has taken off. Once the car is clear of the airstrip, he'll ask Middleburg Police by car-phone to pass the message to us.' The Brigadier's eyes switched suddenly from the crystal ball to Le Roux. 'Have you given Van der Walt the plain language code for that?'

'Yes, sir.'

Nodding approval the Brigadier had returned to his brief. 'If Wessels wants to know who Van der Walt is, you, Pienaar, will say he's from your company's Middleburg branch.'

Thinking back on that briefing it was evident to Pienaar that the Brigadier had thought it likely that Johnson would have wanted to drop him off at Dullstroom. But according to Trudi the Cessna was to fly direct from Maputo to Johannesburg, so it didn't look as if any drop could have taken place on that trip – unless Trudi was an accomplice. So the mystery about her remained.

Pienaar had liked Johnnie Johnson. He was a good-natured, friendly, outward giving man; yet tough, practical and direct. A good man to have around in trouble. Though he had known Johnson for less than twenty-four hours he found it difficult to accept the Brigadier's theory. Wessels, also, had a high opinion of Johnson and he knew him well. But Pienaar had learnt from long experience that it was unwise to judge by appearances, particularly in matters of national security. It was the facts that counted. He had spent a good many years of his life searching for them, sometimes with astonishing results.

When Trudi retired that night to the leafy bed in her *boma* she lay awake thinking about the twist in her fortunes. She was no longer alone, she had two men with her now. Afrikaners who knew the bushveld; strong resourceful men, determined to survive. She had only one reservation about them and that was their apparent dislike of each other. It seemed that adversity had not drawn them together; on the contrary they argued often, sometimes about trivialities, and she sensed that a leadership struggle of sorts was developing.

Wessels, the younger man, was clearly the stronger character and it was this she imagined which upset Pienaar, particularly as Wessels was not altogether tactful, tending to make decisions without consulting his companion. It had also become apparent to her that an already-soured relationship had been further complicated by her arrival on the scene; both men competed, in small, sometimes pointless ways, for her attention. She tried to deal with this by concealing her preference for Wessels, but she doubted whether her efforts were convincing. In the course of debating the issue she fell asleep.

The new arrivals' second day on the island was by no means as uneventful as the first.

It was after the morning meal, when Pienaar had gone behind the bushes set aside for the men, that she approached Wessels.

'I've a problem,' she said, showing some signs of agitation. 'It's Piet Pienaar. He frightens me and I don't trust him.'

Wessels was puzzled. 'How come? What's happened?'

Looking over her shoulder to make sure that Pienaar was not on his way back she blurted out her story: in the early hours of that morning she had been awakened in the *boma* by something touching her. Petrified, thinking it was a snake, she was about to scream when a hand was placed over her mouth and a voice whispered, 'Take it easy, Trudi – it's me, Piet.' Frightened and furious, she had told him to clear off and he had gone. But now she feared him. Something like that could happen again.

Wessels had reassured her, said that he would see to it that she was not troubled again. He told her he had been vaguely aware of Pienaar leaving the *boma* during the night, but had assumed it was to relieve himself.

'Well, all I can say, Jan, is that under no circumstances will I remain here alone with Pienaar.' She shook her head vigorously. 'He's a sinister sort of man and I'm dead scared of him.'

Later that morning, an opportunity having presented itself, Wessels took Pienaar aside. 'Look,' he said. 'What's this Trudi tells me about you going into her *boma* around four o'clock this morning?'

Pienaar's eyes narrowed, their characteristic hostility accentuated. 'So she told you, did she?'

'Yes. You frightened her, man. What the hell were you up to?'

'Not what you think, anyway. If you really want to know it was the Mauser. It was on the ground next to her.'

'The Mauser? You mean to say you were going to take that from her while she slept? You must be crazy.'

Pienaar turned, began to move away, spoke over his shoulder. 'Why don't you try minding your own business some time?'

Wessels moved quickly, put a hand on the other man's

shoulder, spun him round. 'It *is* my business. What did you want that Mauser for?'

With angry eyes Pienaar wrenched himself clear of Wessels' grip. '*Pas op! Moenie so maak nie.* Look out! Don't do that,' he warned in a thick voice.

'Answer my question,' demanded Wessels.

Breathing heavily, Pienaar said, 'That Mauser should be with us, not with her. What good can she do with it if there's trouble?'

Wessels shook his head. 'So you decided to steal it. Why didn't you talk to me about it? Say what you felt? If we had a good case we could put it to her. She'd probably agree. But you go creeping into her *boma* in the dark like a thief and try to steal it. That's not only bloody stupid. It's crooked.'

'Oh, balls. Don't you lecture me, *Meneer* Wessels.'

The younger man gave him a long hard look. 'You had better watch your step, Piet, or you'll find yourself in trouble.'

'Trouble? Who's going to give me trouble?' Pienaar thrust a stubbled chin at Wessels in a gesture of aggression.

'I am,' said Wessels evenly. 'I'll give you plenty of trouble if you try that sort of thing again. *Pas op, my vriend* – look out, my friend.'

'I'm not your friend, thank God.' Pienaar spat the words at Wessels.

Walking away from the clearing in a sullen mood, and with no idea of what he intended to do, Pienaar brooded over the row with Wessels. His object in entering Trudi's *boma* while she slept had been to get the Mauser, not to interfere with her personally.

It had been in his mind, he admitted to himself, that there was just a chance she might encourage him in some way once he was physically close to her, but that had been very much a fringe consideration. He wanted the Mauser

157

because once it was in his possession it would enable him to challenge Wessels' assumption of the leadership.

Ever since that first day after the capsize it had rankled with him that Wessels had set himself up in the role of leader. In the days that followed the irritation had grown into an obsession, exacerbated now by the presence of Trudi who from the start had not concealed her preference for Wessels.

In some vague undetermined way Pienaar believed that the Mauser would change all that; a firearm was a badge of authority, it commanded respect, fear and obedience; it would confer on him a special status. In the last resort he would not hesitate to use it. There would be no evidence, no witnesses, he and the crocodiles would see to that. As it was, he had failed to get the weapon; the woman had talked, and Wessels had insulted him. Somehow, he decided, he would get his revenge for the humiliation – how, when and where, time would show.

The notable event of the day occurred in late afternoon when the men were collecting mussels at the rivermouth. A shouted, 'Christ, look over there,' had come from Pienaar who was standing on a rock pointing to the headland. Wessels, busy prising mussels from the rocks with his sheath-knife, had looked up to see the thin column of smoke spiralling into the sky beyond the rocky headland which hid the view to the south. Their first reactions were mixed. The smoke was only a few kilometres away, but did it mean rescue or danger? They agreed that only a reconnaissance could answer that question.

After a hurried exchange of views they cut short mussel gathering and went back to the island where they found Trudi collecting fruit. In a state of excitement which soon communicated itself to her, they told her about the smoke spiral.

158

'A ship perhaps,' she suggested.

Pienaar was not impressed. 'No way. It was stationary and quite a bit inland.'

'We don't know how the coast runs south of the headland,' said Wessels. 'Maybe there's a bay there, in which case it could be a ship. But I doubt it. Unless it's at anchor.'

'What the hell does a ship want to come there for?' Pienaar's tone conveyed ridicule.

'I don't know,' said Wessels. 'But it's too late to find out now. The sun's nearly gone. We can't climb that rockface in the dark. We must tackle it in the morning as soon as the tide's low enough.'

Sadly Trudi said, 'If it's a ship it may have gone by then.'

The discussion went on, eagerly at times, hotly at others, and at the end of it there was agreement that one of the men would carry out the reconnaissance the following morning. It was evident that neither man was going to volunteer for the task; Trudi thought she knew why: Wessels because he knew she would refuse to be left alone with Pienaar, and Pienaar because he was obsessively jealous and would not want to leave her alone with Wessels. She then suggested that perhaps they should all go, but the men rejected this. Wessels pointed out that absolute silence and stealthy movement were essential to a successful reconnaissance. Three people had no chance of achieving that. Pienaar, not to be outdone, added, 'If things go wrong only one is in danger.'

It was already dark and, anxious to find the answer to the problem before they turned in for the night, Trudi urged them to make a decision as to who should go. When they still showed no keenness she decided as a last resort to fall back on a feminine ploy.

'Very well,' she said severely. 'Somebody's got to do that reconnaissance and if you two are not keen I suppose I shall have to go.'

The men at once protested that there was no question

of letting her do it, it was just the problem of deciding who should go. Pienaar had added, 'The fittest, strongest man should go.'

The embarrassing silence which followed was broken by Trudi. 'I've an idea,' she said. 'You two should draw lots.' She knew what Wessels would be thinking – if he had to go she would be left alone with Pienaar – but she'd already decided how to avoid that eventuality; so in the darkness she patted Wessels' knee, hoping he would realise that it was a signal that he should support her proposal.

It was clear that he did, for both men then agreed that lots should be drawn. Trudi's suggestion that the method should be decided in the morning was accepted.

When the drawing of lots was under discussion Pienaar had been preoccupied with the problem of how he could turn the situation to his advantage if he drew the short straw and had to go. Because the recent humiliation over the Mauser incident was much in his mind, it was the Mauser that presented itself as the solution to his problem.

Before lots were drawn he would insist that whoever had to go should take the Mauser with him. It was a sensible, a reasonable proposition. The Mauser would be for self-defence. Armed with it the man making the reconnaissance would be able to reconnoitre with greater confidence and more thoroughly than if he were unarmed. Even Wessels would have to agree to that. But, if for some reason he did not, there would be no drawing of lots. That in itself should ensure that he would agree.

Pienaar now hoped to draw the short straw for that would give him possession of the Mauser. He had been brought up since childhood to understand the simple truth that a man was stronger with a gun; a truth often confirmed during his long experience in the South African Police. But what if Wessels got the short straw? That was a problem, until a solution suggested itself. If he, Pienaar, drew the long straw he would argue that as winner he would have the right to decide who should go and, in that case, he would insist on going himself. Apart from getting the Mauser, he would be showing Trudi that he had more guts than Wessels. He was a little confused on the point but decided he would sort it out with some hard thinking during the night. Whichever way he looked at it, however, prospects now seemed brighter – and especially if the smoke came from friendly sources for that would mean rescue.

He felt a sudden sense of relief, an easing of the tensions within him.

NINETEEN

That evening while Pienaar was away in the bushes, Trudi reminded Wessels that she was not to be left alone with him.

'I've been thinking about that, Trudi. I don't see how we can avoid it if we're going to draw lots.' Wessels looked bewildered. 'If I get the shorter straw I have to go – no argument. In that case you're left alone with Pienaar. But I wouldn't be away for long, he knows that, and you'll have the Mauser. Not that he'll try anything now that I've spoken to him. Anyway, it's a fifty-fifty chance. Just as likely that he'll have to go.'

'Well, I just want you to know that I'm not staying alone with him, Mauser or no Mauser.' Her eyes flashed. 'That's not on, Jan, so you can forget it.'

'What do you do, then, if I draw the short straw?' said Wessels quietly.

'There aren't going to be any straws. It's going to be pebbles. It's going to be a guessing game.'

'What difference is that going to make?'

'Listen, Jan. I'll explain. We take five pebbles from the river. With my hands behind my back I hold out one hand and each of you in turn must guess how many pebbles there are in it. I'll do it five times, so you each have five guesses. The one with the highest score wins.'

Wessels was quick to reply. 'Same chance for both. I can still lose. If I do you're still left with Piet.'

'You won't lose.' Trudi paused. 'Unless you have a bad memory.'

'What d'you mean?'

'Five-two-four-one-three. Don't forget it.' She repeated the numbers slowly. Soon afterwards they heard Pienaar coming back, and she lowered her voice. 'That's how many stones I'll be holding. Five the first time, two the second, and so on. Five-two-four-one-three.'

'That would be a dirty trick, Trudi.' Wessels sounded unhappy. 'But okay. I suppose I'll do it.'

They agreed that for added credence he would propose the drawing of straws, but would later support Trudi's proposal when she made it.

Getting up with the sun next morning, they made for the seaward end of the island to get a clear view of the headland. The excitement of the occasion was marked by laughing chatter as they made their way towards the sea through the trees and undergrowth. But the gaiety was short-lived for when the headland came into view the smoke spiral had gone.

Trudi groaned. 'So it *was* a ship.'

'Could have been,' said Wessels. 'But I doubt it.'

Pienaar agreed. 'It looked like woodsmoke to me. Camp-fire, I reckon.'

In the discussion which followed the campfire theory was favoured; but whose fire? Renamo guerrillas or a Frelimo patrol? Or simply wandering Africans, refugees whose villages had been destroyed, making their way south to safer country? Only a reconnaissance could answer those questions, but was there now any point in making one?

Wessels said, 'Look, we've already decided to continue the trek to Pomene tomorrow. That means crossing the river and climbing the headland to reach the beach on the far side. Before we do that I reckon we have got to check that there's not a guerrilla camp where that smoke came from. A reconnaissance is a must.'

His suggestion having been accepted, it was decided that the river should be crossed when the tide was low, somewhere between ten and eleven that morning.

To Trudi's surprise her suggestion that lots should be drawn after the morning meal was at once accepted, the objections she'd expected from Pienaar failing to materialise.

With these matters settled the survivors made their way back to camp. It was during that walk, when Wessels was well ahead, that Pienaar apologised to her: 'I'm sorry about the other night,' he said. 'When I came to your *boma* I just wanted the Mauser for the safety of all of us. I'd heard a queer noise in the bush shortly before.' He paused, took a deep breath. 'Jan and myself understand firearms. We are Afrikaners, brought up with guns, and we're used to living in the *bundu*. We sleep always with one eye and one ear open. If a guerrilla or a leopard or something like that comes into the camp at night we can do better with the Mauser than you can. Understand?'

'Why didn't you wake me? Tell me that?'

'I was going to tell you in the morning. Didn't want to disturb you. But you woke up and wanted to scream and I thought that could be bad if the noise in the bush was Africans. Then you told Jan what had happened and he misunderstood the situation and we had one helluva row. I'm sorry, Trudi. It was a misunderstanding.'

The apology was abject and she had no hesitation in accepting it. She finished by saying, 'I only told Jan because I was scared. I thought you wanted to get fresh.'

Pienaar looked shocked. 'On my oath, Trudi. It wasn't like that. But I now see what you could have thought. It was daft of me.'

The meal that morning was an unusually harmonious affair, speculation about what the day might bring dominating the conversation. At its end Trudi said, 'Now, what about drawing lots?'

Wessels rose to his feet. 'I'll get some straws.'

'There's a better way than straws,' she said. 'We used it when I was at school. We called it the Five-Pebble Game.'

His eyes glinting with suspicion, Pienaar said, 'How do you mean, *better* than straws?'

'It's possible to cheat with straws.' Trudi's manner was authoritative. 'At least psychologically,' she added. 'The person holding them can make one straw look longer than the other. With pebbles that's not possible.' She went on to explain the five-pebble method in detail. Pienaar agreed that it sounded better than drawing straws. Wessels was reluctant at first, but agreed eventually.

'All we need now are five pebbles,' she said cheerfully.

Pienaar stood up. 'Okay. I'll get them.'

'Good,' said Trudi. 'There are plenty where we draw our drinking water.'

While Pienaar was away she spoke to Wessels in an undertone. 'Remember, five-two-four-one-three.'

'I still think it's a lousy trick,' complained Wessels. 'Downright cheating.'

'The end justifies the means,' she said with confidence, adding in an undertone, 'Look out, he's coming back.'

Moments later Pienaar returned. 'Here they are,' he said.

She took the pebbles, examined them carefully. 'They're fine. You two ready?'

'There's a couple of things to settle first,' said Pienaar.

She frowned at him. 'Oh, and what are they?'

'I reckon the man who goes must take the Mauser. If he's to do a thorough reconnaissance he must be armed. For self-defence, you understand. In case things go badly.'

Suspecting the other man's motives, Wessels at once disagreed.

Pienaar played his ace. 'I'm not going without a gun,' he insisted. 'Nobody knows who is on the other side of that headland.' It was evident he meant what he said.

165

To Wessels' astonishment Trudi sided with him. 'I think Piet's right. It would be unfair to send one of you off unarmed on what could be a dangerous mission.'

Wessels stared disapproval at her, but she was unmoved, knowing that he was unaware that Pienaar had apologised for the *boma* incident, that she had been impressed with the sincerity of the apology, and that she was determined not to let anything interfere with Pienaar's going.

She stood facing them, hands behind her back. 'Who's first?'

The men looked undecided.

'All right,' she said. 'If you two can't make up your minds I suggest you guess in alphabetical order. P comes before W, so it's you first, Piet.' She put out her right hand. 'How many?'

Pienaar stared at the clenched fist. 'Five.'

She opened her hand. 'You're right. One to you Piet.' Both hands went behind her back again and she juggled with the pebbles before thrusting out her right fist. 'How many, Jan?'

'Well, let's see.' Wessels appeared to be thinking hard. 'I'll say five.'

She unclenched her fist. 'Five it is. Goodness, how smart you two are. One to each of you.'

And so the charade went on until she declared Wessels to have won by four to three. What she believed to have been a worrying lapse of memory on his part had been due to the deliberate error he'd made towards the end when he had already established a margin which ensured that he would win.

To their surprise Pienaar seemed happy with the result.

They reached the seaward end of the island, and the head-land came into view through a gap in the trees as Pienaar,

leading the single file, let out an excited shout. 'Look –
the smoke again.'

And there it was, a thin white column curling into the
blue sky. The sight of it triggered a new wave of euphoria;
there had to be people on the far side of the headland and
people meant rescue.

Trudi handed Pienaar the Mauser and spare ammunition
clip. 'Take care, Piet. Come back soon with good news,
please. And take these.' She handed him the plastic bottle
which she had filled with fresh water, and some biltong,
raisins and biscuits from the iron rations.

'Thanks. I'll do my best.' His lined face grim, Pienaar
pocketed the iron rations and tucked the Mauser into his
shorts.

'*Hamba gahli*, go carefully, Piet.' Wessels' face showed
his concern. 'Looks like there's a camp there. Check
thoroughly before you go in. Remember what Charles
Scott told us. If they're Frelimo they'll have Kalashnikovs
– AK47s. If they're Renamo their weapons will be Heckler
& Koch G3 assault rifles. And Frelimo have military
vehicles, APCs and trucks. Marauding guerrillas mostly
operate without transport, especially in this area.'

Pienaar nodded. '*Ja, moenie bekommer nie. Ek sal baie
versigtig wees* – Yes, don't worry. I'll be very careful.' With
sarcastic emphasis he added, 'After all, Jan, why must you
worry? It's my skin that's at risk.' With that he left them.
It had been agreed that he could not give a time of return.
'I'll do the recce tonight, hopefully come back tomorrow,'
he had said. 'Depends on what I find.'

Once over the sand gully he walked along the bank,
stepped down on to the sandbar and began the journey
across to the reeds. On reaching them he stopped, gazed
into them before moving tentatively ahead, Mauser in
hand.

'He's scared of crocodiles.' Wessels chuckled. 'Don't
blame the guy. But we haven't seen any at this end. Too
salty, I reckon.'

'Ugh! Horrible. How can you laugh?' She made a face. 'Can't wait until he's got on to that rock face.'

They watched anxiously as Pienaar made his way slowly through the reeds, reached the rock face and began the climb; feeling for hand holds, searching with his toes for foot holds, then pulling himself up. It was a slow business.

'The rocks must be hot now, and his hands and feet are bare,' explained Wessels.

'God! I hope he'll make it, Jan.'

'I reckon he will. But it's not easy. You'll know why when we have to climb it.'

Pienaar had almost reached the top when he stopped, turned towards them and waved. They returned the wave. 'He's okay,' said Wessels.

'Good for him. He's tougher than I thought.' She laughed nervously.

'He's an Afrikaner, Trudi. What he's doing now is deep in the blood.'

Determined not to show himself against the skyline, Pienaar moved cautiously along the estuary side of the summit until he came to a gap in the ridge through which he could see the country to the south. A cursory glance told him that the coast on the far side of the headland continued its north-south line, but it was the smoke which commanded his attention. It curled up from between tall trees surrounded by thickets of brushwood. Beyond it a *koppie* stood out above an undulating landscape of bush-clad sandhills stretching south along the coastline as far as he could see. The southern side of the headland itself was less precipitous than the side he had climbed; to go down it, he decided, would be more of a steep scramble than a climb.

The source of the smoke, no more than a few kilometres from where he crouched, was closer than he had expected. To go down the headland in broad daylight was, he felt, too risky. He would almost certainly be seen. He would wait until dusk before making the descent. The final approach to the camp would have to be made under the cover of darkness. That would be an advantage. There would be no moon until towards eleven, but he believed the star-filled southern sky would provide enough illumination for his task.

Because it was insufferably hot on the rock face, he went to its seaward end where he made himself comfortable in the shade of bushes which grew from a fissure in the rocks.

He had not suffered from the climb as much as he'd feared: days of hard living in the bush, of walking on bare feet and breaking branches with bare hands, had toughened him. But he was tired, and he slept intermittently during the afternoon. Towards evening he ate some of the iron rations and drank a little water from the plastic bottle.

TWENTY

About a week after news of the Cessna's disappearance had reached Mutare, Titus Luena flew from Harare to Mauritius where he booked in at an unpretentious hotel in Port Louis, the principal port and administrative capital of the island. Briefed by the Department of Agriculture in Harare, and supplied by them with the necessary documentation, his official mission was to discuss requirements, if any, for grain and tobacco imports from Zimbabwe during the forthcoming year and, conversely, Zimbabwe's requirements of refined sugar from Mauritius during that period.

The real purpose of his mission had been outlined to him by Greg Nielsen some days before he left. Leaning back in the swing-chair in the small office in Harare, bush-hat on the back of his head, cigarette hanging from his lip, the American said, 'Listen, kid, you've been bellyaching a lot about not getting field assignments. Well, I have news for you.' Nielsen stubbed out a cigarette, fumbled in the pockets of his safari jacket, fished out the crumpled packet of Camels, took one from it, and examined it with exaggerated care before putting it in his mouth and lighting it.

Luena sighed loudly. 'Now that you've completed that ritual, Greg, perhaps you'll give me the news.'

Nielsen nodded affably. 'The Minister and I feel you should have some experience of the teeth before you begin wagging the tail.'

'So what is it? Check out public conveniences?'

'Titus, boy, as a wit you are the greatest. No – I said wit. Fact is we're sending you into the lion's den.'

'Where's that?'

'Mauritius.' Nielsen blew smoke at the ceiling. 'Remember? That's where we pick up the trail again. Back to square one, like I told you.'

'What can I do that Patel can't?'

'Plenty, son. You're not known to Gottwald and Kahn. You're not known in Mauritius. You have a bona fide reason for being there. Zimbabwean civil servant representing the Department of Agriculture – what could be more respectable?' Nielsen stubbed out the cigarette in the big ashtray. 'Patel's role is restricted to providing information about Gottwald's and Kahn's movements. For example, he has just reported that Gottwald flew to Johannesburg three days after the Cessna crashed. From there, on to Zürich. Due back in Mauritius a few days after you get there.'

Luena showed signs of interest. 'You mean,' he said, leaning forward, 'that you actually want me to meet the bastard?'

'Could be that, Titus. But certainly shadow him. Watch him like a bloody hawk – Kahn too. Patel says they never meet in public. Don't acknowledge each other. But they do meet at just one place, deliberately, clandestinely and at night.' Nielsen reached for the crumpled packet, found a cigarette, lit it and blew smoke across the desk. Luena coughed, held a handkerchief to his nose. 'Lousy habit,' he complained. 'So where do they have this clandestine meeting?'

'Patel will put you wise to that in the briefing.'

'He knows I'm coming?'

'That's right. But you two will not, repeat not, be seen together.'

One of Luena's eyebrows lifted. 'So how do we meet?'

'At night, out of town. You'll get the details when you arrive.'

171

'You know, Greg, I'm really happy to go but . . .' Luena fiddled with the computer keyboard on his desk. 'It all sounds a bit woolly. I mean, what are you really after?'

Nielsen tipped his bush-hat forward until it all but hid his eyes. 'When Gottwald gets back from Jo'burg and Zürich he'll have plenty to tell Kahn. Patel is strictly limited in what he can do. He's a respected businessman, never meets Gottwald and Kahn. As you know Gottwald is poison to him.' Nielsen began an examination of his nicotine-stained fingers. 'Now, son, I'll tell you what we hope you can do. It's odds on that Gottwald went to Jo'burg to see about a replacement for Johnson. If he – '

'You know, Greg, you're inconsistent,' interrupted Luena. 'You're always telling me to be objective, to base conclusions on facts.'

'So what's on your mind, young Titus?'

'Johnson is. You have made up your mind that he's involved and you've done it on nothing more than Jake Motlani's uncorroborated evidence. Trudi knew Johnson a lot better than we do – we've never even met the guy – and she believed that he was not involved. She reckoned Mavro Costeliades probably was. I go along with her on that, Greg. I reckon you're barking up the wrong tree.'

'Okay, okay.' Nielsen held up a hand as if to fend off an attack. 'Let's say that *if* Johnson was involved, Gottwald probably went to Jo'burg about a replacement. Mauritius, Gottwald, Kahn, Johnson – or some guy else – Johannesburg. That's the chain. Johannesburg's where it ends. So Gottwald goes there. And Zürich. Why Zürich? When he gets back to Mauritius he's going to tell Kahn what's new – okay?'

Luena said, 'Sure, he'll tell him something.'

'He sure will, and that's where you come in, sonny boy. Your assignment is to try and find out what he tells him.'

'Great.' Luena produced a forced laugh. 'No problem. Dead easy. Just follow them and ask.'

'It's not easy. But it's worth trying. We can go on with present tactics, waiting for them to come to us, hoping we'll get on to something worthwhile that way. But that can be a slow, disappointing scenario, as we already know. Now we try something else. We go to them.'

'You mean *I* go to them.' Luena's grimace revealed strong white teeth. 'But it would be nice to know just how I'm supposed to do that.'

Nielsen stubbed out the Camel, began the routine of replacing it. 'Patel will fill you in on that. He's going to give you a one hundred per cent local briefing. Something I can't do. When he's done that, ways and means of getting on with the job should suggest themselves.'

'And if they don't?' Luena fiddled with a paperknife. 'If it's mission impossible?'

'That's up to you, son. Depends on how you handle things. A good agent has to have brains, flair, imagination – on top of that he must be a convincing liar.' Nielsen sniffed, his nose twitching. 'I reckon you fill the bill nicely.'

'Thanks. I like the compliment.'

'My pleasure.'

The younger man was thoughtful. 'It sounds a bit dodgy. Could it be dangerous?'

'Could be. Depends on how you play it. Operators in the Kahn-Gottwald line of business aren't too fussy about eliminating trouble-makers.'

'So, if the elimination scenario comes up how do I deal with it?'

'Wait for Patel's briefing. He'll have some of the answers.'

Dusk had given way to darkness by the time Pienaar finished the descent from the headland. In late afternoon he had seen the smoke column grow thinner and all but disappear. The fire would be stoked up for the evening meal, he told himself. While on the headland he had taken careful note of the direction of the tall trees and the *koppie* beyond; it was a precaution which had paid off well during the journey through the bush for the *koppie* showed as a dark hump against the star-lit skyline. In the final stages of the approach he slackened his pace, moving forward very slowly, feeling ahead with a bare foot for dry tinder before transferring the weight of his body.

The Mauser in his right hand to some extent eased his fear, but he knew that he was perspiring more freely than the hot night demanded.

When he reached the thorn and brushwood which lay between him and the tall trees, he glimpsed for the first time the glow of a fire. Edging forward cautiously, he went down on his knees and crawled, elbow by elbow, knee by knee, until he heard voices speaking in an African dialect. He stopped for a few minutes to listen, then crept on again until he could see the fire through a gap in the undergrowth. Sitting round it on their haunches were a number of Africans in combat camouflage, staring as men do into the flames.

The fire cast occasional light on vehicles in the background, some of them camouflaged; near them two armed men paced slowly to and fro. Their automatic rifles were AK47s. Frelimo – Government forces – he told himself with a sense of relief. Pretoria might back Renamo, but he would not have liked the task of explaining to guerrillas why they should, for that reason, treat kindly a bedraggled Afrikaner wandering alone in the bush.

He was watching, curious, apprehensive, undecided as to what he should do, when he heard the rumble of a heavy vehicle approaching, the beam of its headlights thrusting into the night as it neared the camp. It came into the clearing and he saw that it was a camouflaged armoured personnel carrier. It stopped and a number of armed Africans in combat camouflage climbed out. There were shouted exchanges between the new arrivals and the men round the fire while equipment was passed down and carried to a truck parked in the shadows.

Three men came from the driving compartment of the APC; two were Africans carrying Kalashnikovs, the third was a tall, thickly-bearded white man in combat camouflage; he was wearing sunglasses and a peaked commando cap. A heavy calibre revolver bulged from the holster at his side. Pienaar at once classified the Castro-like figure as a Communist, and watched, fascinated, as the big white man spoke briefly to the men round the fire before walking across to a make-shift tent, a tarpaulin stretched down from the side of a truck. A few minutes later he emerged from the tent and joined those at the fire.

Reassured by the presence of the white man, who was evidently in charge of the camp, and indications that some sort of discipline prevailed, Pienaar decided to make his presence known. Abandoning any attempt at silence he walked round the undergrowth and made for the clearing. He had not gone far when he was startled by a sudden shout from the bushes to his left. Unable to understand the word but assuming it was 'halt', he stopped in his tracks. He was aware of a dark shape moving towards him. Moments later, silhouetted against the light from the fire, he saw a man with a rifle at the ready a few paces in front of him. For an instant Pienaar's hand went towards the Mauser, then he thought better of it and raised both hands above his head. Frightening seconds passed as the dark shape came closer, reached him and pressed the muzzle of the rifle against his stomach; a thick voice said something in Portuguese, followed by words in broken English which sounded like, 'What for you make here?'

Conscious that the sound of voices from the men round the fire had given way to an eerie silence, Pienaar said, 'I come for help.' At that moment two more armed men appeared; there was a quick exchange between the man who had stopped him and a tall black man with a flattened nose. On this man's barked instructions, Pienaar's arms

175

were seized and with the sentry behind him and an armed man at each side he was frog-marched into the clearing and on towards the fire. His escort halted him in front of the bearded white man. Making no attempt to get up from the canvas stool on which he sat, he stared at Pienaar through dark sunglasses, and in total silence. The canvas stool appeared to be a badge of office for like the rest of his men he wore combat camouflage without badges of rank. The others at the fire continued to sit on their haunches, forearms on their knees, hands clasped in traditional African style.

The black man with the flattened nose and the bearded white man had a brief conversation in Portuguese after which the African turned to Pienaar. 'The Commandante asks who you are? What you make here?'

Aware that all eyes were on him Pienaar answered the questions as briefly and directly as he could, after which he waited nervously while the African again spoke in Portuguese to the Commandante whose only response was an affirmative nod. At that the African turned and in a sudden movement snatched the Mauser from Pienaar's waist.

Taken aback at what looked increasingly like a hostile reception, Pienaar protested.

'Thees guerrilla country,' said the Commandante in broken English. 'We not like strangers with gun in camp.'

Pienaar's surprise showed in his face. 'You speak English?'

The white man stared at him, nodded. 'I spik Engleesh.'

Sitting on his haunches by the fire, Pienaar told the story of the disastrous fishing trip, the meeting with Trudi after the Cessna crash, and the refuge they had found on the island where he had left them. The Commandante listened in silence, after which he announced that his name was Vasco Ferreira. Indicating the African with the broken nose he said, 'Alfonso Querrime. My deputy.' It was apparent that the Commandante was a reserved, taciturn man, unsmiling and severe in looks and manner. He spoke in Portuguese to Querrime and the two young half-castes who were, he said, his field assistants. To the Africans he talked in a local dialect in which he was evidently fluent. In response to a question from Pienaar he explained briefly that he and his assistants were carrying out a geological survey on behalf of the Mozambique Government. The military escort was necessary because of the bush war.

While these exchanges were taking place Pienaar had observed that there were three groups of men in the camp: those round the fire with Ferreira, and two other groups round smaller fires near the parked trucks and APCs. From the smaller fires came the welcome odours of food cooking.

Soon Pienaar was enjoying his first real meal for a long time: grilled impala steaks and *putu* – balls of ground maize dipped in gravy – with coffee. Little was said during the meal other than occasional asides between Alfonso Querrime and the Commandante. The latter ignored Pienaar's attempts at conversation.

After the meal he said, 'You sleep by thees fire tonight. Querrime give you blanket.' In a severe tone he added, 'Sleep quiet. Make no trouble. Frelimo sentries keep watch.'

Pienaar's fear that Ferreira was not happy with his story was confirmed when the bearded man looked at him long and hard across the fire. 'We go find your friends tomorrow,' he said. 'See what we can see, but – ' The eyes behind the dark glasses continued to stare, ' – eef you Renamo, an' they make ambush,' he shook his head emphatically, 'you, Senhor Pienaar, will die.'

Pienaar at once strenuously denied that he or the other survivors were in any way connected with Renamo.

'We shall see,' said the Commandante ominously. 'Tonight I talk with Maputo. Tell them of you.'

Pienaar looked pleased. 'So you have two-way radio?'

Ignoring the question the Commandante continued to look into the fire.

Some time after the meal had finished the Commandante and Alfonso Querrime stood by the Land Rover talking in low voices. The African was explaining that he had listened carefully to the Afrikaner's story. 'I do not trust this man, Senhor Vasco. He can be with Renamo. Maybe he tries to make ambush for us. I think it is better to kill him. In the night I can arrange for this.'

'No. You will not kill him, Alfonso. We shall see tomorrow if he speaks the truth. If he does we must help him and his friends. If not,' the Commandante shrugged, 'you can deal with him as you wish.'

'Will you report to Maputo that he is an Afrikaner?'

'Yes. Tonight.'

TWENTY-ONE

For Pienaar, lying on a palliasse near the fire, his blanket cast aside, it was a hot, restless night both because of his thoughts and because of the constant movement of sentries and other sounds in the camp including the departure of a truck near midnight and its return half an hour later.

As to his thoughts, they concerned the Commandante's and Querrime's unconcealed hostility towards him, something which caused him considerable anxiety. The other matter much in his mind was River Island. What was going on there between Wessels and the girl? It was obvious that they liked each other and now they were alone. What an opportunity for Wessels. All sorts of erotic fantasies chased through Pienaar's mind, fuelling his jealousy.

Wessels' farm in Dullstroom was in the territory allocated to Pienaar by the firm of agricultural machinery distributors he represented; in the course of his sales and customer service duties he had called there at regular intervals during the last few years.

He had got on well with Wessels and his wife Tina, and with their children; the friendship which had followed had led to his business visits often including nights on the farm as their guest. It was this friendship which had made possible the fishing trip which the Brigadier had pressed Pienaar to suggest when the latter mentioned Wessels' flying visits to Mozambique with Johnson. Until the *Sunfish* disaster Pienaar had liked Wessels though he had always envied the younger man. Wessels came from a wealthy, long-established farming family, had enjoyed an expensive education, graduating from Stellenbosch and, later, from an agricultural college. The Dullstroom farm, with its thousands of morgen, attractive farmhouse, tennis court, swimming pool and airstrip, had been bought by Wessels with family money; a successful and hard-working farmer who concentrated on afforestation, he had in due course become a wealthy man in his own right.

His privileged background and lifestyle were very different to Pienaar's and it was consciousness of this, among other things, which had bred something like jealousy in the latter's mind. Since *Sunfish*'s capsize that jealousy had turned to dislike and subsequently, during the struggle to survive, a feeling closer to hatred. Not only had Wessels been responsible for the disaster but he was younger, bigger and stronger, and this to Pienaar was further evidence that the dice were loaded against him.

He was thankful when daylight brought to an end the uneasy night and he was able to enjoy the luxury of washing with soap in a bucket of water drawn from a watertrailer which supplied the needs of the camp. After a breakfast which was much the same as the meal of the previous night, preparations began for the journey to River Island.

The Commandante, familiar with the surrounding country, had remarked that he knew the estuary and its island which lay within the area of his geological survey. But for imparting this information he had not spoken to Pienaar; instead he had after breakfast sat writing at a small table outside the canvas shelter where he slept.

It was Alfonso Querrime who told Pienaar that they would be leaving later that morning: 'The Commandante has important work first,' he said. Instructed by Querrime not to move from the fire, Pienaar filled in time walking slowly round it, observing the camp and its surroundings

180

as he did so. Earlier he had seen four armed men leaving the camp, each going in a different direction. Soon afterwards four others had come in from those directions; sentries being relieved, he assumed.

There were more vehicles than he had at first thought. Two APCs, three trucks, one with a telescopic pole aerial, two trailers, the steel water-barrel on one of them, and the Land Rover. In all he thought there were about thirty men in the camp, some cutting firewood, others cleaning rifles, a number sitting in a circle round an African who appeared to be an instructor.

In mid-morning the Commandante abandoned his writing to confer with Querrime, whereafter orders were given and in due course a party of soldiers mustered alongside an APC.

On instructions from Querrime, Pienaar went to the Land Rover and got into the back where he was joined by three uniformed Africans, all armed with AK47s. One of them, a small wiry man with a big head, stared at him with large, frightened eyes.

Two armed soldiers sitting in the front seat of the Land Rover were joined by the Commandante who took the driving seat; he had a final word with his field assistants, they stood back and the Land Rover moved off, followed by the APC where Querrime sat next to the driver.

The two vehicles followed a rough, barely-discernible track through the bush, stopping at times to clear undergrowth which overhung it so that progress was slow. It was some time before the Commandante broke the silence in the Land Rover. 'There is place to cross upstream, on broken causeway of old track,' he said, looking straight ahead. 'Your Renamo friends break with mines.'

'Not *my* friends,' protested Pienaar. 'I support the Komati Accord.' It sounded feeble but was the best he could manage in the circumstances.

'Your country does not,' said the Commandante abruptly.

'What d'you mean?'

'Four millions peoples in Mozambique starving. One child die every few minutes. The Renamo guerrillas burn the villages, kill the people, steal the crops and cattle. Without Pretoria support, Renamo can be finished already long time ago.'

It was a lengthy statement for the Commandante, and one which Pienaar made no attempt to answer. The last thing he wanted was an argument with this large and formidable man whose help was essential to survival.

The journey through the bush seemed endless, the Land Rover jolting and bumping, turning and twisting, its sides constantly scraped and scratched by thornbushes and mopani trees. The APC lumbered along behind, the roar of its engine a comforting sound to Pienaar who had recollections of the brief fire-fight on the journey to Maxixe. He hoped and prayed that would not happen again. There was no longer a friendly helicopter patrolling ahead to flush out guerrillas.

The uncomfortable journey continued through arid bush with little game other than occasional glimpses of impala. Once a small herd of wildebeeste blocked the way, staring with curious, mystified eyes until fear took over and they galloped off into the bush, a cloud of dust behind them.

In time the larger trees lining the river came into view; after running parallel to them for a short distance the damaged causeway was reached. The Land Rover stopped, the Commandante issued orders and the men climbed out, their AK47s at the ready. Before beginning his close examination of the causeway the wild-eyed African had cast round the roughly-repaired structure like a gun-dog. Apparently satisfied, he signalled to the Commandante to come forward. Growling in low gear the Land Rover moved on to the causeway, the logs and boulders with which the structure had been repaired creaking under its weight. The river at that point, though shallow, was too deep for the Land Rover but it was no problem for the amphibious APC which motored steeply down the near bank, ploughed across the water and climbed the far bank in a noisy but impressive performance.

Safely across, the vehicles turned east and made for the coast. Without a track to follow progress was now slower than before but they pushed on, threading through the bush and making wide detours where it became impenetrable.

Apart from occasional radiophone exchanges with Querrime in the APC, the Commandante was uncommunicative; after several failed efforts at conversation Pienaar lapsed into a gloomy silence, occupying himself with mental pictures of Wessels and Trudi on River Island – part two, in a sense, of the blue film he had been watching the night before.

The rescue party began the final approach to the estuary in mid-afternoon. With the possibility of ambush much in mind, the Commandante sent three men ahead to reconnoitre, the wiry, wild-eyed African in charge. Darting left and right he stopped at times to check the ground and undergrowth, his men covering him with their AK47s. Moving silently the advance guard was soon lost to sight as combat camouflage and bush merged into one.

With its heavy machine guns and mortar-throwers manned for action the APC moved ahead of the Land Rover, travelled a short distance and stopped. Only when the wild-eyed African reappeared ahead and waved did the vehicles move forward, travelling a hundred metres or so before stopping, after which the process was repeated, the advance guard disappearing once more into the bush.

Pienaar said, 'That small black, the one with the mad eyes. What's he? Sergeant or something?'

'Gumede the tracker is not mad,' said the Commandante brusquely. He turned away as if to signal the end of the conversation, which indeed it was.

Before long water showed up through the bush, the estuary reflecting the light of the sky like a mirror. The vehicles were halted, a party of armed men climbed down from the APC and headed for the estuary, Querrime leading. Those in the Land Rover disembarked. The Commandante took the big revolver from his holster, stared at Pienaar with eyes which were inscrutable behind the dark sunglasses. 'You lead, I follow,' he said.

They set off in single file, an apprehensive Pienaar leading, the Commandante following, four armed Africans bringing up the rear. The bank of the sand gully was reached, the island immediately beyond it. Spread out along the bank with their automatic rifles and mortars the advance guard was scarcely visible, even at close range. Beyond them the rising tide had covered the gully.

For several minutes the Commandante searched the far bank with binoculars. Saying something to Querrime, he passed the glasses to the African. Querrime held them steady on a section of the island to his right. He nodded, passed them back.

The Commandante turned to Pienaar. 'Show yourself. We see people there. Tell them must come forward.'

Pienaar hesitated, stood up and stepped away from the thornbush behind which he had been crouching. He cupped his hands, shouted, 'Hey, Trudi, Jan. It's okay. These are Government people. We've come to fetch you.'

There were signs of movement on the far bank followed shortly by Wessels' and Trudi's appearance. Their excited exchanges with Pienaar were interrupted by a gruff order from the Commandante. 'Tell them must come this side.' Pienaar repeated the order.

'What about crocodiles?' Trudi shouted, pointing to the reeds.

'Nothing at this tide,' shouted the Commandante. He gave an order to Querrime. Two Africans raised their AK47s, fired short bursts into the reeds. There was no response. 'You see – nothing,' called the Commandante. When Trudi had rolled up the legs of her slacks, she and Wessels climbed down into the gully and waded across, the water up to their knees. They clambered up the bank and there were introductions, the newcomers excited and grateful.

The Commandante had directed a frowning stare at Wessels when Pienaar introduced him. To Pienaar it seemed that the heavily-bearded Portuguese was suspicious, puzzled, as he stared at Wessels in silence. Satisfied apparently that there was no ambush the Commandante led the way back to the vehicles followed by Wessels and Trudi who were engaged in a rapid exchange of news with Pienaar.

'When we heard the sound of engines,' she was saying, 'we left the camp and hid in the bushes, trying to see what was happening. We caught glimpses of soldiers in the bush. We thought they could be Renamo. It was really scary. Then you stood up Piet and – oh, I can't tell you.' She broke off, tears in her eyes. 'Sorry.' She wiped them away with her fingers. 'But it's so marvellous to have been rescued.' An instant later she added with feminine practicality, 'My things are still on the island. Clothes, shoulderbag, etcetera. I must get them.'

'Me too,' Wessels grinned. 'A hatchet and a fishing bag.' He had a word with the Commandante who said yes, they could fetch them; he gave them ten minutes and an escort of two men.

When Wessels and Trudi returned, the Commandante led the way back towards the vehicles. On reaching them he took Querrime aside. Speaking in Portuguese he said, 'It seems that the man Pienaar's story is correct but it is necessary to check it out. We must find the aeroplane. See if it crashed where the woman says.'

185

The African nodded. 'Yes, Senhor Vasco. This is good plan. She says is not too far.'

The Commandante told the survivors of his intentions. 'Now we go find the Cessna,' he said.

'What for?' asked Wessels. 'What's the point?'

The Commandante stared at him for some seconds before saying, 'I say so. That is point.'

Trudi looked pleased. 'If my note has gone we'll know JJ came back. Besides,' she added firmly, 'my clothes, my luggage, are there.'

The Commandante questioned her about the direction from which she had come when she first reached the island, the time it had taken to make the journey from the Cessna. How fast had she been walking? She explained that for much of the way she had kept to the beach. Could she remember at what point she had joined it? She told him of the clump of palm trees and the pool in the rocks: 'I'll recognise those, all right,' she assured him. The Commandante, having announced that she would take the place of one of his men in the front seat of the Land Rover, gave orders to proceed.

With Pienaar and Wessels in the APC, the vehicles set off on the journey down the beach, keeping close to the sea where the sand was firm, and making detours inland where outcrops of rock blocked the way. The footprints left by Trudi and the *Sunfish* survivors were still visible in places where the tide had not washed them away. In late afternoon the rock pool and palm trees showed up and the vehicles turned inland.

At that point Gumede the tracker took over, following the spoor Trudi had left, footprints, scuffed earth and recently-broken undergrowth, but progress was now so slow that shortly before sunset the expedition had covered little more than half the distance to the Cessna if Trudi's estimate that her journey had been about twenty-five kilometres was correct.

Camp was made for the night, a fire was lit, sentries were

posted and a meal prepared. The Commandante produced a plastic washbowl, hot water, soap and towel. 'For the Senhorita,' he said, his broken English lending to the statement a touch of gallantry. 'The men must make for themselves.'

Before the evening meal he took Trudi to the Land Rover. There, sitting together in the front seat, he questioned her closely. The story she told him was precisely that which she had told Johnson the day they met on the verandah of the hotel in Mutare; to it she added an account of how their brief friendship had resulted in his offer to fly her back to Johannesburg in the Cessna. Suspicious at first, the Commandante appeared to be satisfied by the time she had finished.

TWENTY-TWO

With maps and literature from the local tourist office, Luena spent his first day in Mauritius making a reconnaissance of Port Louis in a hired Renault. It included the premises of Gottwald, Matchett, Liebson & Co Ltd, the harbour and its environs, and the principal restaurants, hotels, parks and sporting facilities in and outside the town. He also had a brief telephone conversation with Ranjut Patel.

Most of the next two days was spent in Government offices discussing import/export possibilities in general terms. After dinner on the second night he drove out on the Curepipe road, turned left about a couple of hundred metres after the layby indicated on the sketch Patel had sent him, and followed the dirt road bordering cane-fields for about a kilometre before stopping in the shadows of a pile of boulders which lay beyond a grove of tall trees. There he turned the Renault and backed into the shadows, facing the way he had come. There was no other car to be seen but he had arrived early and was not surprised. He filled in the time recalling what Nielsen had said about the Hindu.

A year before Ranjut Patel had been in Harare on business. He had at that time given certain information to a senior government official; this had been referred to police HQ whence it had been passed to Nielsen's new unit for necessary action.

Nielsen had at once arranged a meeting with Patel. The Hindu had told him of certain activities in which he believed Gottwald and Kahn were engaged. He had sketched in their backgrounds, the salient points of which

188

were the German's dubious business reputation, and the fact that despite their clandestine relationship they had no overt social or business connections with each other. Kahn, he said, was the Mauritian representative of a Karachi textile firm, his business of considerably less importance than Gottwald's.

Finally, Nielsen had obtained from Patel answers to two matters which had worried him during the discussion: why was he so anxious to give damaging information about Gottwald and Kahn, and how did he know about the German's covert relationship with Kahn and details of their travels abroad?

The answers were comparatively simple: some years back, at a time when the two men had been business acquaintances, Gottwald had introduced Patel to a visiting Swiss entrepreneur. The latter had proposed a business venture which entailed buying a 'shell' company to be used as a vehicle for property development in Mauritius. Impressed by Gottwald's enthusiasm for the project and the profits it offered, Patel had invested a substantial sum of money. Not long afterwards the Swiss had left on a visit to Zürich from which he never returned. With him had gone every penny of Patel's investment. In the course of enquiries in Zürich the Hindu had learnt that the entrepreneur was a cousin of Gottwald's; something the latter had omitted to mention.

As a result, Patel had severed his relationship with Gottwald, refused ever to speak to him again and – at this point Nielsen had quoted the Hindu's own words – 'To show up Herman Gottwald, to get even for the financial loss and humiliation he caused me, has become an important part of my life. You can call it an obsession if you like. But that is why I tell you these things and offer you my assistance.'

The assistance – valuable as it was – had been due to a fortuitous circumstance: a young woman, Sushila Chopra, had been nursed through a dangerous illness by Patel's wife in earlier days when the latter was a nursing sister. Some years later Miss Chopra had become switchboard operator and receptionist in the outer office of Gottwald, Matchett, Liebson & Co Ltd.

Sushila Chopra, eternally grateful to Mrs Patel and disapproving of Gottwald for a number of reasons, had become an invaluable source of information.

Luena was thinking about the Gottwald-Patel saga when he saw in the distance the lights of a car coming up the dirt road beside the cane fields.

Sitting round the fire that night the Commandante was for the most part silent. Listening to the chatter of the survivors he sensed the tension between the two Afrikaners, Pienaar displaying petulant signs of jealousy and irritating Wessels and the girl with silly innuendoes about their night on the island alone. Her attempts to change the subject by making conversation with the Commandante made little headway until she got on to the subject of Gumede. 'I was watching him this afternoon,' she said. 'It was fantastic how he followed my tracks, especially in thick bush. How on earth does he do it?'

'Gumede is Shangaan,' replied the Commandante. 'For many years he work in Kruger Park – for game ranger. In this way he learn to follow spoor. Now he is – how you say? – a genius of tracking.'

'Sad looking man, isn't he? Such haunted eyes.'

'For Gumede there is bad things this year.' The Commandante stared into the fire. 'The wife, children, also old mother, brother – Renamo guerrillas kill all. First rape the women, then kill them. Also burn the huts, take the cattle, the crops. For Gumede everything is finish.'

'Oh, poor man.' She closed her eyes. 'How absolutely ghastly.'

*

Later that night heavy clouds shut out the moon and the stars and there were distant rumbles of thunder. The Commandante thawed, said that it was good, rain was vital to Mozambique because of the long drought. He insisted that Trudi should sleep in the Land Rover, the men would have to sleep by the fire. 'If storm come,' he told Wessels and Pienaar, 'you can go in APC. My men like the rain. They will wish to enjoy it. In their language it is the water of God.'

The Commandante stayed by the fire for some time after the others had left, his mind disturbed by unpleasant thoughts. The voice, the accent, had evoked long-buried memories of troubles, terrors and fears, recalling with chilling clarity the humiliation, the pain and the despair of the chalk circle.

To escape from them he switched his thoughts to the survivors' stories. Wessels had confirmed Pienaar's account of the *Sunfish* disaster and the subsequent struggle to survive, but that did not necessarily mean the story was true.

And the woman's story of the air crash? How she had trekked through the bush, taken refuge on the river island where she'd been joined by the men a few days later. Wasn't that a bit too much of a coincidence? Wessels and Pienaar could be SAAF aircrew shot down while dropping supplies to Renamo, or carrying out clandestine air reconnaissance, the woman with them as cover? The Cessna might provide the answer. Had her questions about Gumede's tracking been motivated by fear that the Cessna *would* be found – and in it incriminating evidence?

He had taken the truck up the hill above the camp the night before to report by radiophone the arrival of Pienaar. At the Maputo end d'Abreu had confirmed that two South Africans named Pienaar and Wessels had been passengers in the *Sunfish* posted as missing by Inhambane, whence it

191

had sailed. 'You tell me Pienaar says he left his passport in the hotel at Maxixe. Don't accept that story until we've checked it,' d'Abreu had warned. 'If he and his friends *are* Renamo they could have heard about the missing boat and the names of the occupants. The news was broadcast on Mozambique radio and on SABC. The same for the missing Cessna.'

The Commandante assured d'Abreu that he would check and report back. Since that conversation Wessels and Trudi Braun had come into the picture. The Commandante had seen her passport and it appeared to be in order. Wessels, like Pienaar, said he had left his in the hotel at Maxixe. He claimed to be a farmer in the Dullstroom district and confirmed that Pienaar was an agricultural machinery salesman. Both could be lying. It would be for d'Abreu to sort that out.

Whether they found the Cessna or not he would have to get the survivors down to Maputo by way of Pomene and Rio das Pedras. That meant an armed escort of several men. At Rio das Pedras the survivors could be taken on by military convoy to Maputo. Once there they would become d'Abreu's problem. But would they get to Pomene, let alone Rio das Pedras? Querrime would have told the others of his suspicions about Pienaar, the Afrikaner. The Africans were seeing their country, their villages, their families and crops devastated by Renamo guerrillas. Their media constantly told them that Renamo enjoyed the covert support of South Africa. No, it would be too dangerous, decided the Commandante. He himself would have to go with them, even if it meant the loss of important time.

He had left the fire to check that the sentries were at their posts when the storm broke with equatorial violence, the rain, driven by the wind, beating down in swathes, its hissing roar broken only by the crack of lightning and the roll of thunder.

*

192

In the cheerless, bleakly furnished office high in the grey building in Johannesburg a mood of frustrated excitement beset the pink, bespectacled Captain Le Roux as he read the telex message from Maputo:

> *It is understood that a survivor from the missing motor launch* Sunfish *has been found by government forces somewhere in Inhambane Province. The possibility exists that the rescued man may be able to assist in regard to the whereabouts of another survivor from the* Sunfish *and also one from the* Cessna *which disappeared ten days ago while on a flight from Mutare to Maputo.*

The telex had been sent by Carvalho in plain language to Charter Couriers RSA Ltd at Grand Central Airport. Its contents had been phoned through to the Brigadier's office by Lategan.

Le Roux's excitement at the news was to some extent dampened by irritation. It was important that the Brigadier should be made aware without delay of this latest and surprising development, but though it was past ten o'clock in the morning he had not yet arrived. Le Roux had telephoned his residence only to be told by an African servant that the Brigadier and his wife had left the house at nine o'clock that morning; the African did not know where they had gone.

Le Roux was reflecting that this was most unusual behaviour on the part of the Brigadier who was punctilious in letting his staff know his movements, when that officer strode through the outer office with a curt 'More – morning,' and went on into his own office.

Le Roux at once phoned through for permission to bring in an urgent message from Maputo. He had hoped the Brigadier would ask what it was about, but instead he had snapped, 'Yes,' and put the phone down, thus robbing Le Roux of the opportunity of adding a touch of drama to the occasion with something like, 'It's about a survivor from the *Sunfish*, sir.'

With Le Roux eyeing him anxiously the Brigadier read the message a second time before looking up with a portentous frown, the cold grey eyes reflecting displeasure. 'Why can't Carvalho be specific? What the devil does all this mean?'

The Brigadier quoted from the message sheet: 'A survivor . . . government forces . . . somewhere in Inhambane . . . the possibility exists . . . maybe able to assist . . . another survivor . . . one from the Cessna.' He slammed the message sheet down on his desk. 'Why no names, no details, all this secrecy?' he demanded of the apprehensive Le Roux as if he were in some way responsible for the message.

'Is it not possible that that is the only information so far issued by the Mozambique authorities?' he suggested. 'It is typical of these African bureaucrats to frame a message in such vague terms. They like to beat about the bush.'

'Pity they ever came out of it,' snorted the Brigadier. 'There were five men in the *Sunfish* – three whites and two blacks, according to the Inhambane report. So we've a one-in-five chance that Pienaar is the survivor.'

'Does it matter, sir? Now that *Doodslaan* is cancelled.'

The Brigadier looked up from the crystal ball upon which he had been focusing. 'Of course it matters. If Pienaar is the survivor he may have learnt something from the Cessna survivor. He might have found the crashed aircraft, possibly seen what Johnson had on board. If the woman was the survivor, Pienaar may have learnt something important from her, or by inspection of the crashed aircraft.'

'Yes, sir. But one-in-five is not very good odds.'

With an impatient gesture the Brigadier pushed the crystal ball away from him. 'For God's sake, Le Roux,' he admonished, 'don't always emphasise the obvious. Of course they're not very good odds – but think positively,

194

man. There's no future in being negative. Not for the department, nor,' the Colonel glared ominously,' nor for you.'

'Yes, sir. Of course.' Le Roux's forefinger tapped nervously at his spectacles. 'Is there anything else, sir?'

The Brigadier slid the message sheet across the desk. 'Yes, take this. Tell Lategan to let Carvalho know that I am not pleased, that I want definite information from him – and I want it quickly.'

With a subdued, 'Ja, Brigadier,' Le Roux picked up the message sheet and left the office.

TWENTY-THREE

Curled up in the driving compartment of the APC in uneasy sleep the Commandante was visited by the nightmare which had troubled him over the years; the details changed but the setting, the principal characters, remained the same.

He was standing in the chalk circle high in the building. He had been standing there for hours: knee, leg and back muscles rigid with pain, his mind confused by the harsh voice mouthing endless questions, insults, sarcasm, abuses, sometimes with physical reminders of his helplessness, a slap in the face or a knee in the groin.

Someone was shaking him and he supposed that once again he had lost consciousness and fallen to the floor. So he lay waiting in miserable expectation of the sluice of cold water knowing that soon, limp and shattered, he would be taken back to the dimly-lit cell to wait in solitary confinement for the next session. Fearful of these things he had cried out in his sleep. But it was only Querrime shaking him, saying, 'You make bad dream, Senhor Vasco. Do not worry. I am here. It is only dream.'

The nightmare had been too vivid, triggered too many memories for sleep, so for a long time he lay thinking, the reality behind the dream returning in all its detail: the smell of the room, a synthesis of floor polish and disinfectant, an odour which masked others: vomit, urine, sweat and blood? The walls a mournful green, their shine removed by frequent washing. The brown linoleum floor showing signs of wear. A desk, a filing cabinet, a small scrubbed table scarred with cigarette burns and unexplained dents and scratches. But for the chair at the desk, hard-backed wooden chairs; simple, austere, barrack-like, two of them. But not for him. For him the chalk circle. Just big enough to stand in clear of the wall; to stand in for long minutes which drifted into longer hours. Mostly with *them* there, sometimes alone, but always watched. The window at the far end was shut, its sash screwed into the sill. Once when he had begged for fresh air the Lieutenant had said, 'No, my boy. We don't fall for those tricks. This is six storeys up. In the past some of you buggers have jumped. And we got the blame. Must have been torture, your *rooinek* papers said. So we're in trouble then. Not bad trouble, you understand, but trouble enough. Worse was that they couldn't tell us what we wanted to know once they'd jumped. They were okay, you see. No more trouble for them. But they jumped and we got the shit.' The Lieutenant's voice rose. 'That's why that window's screwed down. Now, come on, man. We know what you know. And we know that you know a lot more than you've told us.'

So the sessions of standing in the chalk circle went on, day after day and sometimes long into the nights.

At that time life had only two dimensions, two environments: the sessions in the chalk circle alternating with solitary confinement in the dimly-lit cell, unfurnished but for the sanitary bucket, the blanket and the palliasse.

But it was the sessions in the chalk circle which destroyed a man. The endless questions. Questions put sometimes in a quiet voice, sometimes in a friendly cajoling one, at others threatening shouted questions loaded with insults; there were sly questions, puzzling questions, and stupid ones. Then the switches, sudden, unexpected: the slap in the face, the head banged against the wall, the knee in the groin, mostly things which left no physical mark. The persuasive technique would follow: 'Come on, man. We know what you must know. Your mates have talked, you see. They're not all awkward bastards like you. Come on, it's best for you to tell us the truth. Play the game. Just answer the questions.' The Lieutenant would stand up, light a cigarette, walk the few feet to the window, sigh loudly, then turn and come back. 'You know we don't like this business any better than you do. We have to act like this. It's our job. Just doing our duty. That's all, doing our duty. The same way security police do it anywhere in the world. But we're civilised. Not like your black friends. Not like the Idi Amins or the Bokassas. We don't cut off your balls. We don't eat nuns or necklace our political opponents. We don't maim or kill you. We play the game according to the rules. And that's all we ask you to do. Just co-operate with us and you'll be fine. Just answer the questions. Outside this situation we could be friends. You know that, man. So let's settle things in a decent civilised way.'

A long silence before the next switch of tactics. 'Okay, *kerel*. If that's the way you want it.' The Lieutenant's voice would thicken, threaten. 'If you want to play tough. Okay, my Commie friend. You want it like that you get it like that.' Shouting now, his face dark with frustration, the Lieutenant comes closer, his mouth exuding warm, cigarette-laden breath. 'You won't talk, hey? So you make me force you to talk? Is that it?' The Lieutenant's elbow struck into his kidneys, throwing him off balance. The room had begun to swim, his knees to sag. He fell against the wall clear of the chalk circle.

Then the return to consciousness, hastened by a sluice of cold water. The Lieutenant's voice droning in through a misty haze. 'Come on. Get up, man. No good playing that game. We know you haven't fainted. Get back in that fucking circle. Quick, unless you want your balls squeezed.' The Commandante remembered as if it were yesterday the struggle to get up, the aching pain in his knees and ankles, leg muscles set from long hours of standing, hands wet with vomit scrabbling against the green wall, slipping on its smooth surface.

At last the scrape of chairs, dim shapes rising, the Lieutenant's voice. 'Come, Sergeant. Time for coffee, man.'

'Fine,' says the Sergeant. 'I can do with that.'

'And you – you stay in that circle. Don't forget you're always watched.' The Lieutenant looked up at the TV lens high in the wall. 'It never sleeps.' He smiled at the Sergeant, who nodded. 'And remember, Constable Gerricke's on the door. You don't like Gerricke, do you? I think he also doesn't like you.'

And of course in time he'd broken. Told them what they'd wanted to know in a humiliating, hysterical session. Anything to get away from the endless bullying, the deadly hours of standing, the long periods without sleep. No man could take much of that for long. So in the end he had told them what they wanted to know realising as he did so that he was guilty of betrayal.

Refreshed by the rains of the night before, the bush next morning seemed more alive, more vital, the bird songs louder, the smell of the undergrowth stronger. The mood of the Africans had lifted, there was happy chatter and laughter and this communicated itself to the survivors for whom the future seemed somehow brighter. Only the Commandante, whose manner was even grimmer and more silent than usual, appeared unaffected by the rain.

An early start was made, the morning meal of *putu* and black coffee finished soon after sunrise when camp was struck and the expedition moved on. As before, the Land Rover was driven by the Commandante, Trudi and an armed African sharing the front seat with him.

Gumede the tracker and his escort walked ahead but tracking proved difficult, the rain having washed away much of the spoor left by Trudi. To add to these problems, the bush was so thick in places that the vehicles were unable to follow the tracking party and had to make wide detours. There were long pauses at times when the spoor was lost, Gumede again casting round like a gun-dog, seeking broken twigs in the undergrowth or the remnants of footprints still visible to him in spite of the downpour.

Questioned by the Commandante, Trudi told him that she could recall few landmarks on her trek down to the coast. 'You know what the bush is like, Vasco. It's monotonous, looks the same wherever you are if you're on foot. One clearing isn't very different to another.'

The dark glasses hid the expression in his eyes but she knew he was staring at her and she found it disconcerting. 'Where the Cessna crashed?' he said. 'You say palm trees break off wings. That place. Can you know it from far?'

'Yes, definitely. The line of sandhills the Cessna had to cross before the clearing, and the tall palms and other big trees on the far side. Yes, I'll recognise them from quite far off.'

He continued to stare. 'We shall see,' he said.

She thought he sounded doubtful.

As the morning progressed and the expedition penetrated more deeply into the bush scatterings of game appeared: wildebeeste, zebra, impala and warthogs. A solitary porcupine challenging Gumede on a game-path, its quills extended and quivering in brilliant sunlight, drew raucous laughter from the Africans who shouted advice and encouragement to the little man. Once, when the Land Rover rounded thick bush, and a small herd of impala was seen grazing in a clearing, the Commandante put on the brakes, climbed down with his rifle and shot an impala ram.

'Oh, why, Vasco?' protested Trudi. 'Why kill such a beautiful creature?'

'We must eat,' he said. 'Before the war is lot of game. Now the war, also no rain, makes different. The people starve. We are fortunate. We have plenty *putu*. But for meat we must take what we find.'

It was a long speech for the Commandante, so defensive in tone that she realised she had hit on a raw nerve.

It was past noon and by the Commandante's reckoning the crashed Cessna should have been reached. Gumede, however, continued to find enough spoor to follow, so the Commandante assumed that the woman's estimate of distance was at fault. By not too much, he hoped; since tracking on the return journey would be unnecessary a fair pace would be possible and he intended to get back to the base-camp that night. Undue delay in finding the Cessna could make that difficult.

With this in mind he was wondering how much further they had to go when she touched his arm. 'Look, Vasco – there they are.' Her voice trembled with excitement. 'The sandhills and the trees.' She pointed. 'Look. When we're through the bush ahead you'll see the clearing. And the poor old Cessna.'

The crash site looked exactly as it had when last she'd seen it, the damaged palm trunks, the scored undergrowth, the Cessna's severed wings and fuselage shining perhaps a little more brightly than she remembered. Washed clean by the rain, she supposed.

Wessels and Pienaar had left the APC and were walking towards the Cessna when the Commandante, accompanied by Trudi, waved them back. 'Keep away,' he shouted brusquely. 'We make examination.'

The two Afrikaners looked at each other in surprise, shrugged and turned back.

The Commandante climbed awkwardly into the wrecked cockpit, his size complicating the operation. Trudi followed, her first concern the note she had left; soaked and illegible in part, it was where she had put it.

Querrime came over to the wreckage for a hurried consultation with the Commandante. Soon afterwards Gumede with two men, AK47s slung over their shoulders, left the clearing.

'Where are they going?' Wessels asked Querrime. The African pointed to the black shapes circling in the sky to the west. 'They go to see what the vultures see. Can be lion kill. Can be wounded guerrilla, or Frelimo. The vultures watch and wait.'

The Commandante questioned Trudi about the Cessna, its layout, what she remembered of the crash, and what she and Johnson had done immediately after it. With his permission she took her grip from the luggage-locker and put it in the Land Rover. She was there talking to the Afrikaners when the Commandante came back to them. 'Daylight still plenty,' he said. 'When Gumede and others come back we go. Journey must finish before dark.'

'Aren't you going to report finding the Cessna?' Pienaar's face showed concern. 'Tell them Johnson's not there? That he headed for Cheline but didn't come back?'

The Commandante shook his head. 'Thees guerrilla country. Not good to make radio talk until base-camp.'

It was some time before Gumede and his men returned in a sort of triumphal procession; in addition to their Kalashnikovs, one was carrying a sporting rifle, the other a pilotcase, the pink strap over his shoulder, while perched high on Gumede's head was a bush-hat with a leopardskin band.

'Oh, my God,' Trudi shrilled. 'Those are JJ's things.'

The Commandante directed a surprised stare at her before speaking to Gumede. After the question and answer session which followed he turned back to her. 'Yes. They find him. The things by the body. Not far. Two kilometres, they say.'

'You mean he's dead.' Her voice had in it an uncertain quaver.

'Yes. Not much left. Jackals still with carcase. The vultures wait.'

She buried her face in her hands. 'Oh God! Poor JJ. How horrible. He was such a nice, kind guy. Really nice.' She shook her head in disbelief. 'He was still so close. What can have happened? I can't bear to think of him lying there alone. If I'd known I could have helped him. At least stayed with him until he died.' She looked up, her eyes filled with tears. 'What killed him, d'you think?'

'The crash?' Ferreira shrugged. 'Can be fractured skull. You say he bleed from nose and mouth . . . speak in a funny way?'

She nodded. 'Yes. He should never have gone. Poor JJ. How he must have suffered.' She was deep in thought. 'What will you do with his rifle and pilotcase?'

'Give to government people in Maputo. The Cessna crash in Mozambique territory. They will send his things to his company.'

Pienaar spoke to Wessels in Afrikaans after which he turned to the Commandante. 'We'll take charge of them if you don't mind. The aircraft, its owners, the pilot – ' He looked at Trudi, ' – and the passenger were all South Africans. We'll be returning there in a day or so . . .'

'Will you?' interrupted the Commandante, his voice heavy with doubt.

Pienaar's head came up suddenly, a startled expression on his face. 'Yes. Why not? Now that – '

Wessels interrupted. 'We don't have to be responsible for the rifle and pilotcase, Piet. Forget the bloody things. We have every reason to be grateful to Vasco. But for him . . .' He shook his head. 'Who knows?'

Pienaar gave him a sullen, disapproving look.

'Tell me, Vasco,' Wessels asked. 'What *are* your plans for getting the three of us back to South Africa?'

The Commandante looked into the distance, fingered his beard. 'We go to base-camp now. I speak with Maputo tonight. They tell me. In the morning you will know.'

TWENTY-FOUR

The Commandante's search party did not get back to the base-camp that night.

When they reached the river in late afternoon Gumede once again checked the causeway for mines, declared it safe and the Land Rover moved on to it. It was some way across when, with a final creak and groan, the structure collapsed. The Land Rover descended with it, settling into the river on top of a jumble of logs and boulders, its partly-submerged wheels trapped by them. An attempt by the APC to haul it clear failed. Concerned that further efforts might break the towing chain or damage the vehicle, the Commandante ordered his men to clear the logs and boulders which held the wheels.

This entailed working in waist-deep water in failing light, a task made more difficult by the Africans' fear of crocodiles. After various difficulties, and rather more than an hour's work, the offending debris had been removed and the APC hauled the Land Rover up on to the bank on the far side. It was then necessary to work on the engine and by the time it had been restarted the Commandante announced that camp would be made for the night in a nearby clearing.

It was evident from his demeanour that the Commandante's mood had not been improved by the incident, for while the camp was being made ready he was noticeably short with Querrime and his men.

The meal round the fire got off to a gloomy start, Trudi preoccupied and miserable about Johnson's death, the two

204

Afrikaners quiet and thoughtful, occasionally muttering to each other in subdued voices, while the Commandante sat staring into the fire, silent and unapproachable. He went off at one stage to check that the sentries were on their beats; when he returned Wessels attempted to break the ice by thanking him for their rescue. 'But for you, Vasco,' he said, 'God knows what would have happened to us. We sit here round the fire, well fed and in safe hands. But for you it would be very different.' He paused, laughed cheerfully. 'For one thing, Trudi might have been taken by a crocodile.'

The attempt at humour fell flat. The Commandante shrugged, said nothing, but continued to look into the fire, its light playing on his bearded Castro-like face and glinting on the sunglasses which he was never without.

Wessels tried again. 'You know, folks, the first thing I'll do when we get to the Polana is have a real good soak in a hot bath. I reckon I must stink like a polecat.'

'You do, Jan.' Trudi wrinkled her nose. 'I'm sure we all do.'

Pienaar yawned noisily. 'First thing I do when we get there is sink a bloody great lager. Then another and – '

'There's a problem.' The Commandante broke his long silence but continued to gaze into the fire.

'What's that?' challenged Pienaar.

The dark glasses focused on the Afrikaner. 'You,' said the Commandante.

'Me?' Pienaar stiffened on his haunches. 'What are you getting at?'

'You are travelling in Mozambique, in guerrilla war country, under a false name and on a false passport. That will take some explaining in Maputo. Espionage is taken seriously there. Men are executed for it.'

The veins on Pienaar's forehead stood out, pulsed worm-like. 'You're crazy, Commandante. You talk rubbish. We can prove that we came on a fishing trip. Nothing more. For God's sake, d'you think we wanted the boat to capsize, to drift on it for days facing death? D'you think that sounds like espionage?'

'No, Steens Badenhorst – Lieutenant Badenhorst – I'm not crazy. Curious is more the word.'

Pienaar stood up, faced the big Portuguese across the fire, stared at him as if he were a ghost.

Wessels got to his feet, broke the silence which had followed the Commandante's charge. 'What's going on, Vasco?' There was bewilderment in his face and voice. 'What d'you mean?'

'He's getting me bloody mad,' interrupted Pienaar. 'That's what's going on.' The hoarse voice had risen, the stubbled chin thrusting aggressively at the Commandante. 'You better watch your step, *Mister* Ferreira. You can find yourself in bad trouble.'

'Wilkens to you, Lieutenant. Or are you now Major, or maybe Colonel?' The Commandante was still on his haunches, the wide shoulders hunched forward, hands clasped between his knees, his eyes on the fire. 'George Wilkens,' he went on. 'One time detainee in Johannesburg. We saw quite a lot of each other in those days. Me the prisoner, you the interrogator. You haven't forgotten, have you? Or have too many poor devils passed through your hands since?'

The ripple of shock among those round the fire came not only from what Ferreira had said but from the way in which he had said it. The broken English, the Portuguese accent, had gone, their place taken by fluent English, clipped and blurred with a South African accent.

Pienaar continued to stare, the muscles of his face working. 'George Wilkens? I've never heard of any George Wilkens. Nor of Steens Badenhorst. Why should I know Badenhorst? I've never been in the police.'

'You lie, Badenhorst.' The Commandante removed his sunglasses, and turned dark eyes on the Afrikaner. 'Remember the cut your fist made under my left eye? See the scar? Your ring made that. The ring you're wearing now.'

Pienaar moved round the fire, stood over the crouched figure. 'You're trying to make trouble, Ferreira. *Pas op, man* – look out, man. Nobody fools around with me.' The Afrikaner's face seemed to swell, his voice to get hoarser.

'Don't be stupid, Badenhorst.' The Commandante spoke in a tired voice, his eyes once again on the fire. 'You're not impressing anyone.'

The Afrikaner growled, moved closer, a hand on his sheath-knife.

There was a rustle of leaves in the shadows behind the Commandante and Querrime stepped into the light of the flames. He said nothing, just stood there, the muzzle of the AK47 pointing at Pienaar. The Afrikaner stared at the gaunt, broken-nosed African, shook his head and went back to the far side of the fire.

Wessels had been watching the scene with incredulous eyes. 'I've got to have a private word with Pienaar,' he said. 'Okay if we leave the fire for a moment, Commandante?'

'Yes, but don't go far. My men will be watching. They can be trigger-happy.' He turned to Querrime, said a few words in Portuguese. Wessels and Pienaar disappeared into the darkness, followed by Querrime, behind him the shadowy figure of Gumede.

As the approaching car came closer and the sound of its engine grew louder Luena switched on the Renault's parking lights, counted five, and switched them off again.

The lights of the oncoming car dipped twice in succession. Moments later it passed the Renault, turned and parked in the shadows behind it. A dark shape emerged from the driving seat.

Luena got out. 'Mr Patel?' he enquired.

The dark shape extended a hand. 'Yes, indeed – and you are Mr Luena?'

'That's right. Like to sit in the car or talk here?'

'The latter is more suitable,' said Patel, his precise English flavoured by the Hindi accent. 'We are not likely to be seen,' he explained. 'But should a car pass this way it will appear that one motorist has stopped to make an inquiry of another.'

'Okay,' said Luena. 'Where do we begin?'

'I would like first to place this shopping bag in your car. Mr Nielsen asked me to give it to you. I will explain later.'

'Go ahead, Mr Patel. Put it on the front seat.'

Having done so, Patel expressed the hope that Luena's journey had been comfortable, that the Port Louis hotel in which he was staying was adequate, and that his business with local officialdom was progressing satisfactorily. These courtesies concluded, he came to the point: 'I am aware of the real purpose of your visit here, Mr Luena, but I must confess that you face almost insurmountable difficulties if you hope – as I know Mr Nielsen does – to know what goes on between Herman Gottwald and Abdul Kahn. If it were simply a matter of being physically present in Mauritius, I could have solved that problem long ago. But these two men are never seen together, never meet in public. We know that Kahn never telephones Gottwald in his office – and vice versa.'

Miss Chopra, thought Luena, but he said nothing. Nielsen had told him not to refer to Sushila Chopra unless Patel introduced the subject.

'Of course they must communicate. Possibly by telephone from their residences, but more likely by means of public phone-booths. Even so they would not discuss details of, shall we say, covert operations by such means.'

Clouds drifted across the moon and the night grew dark, masking what little Luena could see of the Hindu's features.

'So how do they discuss things, Mr Patel?'

'Ah, I think I know the answer to that but it does not make the problem any easier, Mr Luena.'

208

'So what *is* the answer?'

'Beau Rivage.' Patel was overcome by a sudden fit of coughing. When it had run its course he blew his nose, put away the handkerchief and apologised. 'That is the name of Mr Gottwald's holiday villa. It is situated on the slopes of a hill not far from Mahebourg. They say with a fine view of the sea. It is, I am told, in a quiet, secluded area. Mahebourg itself is on the island's east coast. About fifty kilometres from Port Louis by the direct route.'

'You mean they meet at Beau Rivage?'

'So I understand, Mr Luena. But only occasionally and always at night.'

Miss Chopra again, reflected Luena. What a girl to have around.

'There is reason to believe,' continued Patel, 'that such a meeting is likely to take place this coming weekend. On Sunday night, to be exact.'

Luena could not restrain himself. 'How on earth do you know that, Mr Patel?'

There was a moment of silence before the dark shape beside him answered. 'Gottwald telephoned his wife to inform her that he would be visiting Beau Rivage during the weekend, entertaining a business guest. She asked if he wished her to be present. He replied that, since they would be discussing confidential matters, her presence might be embarrassing. She then said, "Oh, *that* guest. Then I will certainly not come." '

'At that point,' continued Patel, 'Gottwald rang off, having told her that he would not be needing Paul.'

'Who is Paul?'

'A Creole servant. He is sometimes taken up to Beau Rivage to assist over weekends.'

Luena thought for a moment about what Patel had told him before asking his next question. 'How d'you know that the business guest is Abdul Kahn?'

'I suspect it, but do not know it. There was some significance perhaps, in Mrs Gottwald's "Oh, *that* guest".

Furthermore, Gottwald has just returned from a visit to Johannesburg and Zürich. He is likely to have news for Kahn.'

'I see.' Luena paused. 'What you've told me about Beau Rivage is very interesting, Mr Patel. But I don't really see how I can make use of it.'

The moon came clear of the clouds again, casting pale light on the faces of the two men.

'Nor do I, Mr Luena. But that is your problem.' Patel's smile exposed ivory white teeth. 'A solution may suggest itself when you have given the matter more thought. Since they are dining together – and it will be dark then – I imagine between eight and nine on Sunday night would be the most suitable time. Now, I'm afraid I must go. Mrs Patel will be worrying.'

Luena said, 'Of course,' adding, 'The shopping bag? You said you would explain.'

'Yes, indeed. In it there is an envelope containing a map which shows the way to Beau Rivage. Mr Nielsen asked me to let you have the other item. He said it was a toy. That you would not have been able to get it through the airport checks.'

'A toy?' Luena laughed. 'What the hell is Greg up to?'

They walked across to where Patel's car stood in the shadows. The Hindu opened the door, got into the driving seat, and started the engine.

Luena said, 'Thanks for your help, Mr Patel.'

'Not at all, Mr Luena. These are matters of mutual interest.' He lowered his voice as if to ensure that he would not be overheard. 'If there is any likelihood of your being seen in the vicinity of Beau Rivage on Sunday night, it might be advisable to leave for Africa by the first available flight on Monday morning.'

By the time Luena had digested the remark all that could be seen of Patel's car was the loom of headlights as it sped down the road past the cane-fields.

TWENTY-FIVE

Behind a thicket of scrub and mopani trees away from the fire, Pienaar and Wessels held a hurried conversation in Afrikaans. Wessels began by accusing Pienaar of abusing their friendship. Why had he used a false name, never mentioned his time in the Security Police, pretending he had always been in the agricultural machinery business? 'Why do you have to come into Mozambique with a false name and passport? Nobody's going to fall for the story that it was just a fishing trip. You've put me at risk. The authorities are not going to believe I didn't know who you were.'

'I haven't abused your friendship. You know I sell farm machinery.' Pienaar's plaintive protest suggested that he had been done an injustice. 'Christ, man. You've bought it from me. I've been doing it for years. *Ja*, okay. I did change my name when I left the Force a long time back to go into business. I changed it because my life would have been at risk if Africans had known I'd been Security Branch. It had been my job to interrogate terrorists. They would have got me for that, for revenge. You know how they can be?'

'I wonder if you're telling the truth? You were after Johnson, weren't you? You knew that I knew him well. I'd told you he had often flown me and others from the syndicate down to Mozambique on fishing trips.' There was cold anger in Wessels' voice. 'You kept saying you hoped he'd be the pilot. Why? This afternoon you wanted to take charge of his pilotcase. Why? When we were on the island I heard you questioning Trudi about it. Why?

211

Casual questions they seemed at the time, but I can see now there was something behind them. You've not played the game with me, Pienaar.'

Pienaar shook his head emphatically, clicked disapproval. 'That's not right, man. You shouldn't make such accusations. I wasn't after Johnson. Why should I be? What for? I knew nothing about him except what you told me. That he was a first-class pilot and a helluva nice guy.'

'So how do I come out of this?' challenged Wessels. 'Who's going to believe my story: that no way did I know you had another name or that you'd been – may still be for all I know – Security Branch? The truth is, Pienaar, that for me you're bad news.'

The older man put out a hand in the darkness, touched Wessels. 'Sorry, Jan, but I swear that what I've told you is the truth. I came for the fishing, nothing else. It seemed to me only right that we should take care of the pilotcase if Johnson reckoned it was so important. He was a fellow South African.'

'Right, but you'll have to admit to Ferreira that you are Badenhorst. That's for sure. No good trying to bluff a man you've interrogated.' With a note of irony Wessels added, 'From what I've heard it's the sort of experience a man doesn't forget. Also tell him why you changed your name – the story you've just told me. I hope to God he'll believe it. I'm not sure I do.'

Darkness hid Pienaar's expression of fear – and an added hatred for Wessels.

When the two Afrikaners had left the fire Trudi, speaking in a low voice, asked the Commandante about his dual identities. What lay behind the accusation that Pienaar was Steens Badenhorst, and the admission that he – Vasco Ferreira – was George Wilkens?

In a quiet, unemotional way the Commandante told her of the anti-apartheid movement to which he had belonged after graduating from Witwatersrand University, his arrest and months of detention in solitary confinement, the interrogation led by Badenhorst, the trial on charges of sabotage, his conviction and the imprisonment which followed. Years later when he came out of prison he knew there was no future for him in South Africa, since he was not prepared to accept apartheid. Loath to leave Southern Africa, feeling that he could help the people of Mozambique where there was a shortage of men with his qualifications, he had contacted the authorities there, offered his services as a geologist and been accepted. His mother was Portuguese and he spoke the language fluently. Once settled in Mozambique he had, with the consent of the authorities, taken his maternal grandfather's name – Vasco Ferreira.

Trudi listened earnestly. 'That explains a lot, Vasco. But why the funny accent and the broken English?'

The Commandante laughed. 'That wasn't easy. I suppose it sounded a bit phony. But when we met in the base-camp a couple of nights ago I realised Pienaar didn't recognise me. I've changed a lot in all those years: heavier, tougher, longer hair, plus the beard and sunglasses. I knew I was well disguised. But a voice can give you away, so I did the broken English bit.'

'Would it have mattered if he had recognised you?'

'Yes. I mistrusted the man, I was suspicious. What was he – what *is* he – doing in Mozambique under a false name? I suspected he was involved with Renamo. By concealing my identity I was in a strong position. If he'd known I was George Wilkens at the beginning he'd have been on his guard.'

There was a long silence after that, broken only by the squeaky calls of bush partridges and the murmur of voices and laughter from the Africans.

When the two Afrikaners got back to the fire Wessels said, 'Commandante, I've asked . . .' he hesitated, evidently

213

wondering what name to use, 'I've asked *him* to tell you what he's just told me. I can assure you it's news to me.'

Speaking in a jerky, embarrassed way, Pienaar admitted that he was Steens Badenhorst. He had, he said, left the Security Branch many years before in order to sell farm machinery. At that time, and with official approval, he'd changed his name to Pieter Pienaar. He had also shaved off his moustache, and crew-cut the hair round his bald patch. He had done so because the nature of his previous occupation could have endangered his life. 'A man can make bad enemies if he has to do what I had to do. You know what I mean?'

'I do,' said the Commandante, adding, 'That has to be the understatement of all time.' But for this remark, which sparked a flicker of aggression in the Afrikaner's eyes, he continued to listen in silence as Pienaar explained that ANC agents could have been sent to 'get him' had his identity been known.

'You must believe that, Commandante. As true as God, those are the facts.'

The Commandante's response was a shrug of his shoulders.

This seemed to encourage Pienaar for he added, 'You should understand, Wilkens. After all, you have changed your name and how you look. You must also have a good reason for that. *Nie waar nie* – is that not true?'

Trudi stood up, announced that she was tired and wished to sleep. She made for the Land Rover.

The Commandante followed her, soon caught up. 'What d'you think of all that?' he asked in a quiet way.

'I don't know,' she said, 'I'm confused. I really don't know what to think. But I can imagine what you must feel about him, Vasco.'

He said nothing to that, wished her a good night's rest, and went back to the fire.

*

The brooding silence among the white men after Trudi's departure was overlaid by the chatter and laughter of the Africans and the noises of the bush.

It was Wessels who spoke first. Looking at the Commandante he said, 'Your Africans must have many worries while this bush war continues, but listen to them. They have no reason to be happy but they make the best of things. They talk, laugh, live for the moment. We sit here silent, without laughter, brooding. We are white Africans, they are black Africans. This is something that has always puzzled me. The blacks have nothing like the privileges or material advantages of the white man, but they seem to be happier than we are. Perhaps it is natural to be happy if you have nothing to lose.'

Wessels' observation, intended to provoke discussion rather than state a philosophic truth, was more effective then he had hoped; it sparked an exchange of views and these led inevitably to apartheid.

The discussion soon became antagonistic, a conflict of views between Pienaar and the Commandante, the former steeped in apartheid, in the Afrikaner belief of *die swart gevaar* – the black peril; and the Commandante, the educated liberal, convinced that pigmentation did not entitle a small white minority to determine the lives of the great black majority. As they argued the tension grew: the Commandante cold, distant, wary – Pienaar sullen, adversarial, mistrustful.

He defended the methods used in interrogating prisoners, said it should never be forgotten that the interrogator was dealing with men suspected of terrorism; he was obeying orders, doing his duty to his country, defending his people.

Ferreira took off the dark sunglasses, directed a hostile stare at the Afrikaner. 'The trouble with you, Badenhorst, is that you enjoyed what you were doing. And you made no effort to conceal that enjoyment. You enjoyed shouting, threatening, hitting, humiliating and insulting.' In

215

the firelight the Commandante's eyes glinted with sudden anger. 'Know why, Badenhorst? Because you're a sadist.'

The Afrikaner frowned, his eyes narrowed. 'What d'you mean?'

'In simple language, you were a bullying shit who enjoyed being just that.'

Speaking quietly and without emotion Wessels put in a defence for Pienaar, stressing the advantages of education and opportunity which he and, he assumed, the Commandante had enjoyed compared with those which had been Pienaar's lot. 'He was the son of a *bywoner*, a squatter in the Western Transvaal,' explained Wessels. 'He left a dorp school to work on the land for his keep. Don't be contemptuous of him.'

Wessels went on to defend apartheid as something which had been necessary in its time. Important changes had already taken place and he conceded that there must be continued reform, leading perhaps to a federal system. But never, he emphasised, a unitary state based on one man one vote. 'That would sink the white man in a sea of blacks, destroy his culture and, if experience elsewhere in Africa is any guide, impoverish the country.'

The Commandante interrupted with a throaty 'rubbish', but Wessels went on undeterred. 'Unlike the English-speaking population, we Afrikaners have no mother country to run to in time of trouble. We have fought for our country for more than three hundred years. Fought against African tribes, against the British. We will go on fighting for it, for our way of life and our culture. Most of us would rather die fighting than place ourselves under black rule. Unless you understand that you don't begin to understand the South African situation.'

In tones which were now as calm and controlled as Wessels', the Commandante countered briefly by stressing that there was no moral basis for apartheid. 'You are not only fighting against the great majority of your own

216

countrymen because they happen to have darker skins, but you are fighting world opinion and, increasingly, world action. Most formidable of all you are fighting morality itself. That is why apartheid is doomed. It can't succeed. No more than Hitler's mad Aryan dream of a Thousand Year Reich and his gas chambers succeeded. Given time, evil destroys itself. Apartheid will go. Not this year, not the next, maybe not in ten or twenty years, but it will go and if the white man co-operates in getting rid of it he has a future. If he doesn't . . .' The Commandante paused, stared into the fire. 'Then God help him.' He stood up, stretched his arms. 'Time for sleep,' he said.

Wessels held up a restraining hand. 'Before you go, Commandante. What is to happen to us, we survivors?'

'I've already told you.' There was a hint of irritation in the reply. 'You will know after I've spoken to Maputo.'

'Yes. But what do you think will happen?'

'I expect you'll be sent down to Rio das Pedras under armed escort, then handed over to a military convoy for the journey on to Maputo.'

'After that?'

The Commandante was thoughtful. 'If your passports are in order and your stories are confirmed I imagine you and Trudi will be sent back to the Republic.'

'And Piet Pienaar?'

The Commandante looked up from the fire, frowning. 'I can't say. The false name and passport aren't going to help.'

Pienaar, having watched them in gloomy silence, shook his head and walked away.

'You'd better tell him I'm doubling up the sentries to-night,' the Commandante said to Wessels. 'I don't want him shot.'

Before unrolling a palliasse to sleep near the Land Rover the Commandante did the sentry rounds with Querrime.

As a result of what the African then told him he was satisfied that Wessels was not involved in Pienaar's mission, whatever it might have been. Querrime and Gumede had been in the mopani thicket not far from the two Afrikaners when they'd left the fire for their private discussion. They had spoken in Afrikaans, a language in which Querrime was fluent, having for some years worked on a farm in the Eastern Transvaal.

He told the Commandante that from the conversation he had overheard – 'They talk in low voices, Senhor Vasco, but I hear' – he was satisfied that Wessels had no idea of Pienaar's former name and employment. 'He is angry with this man Pienaar,' said Querrime. 'Very angry.'

Disturbed by what he had privately decided to do with Pienaar, the Commandante found sleep difficult that night. Was he entitled to have made the decision? Was the Afrikaner's story about his change of name anywhere near the truth? Or was he an undercover agent, in Mozambique on some intelligence gathering operation? There *had* been a disastrous fishing trip, Wessels had confirmed that and he believed Wessels. But what lay behind the fishing trip? Was it no more than Pienaar's excuse for his presence in Mozambique? He conceded the man's right to engage in espionage, that was a matter for his conscience, but he must have known what the consequences might be.

The Commandante doubted whether Maputo would give the Afrikaner the benefit of the doubt, even if he succeeded in arriving there alive. But was he, Vasco Ferreira, doing the right thing in taking matters into his own hands? Was his decision based upon moral grounds or expedience? Or was it, as he suspected, the result of a synthesis of mixed emotions?

TWENTY-SIX

On the Friday following his meeting with Ranjut Patel, Luena drove out from Port Louis in the afternoon through Curepipe and Rose Belle to Mahebourg, a small town on the eastern coast of the island. Using the map Patel had left in the shopping bag, Luena passed through Mahebourg and motored on towards Soutflier. In the course of a discreet and casually executed survey of what was little more than a scatter of holiday homes fronting the beach, he was able to take a long-range look at Beau Rivage.

Standing by itself on high ground, well away from the sea, the white-walled, red-roofed villa, partially surrounded by trees, certainly merited Patel's description: *in a quiet secluded area*. But having seen the villa which lay at the end of a long, high-hedged drive, the entrance to which was signposted *Propriété Privée*, Luena was, if anything, more than ever confused as to how Beau Rivage could be used to obtain worthwhile information about the activities of Messrs Gottwald and Kahn. Was he expected to hide in the grounds, to eavesdrop at an open window, or perhaps present himself at the front door and demand information? Patel had said, *a solution may suggest itself when you have given the matter more thought*. Well, he'd given it a lot more thought, and it hadn't.

Unless – ? The 'toy' in the shopping bag had turned out to be a Beretta .33 automatic in a shoulder-holster: he had assumed it was for self-defence; a reasonable assumption when he recalled Nielsen's briefing in Harare: *operators in the Kahn-Gottwald line of business aren't too fussy about eliminating trouble-makers;* and Nielsen's reply when asked how to deal with the elimination scenario: *wait for Patel's briefing. He'll have some of the answers.*

Luena had, however, taken to heart one item of Patel's somewhat enigmatic briefing by making a reservation on the 0815 flight to Nairobi on the coming Monday morning.

The problem of how he could make a success of what looked like a hopeless assignment occupied his mind throughout the drive back to Port Louis.

What should he do? To return to Harare and report failure would not commend him to the Minister; nor to Nielsen, unless the American had known the mission was bound to fail and had planned it to devalue him. Nielsen had been less than tactful in hinting to others, including Trudi, that Luena was too young and inexperienced to inherit the embryo department once he, Nielsen, had returned to the USA. He had, too, hinted that Luena would never have got the job but for his uncle's influence. Since Luena's uncle was a cabinet minister, the allusion had about it a hurtful ring of truth.

That night a young civil servant, Jean Pierre Lefroy – he had met him in the course of his duties – picked him up at the hotel and drove him out to Curepipe to dine at the house of the senior government official with whose department Luena had been discussing trade matters.

It was a pleasant, informal occasion: an interesting dinner of French-Creole dishes, followed by dancing to taped music with the host's daughters, while the older people played bridge.

It was some time after midnight when he was taken back to Port Louis by Jean Pierre who lived in the town. They agreed to meet again the next day, Saturday, when the young Mauritian promised to take him to St Geran where there was, he said, fabulous wind-surfing. 'I pick you up at nine o'clock. We spend the day there. On the sea and also at the villa of my family.'

The Commandante having once again ordered an early start, camp was struck after a rudimentary breakfast of *putu* and coffee, and the return journey was resumed. The Land Rover was none the worse for its fall at the causeway and by mid-morning the base-camp was reached and a cheerful and noisy welcome followed. Trudi and Wessels were examined by the Africans with a mixture of curiosity and suspicion, and there was much discussion about them with the men of the rescue party.

The survivors were faced with idling away the rest of the day since at the earliest their journey south could not begin until the following morning by which time the Commandante would have spoken to Maputo.

With a bar of coarse soap at last available, Wessels and Pienaar stripped down to their Y-fronts and washed their shirts and shorts, while Trudi with her luggage-grip was able to do rather better. After a lunch of *putu* balls soaked in impala gravy, followed by wild fruit, the survivors rested in the shade. Around them the clearing pulsed with heat under a relentless sun.

In late afternoon the Commandante left the camp with his field assistants to collect geological samples. He took with him in the Land Rover sample bags, prospecting hammers, and a number of scientific instruments.

It was already dark that evening when he and his men returned. Trudi accosted him as he walked over to his lean-to tent. 'Did you find anything interesting this afternoon?' she asked.

'We always find something interesting,' he said in a noncommittal way.

Determined not to be put off so easily she said, 'What are you actually looking for?'

The Commandante contemplated her in silence before saying, 'Many things, but principally oil. This is vital to Mozambique's economy. The cost of importing it is a crippling burden.'

'D'you think you'll find any?'

'Possibly. Some of the indications are good.'

Trudi smiled sympathetically. 'Oh, that's great.' She liked Vasco Ferreira, and she felt sad about him; such a distant, lonely man. 'What are they?'

He shrugged. 'It's too long a story,' he said, turning away.

But for this brief interlude he scarcely spoke to the survivors that night, spending most of his time with the Africans at their fires.

Some time after the evening meal the Commandante left the camp with two armed Frelimo on the truck with the pole aerial and drove up the hill, following the track his previous visits had made. At the top of the hill he stopped the truck, got out and extended the pole aerial. He got through to Maputo after a delay of several minutes. To the operator there he gave the departmental number, asked for d'Abreu. Several moments later he heard the Chief Secretary's gravelly voice.

'What's the news, Vasco?'

'We've found them,' replied the Commandante. He explained that Wessels and Trudi Braun were now in the base-camp with Pienaar; the crashed Cessna had been found and he had examined it. Johnson's body had been discovered some distance from the plane, with it his locked pilotcase. He gave the names and addresses of the survivors, said he had seen Braun's passport which appeared to be in order but added that one of the survivors, Pienaar, was travelling under a false name and presumably with a false passport. D'Abreu confirmed that such was the case; the proprietor of the *pensão* in Maxixe had found the passports in their room, one in the name of Pienaar, the other in Wessels' name.

D'Abreu agreed with his suggestion that the survivors should be sent to Rio das Pedras under armed escort to await a military convoy for the final stage of their journey to Maputo, and undertook to phone on the following morning at 1030 to confirm the arrangements provisionally agreed. It would not be necessary, he stressed, for the Commandante to come down with the survivors. The geological survey was of paramount importance and should not be further delayed.

Felicia Santos swept across the Polana's lush lounge with the elegance of a yacht under full sail. A body-clinging gown of black silk was set off by the red camellia in her black, piled-up hair, and the carmine lips of her lovely face. Watching her approach, Andrada observed to himself as he had many times before that she was not only a woman of exceptional beauty but one who knew best how to display what nature had given her.

These pleasant thoughts were overtaken by her arrival at the table. With his customary apology for a bad leg he excused himself from getting up. She replied with her customary charge that he was an old fraud. He kissed her hand, she touched his forehead and sat down on the settee beside him.

'You are wearing deliciously seductive perfume, Felicia.'

She raised a critical eyebrow. 'I did not think you would notice it, Andrada. Those awful cheroots.'

She put her evening bag on the table, looked round the lounge, and made a slight gesture with long, tapering fingers to acknowledge a wave from a woman on the far side of the room. 'Hypocritical bitch,' she murmured.

Andrada had noticed the exchange. 'She has much to be envious about, Felicia.' He stubbed out the cheroot. 'It was kind of you to accept an old man's invitation at such short notice. But, tell me, where is Mavro Costeliades?'

She turned her head, her dark eyes on his. 'He had to go up to Jo'burg this morning. Asked me to apologise.'

'A sudden departure, was it not?'

'Yes. It was.' The tapering fingers teased a wisp of hair back into place.

'He seemed very concerned about Johnnie Johnson's death. They were good friends, I think. Both much opposed to apartheid.'

'JJ's death?' She looked startled. 'Do you mean they've found the Cessna?'

He took a cheroot from the brown leather case. 'I believe so.'

'If you believe it, Andrada, it means you know it.' She looked sad. 'Poor JJ. I didn't really know him well, but he was such a nice man. How very sad.'

'Mavro's visit to Jo'burg. D'you think it had something to do with Johnson's death? To see his widow, perhaps?' He lit the cheroot, watching Felicia closely as if to check her reaction.

'No, it wasn't that. He told me he'd had a telex from NBC. He had to go up to Jo'burg and Pretoria to check a rumour that the USA was willing to provide funds for restoring the Cabora Bassa power lines. It seems South Africa wants the power and Mozambique needs the money.'

'I see.' Gouveia was thoughtful; the news of possible US participation had not yet reached the Mozambique Government. Conversation was interrupted by the arrival of a waiter with the drinks Gouveia had ordered. He signed the *conta* and the waiter left.

'You see a lot of Mavro, don't you, Felicia?'

'Yes – why?' She watched him over the rim of her glass.

224

'Interesting chap,' said Gouveia. 'An excellent media man, no doubt.'

'Yes, I think he is.'

'Know much about him? His life before he came here?'

'He has told me of certain things. Wonderful experiences he has had. He was a platoon-sergeant in Vietnam. Incredible things happened to him there.' Her eyes shone with vicarious pride.

Gouveia smiled. 'I'm afraid, dear Felicia, that they would have had to be incredible.'

'Why? What d'you mean *would have had to be*?' She raised a quizzical eyebrow.

'You see, he wasn't actually a platoon-sergeant in Vietnam.'

'But he *was*, Andrada,' she protested.

'I'm afraid not.' Gouveia smiled discreetly, drew on the cheroot, and exhaled blue smoke. 'Let me explain. I have to know a good deal about accredited media men. Soon after Mavro got here, the platoon-sergeant-in-Vietnam story was doing the rounds. I doubted it because of his age. We enquired in Washington. Got a different story. He was an undergraduate at Berkeley, California, during the last two years of the Vietnam war. Prominent, I am told, at campus meetings protesting against it. Later he became a draft dodger, cleared out to Mexico. After the war he went north again, slipped across the border at night. Back in the USA with a different name he took odd jobs before getting into journalism. One of the odd jobs was a bit part in a Vietnam movie. That's as near as he ever got to being a platoon-sergeant in Vietnam.'

'Oh my God! So he's a liar.' She put a hand to her forehead in an exaggerated gesture of shock. 'Why d'you have to tell me that, Andrada? You might have left me with my illusions.'

He put a reassuring hand on her arm. 'Illusions about men can be dangerous for beautiful women, Felicia. But he's still the Mavro you know. A colourful character.

Young men often fantasise about heroic roles. Don't be too hard on him.'

'Colourful character my foot,' she said. 'He's a lying bastard. Wait till I get my hands on him.'

Gouveia chuckled. 'I daresay that will be tougher than being a platoon-sergeant in Vietnam.'

TWENTY-SEVEN

Before dawn next morning the Commandante went across to where Pienaar lay on a palliasse near the ashes of the night's fire. He had thought the Afrikaner was asleep, but leaning over the prone figure he saw the open eyes.

'What size shoe do you wear?' the Commandante asked.

Propping himself up on an elbow Pienaar said, 'Size ten, why?'

'We've got some spare boots in the stores truck. And military socks.'

'So what?'

The Commandante looked round the camp where mist-shrouded objects were taking shape as the light grew stronger. 'We can't talk here,' he said. 'We'll go for a walk shortly. I've news for you.'

'What sort of news?' Pienaar's red-rimmed eyes filled with suspicion.

'I'm going to help you.'

'How?' It was a hoarse challenge.

The Commandante pulled at the peak of his Cuban combat cap. 'You'll know soon enough,' he said, in a tight-lipped way. 'Come, we'll get the boots.'

They walked out of the camp together, the salmons and golds of the rising sun reflected in the eastern sky. A sentry on the perimeter saluted. He and the Commandante spoke to each other in Portuguese. The man nodded, looked at the panga the big man was carrying, grinned and waved

them on. Over his camouflage safari jacket the Commandante wore the webbing straps of his holster, the handle
of the revolver jutting from it. They walked on in silence,
Pienaar following the Commandante.

Within half an hour they had reached a baobab tree
standing huge and solitary before an outcrop of granite
rocks. The Commandante stopped. 'This will do,' he said
tersely. The two men faced each other like duellists in the
pale light of morning, Pienaar's eyes large with fear as they
focused on the panga.

'So now?' He breathed noisily, like a frightened horse.
'You said we were coming here to – to help me.'

The Commandante stroked his beard as if considering
the matter afresh. 'I'm going to let you go, Badenhorst.'

The Afrikaner's face was a study in disbelief. 'How d'you
mean *go*? Go where?'

'You're going to escape. That will be my story when I
get back to camp.'

'Escape to where? I've got nothing. No food, no gun,
nothing.' His eyes narrowed in sudden understanding.
'So that's the idea. You shoot me and say I tried to
escape.'

'No, I don't. Though that's not a bad idea.'

Pienaar's eyes switched from the revolver back to the
panga. 'So what is it?' Fear lifted the hoarse voice to a
higher key.

'If you go down to Maputo with Wessels and Trudi Braun
escorted by my men, two things can happen. Most likely
they would kill you, saying you had tried to escape. They'd
do that out of sight of the others. It's an old trick. You
must know it.'

'You said *two* things. What's the other?'

'If you did get back to Maputo you'd be charged with
espionage. If you were lucky they would execute you. If
not you would spend the rest of your life in a Mozambique
gaol. There would be plenty of interrogation before that. I
don't have to tell you what that's like.'

Pienaar's eyes flickered. 'So you've told your blacks I was Security Branch?'

'That wasn't necessary. Querrime overheard our conversation by the fire the other night. He'll have told them. I've already informed Maputo that you're here under a false name and passport.'

'That was a lousy thing to do.'

'It was necessary. Querrime would have told them. They would want to know why I had not.'

Scuffing the sandy path with his foot, his eyes on the ground, Pienaar was thoughtful. He looked up, anguish in his face. 'You really mean it. That I must go?'

'Yes. I do.' The Commandante felt in a pocket and produced a map. 'You can have this.' Unfolding it, he held it between them. 'I've marked the route I think you should take. Your best chance is to head west for the Limpopo. About thirty-five kilometres from here you'll hit the main road running north from Inhambane towards Vilanculos.' The Commandante put a finger on the map. 'Here, see.'

Pienaar nodded forlornly. 'Then?'

'Don't attempt to cross in daylight. Head on west through the bush until you come to the road from Manhica which runs through Funhaloura to Marrimane. That's another hundred and forty Ks as the crow flies. There could be Renamo guerrillas there. They might be friendly if they knew you were a South African. But if you can't speak their language you have problems. Better to avoid human contacts. Keep clear of the villages.'

'But if I run into blacks how do I explain being out in the *bundu*?'

'You were sole survivor in the Cessna which crashed. Show them that gash on your cheek. You waited a few days at the crash site, hoping help would come. It didn't, and you'd no idea where you were, so you headed west for help.' The alacrity with which the Commandante answered suggested that he had anticipated the question.

229

'After Marrimane, where then?' The pouches under Pienaar's eyes glistened with sweat.

The shadow of a smile showed on the Commandante's face. He had a sneaking admiration for the Afrikaner's assumption that he would reach Marrimane. Whatever else he thought of him, he had to admit the man had a strong survival instinct. 'Keep heading west. You'll be going through sparsely-populated country with some marshland. But there's been a long drought. The going shouldn't be too bad. About a hundred and thirty-five Ks after Marrimane you'll hit the Limpopo south of Mapai.' Ferreira pointed to the spot on the map. 'Here – then go north up the eastern bank towards Mapai. It's a small African village. Maybe empty, maybe burned out now. Depends if your Renamo friends have called. There's a bridge or causeway across the Limpopo a few kilometres west of Mapai. Because of the drought the river will be low. Hide near the bridge in daylight, cross at night. Forty Ks west of the Limpopo you come to the Kruger Park game fence. South African border guards may pick you up. If not get through the fence. About twelve Ks west of it you'll find the Shingwedzi–Punda Maria road. There'll be some traffic on it, even at this time of year.'

Pienaar looked worried, ran a hand over his balding head. 'Christ, man. It's a long trek. Bushveld, guerrilla gangs, big game, the lot . . .'

'You're an Afrikaner,' said the Commandante. 'You know how to handle the bush. Most of the big game will be well to the west, towards the Kruger Park. Refugees making for the Park, and wandering guerrillas, have made the game wary of man.' He looked at Pienaar's feet. 'And at least you've got good boots.'

'I can look after myself in the bush.' Pienaar's manner had become defiant. 'But not without a gun. How else can a man get food and protect himself?'

'Wild fruit.' The Commandante's laugh was sardonic. 'But it's not as bad as that. Come over here.' He went across to the granite outcrop, moved a loose rock from a crevasse, reached in and pulled out an army rucksack. He gave it to Pienaar. 'There's a full water-bottle in there, some biltong, mealie-meal, raisins and nuts. Keep them as emergency rations. Live off the country. There's plenty of wild figs, bird plums, marulas, nuts and other wild fruit. There's a billycan in the rucksack. Boil the water you use. Take this lighter.' The Commandante handed it to him.

Pienaar looked at him in a strange way. 'When did you put that rucksack there?'

'Yesterday afternoon. When I was out in the Land Rover.'

The Afrikaner shook his head. 'Christ, I never thought the fishing trip was going to end like this. My chances are not too good, hey?'

'Better than if you don't go.'

Pienaar shrugged. 'I suppose so.'

'Better take this. You may need it.' Ferreira handed him the panga. 'Trudi's automatic is in the rucksack. Also two clips of ammunition.'

'That's the best bit of news for a long time.' Pienaar's stubble-bearded face broke into a grin. 'Aren't you scared I'll shoot you?'

The Commandante didn't return the grin. 'You'd be dead long before you loaded it.' He touched the holster at his side.

'Well, I suppose I'd better be going.' Pienaar slung the rucksack on to his back, looked at the sky. 'It's a long trek.' As an afterthought he added, 'Sorry about what happened in the past, Wilkens. I was only doing my duty.' He held out his hand. 'Let's shake.'

The Commandante ignored the outstretched hand. 'I accept that you had to interrogate me. It was your job. What I don't accept was the way you did it. That I won't forgive or forget.' He paused, levelled an intimidating stare at the man who faced him. 'I used to hate you, Badenhorst. Fear you. Could have killed you if I'd had the chance. You had the whole power of the State apparatus behind you, and my God you took advantage of it. I know what you

231

did to me. I don't even like to think what you must have done to black prisoners.'

Pienaar shrugged. 'I was doing my duty by my country. But what's the good of arguing or hating now?'

'Those feelings have changed.' The Commandante spoke with casual indifference. 'It isn't hatred any more. It's contempt. Contempt for you and the values you represent.'

The veins on Pienaar's forehead stood out, pulsed, as he stared into the Commandante's coldly hostile eyes. 'You can do this to me now, Wilkens,' he said hoarsely. 'Send me off into the *bundu* alone, insult me. Yes, you can do that to me now, but only because I'm alone, at your mercy.' He looked at the holstered revolver. 'With every man's hand against me.'

The Commandante nodded. 'Yes. Like I was in Jeppe police station when we met. Like I was for the next six years in Pretoria Local. Alone, with every man's hand against me. But there's a difference, Pienaar. Nobody gave me the opportunity to escape. You're luckier than I was.' His voice hardened suddenly. 'Now for God's sake go.'

For an instant the Afrikaner returned the big man's stare, then he turned and set off across the clearing. The Commandante watched until the distant figure had been swallowed by the bush on the far side.

The early light of sunrise played on the baobab tree, casting weird shadows, and from the undergrowth beyond the granite outcrop came the call of bush partridges; like the sound of a squeaky pump, thought the Commandante, as he set off down the dusty track which led to the camp.

He told Alfonso Querrime of Pienaar's escape.

The African laid a finger along his broken nose. 'Yes, Senhor Vasco. I thought when you took the man from the camp that he would escape.' He looked to the west. 'I can take trackers, follow him, Senhor, if you wish. We will kill him quick. He is the enemy of our people.'

232

The Commandante took off his sunglasses, rubbed his eyes. 'No. For God's sake let him go. The journey is long and dangerous. Others may kill him. He will suffer enough.'

'I understand what the Senhor says.' Querrime's tone had become suddenly conspiratorial. 'I will tell the men that the work is too important. There is no time to chase this man. But they will be disappointed. When the Senhor left the camp before sunrise, taking the panga, they hoped to see the vultures circling when the sun was high.'

When Wessels and Trudi came to him before *putu* and coffee that morning to ask where Pienaar was, the Commandante told them what had happened; how he had taken him out of the camp on a short walk to discuss what was likely to happen in Maputo. After that discussion, while he – Vasco – was relieving himself, Pienaar had slipped off into the bush.

Wessels' face was a study in disbelief. 'You mean to say he escaped? Where to?'

'Where on earth could he go?' echoed Trudi.

The Commandante ignored the questions. 'It was his only hope. He would have been in serious trouble if he had got to Maputo – *if* he'd got there.' He explained what lay behind the if.

'But he hasn't a chance, wandering off into the bush like that,' said Wessels.

Stroking his beard the Commandante seemed lost in private thought. 'Somehow he got hold of one of my maps – also Trudi's automatic. Must have stolen them during the night. He complained about his feet when I woke him this morning, so I gave him a pair of boots. He must have been planning a get-away of some sort.' As an afterthought he added, 'You also can have a pair, Wessels.'

'If you reckon your men would have killed him on the journey to Maputo, what about Trudi and me when they take us down there?'

'There's no problem about that. Querrime will see you

233

get there safely. If you two had been travelling under false names and passports it would have been a different story.'

A puzzled Wessels said, 'I suppose he'll head west for the Transvaal. What chance d'you think he has of getting to the border?'

'Better than he had of reaching Maputo,' said the Commandante dismissively.

Later that morning the Commandante left the camp in a truck with three armed men and drove to the top of the hill. The pole aerial was extended, he switched on the generator and adjusted the headset. At ten-thirty d'Abreu's voice sounded on the radiophone. He confirmed that a military convoy would be passing through Rio das Pedras during the afternoon of the following day. 'Get your survivors down there by two o'clock,' he said.

'One of them, Pienaar, has escaped,' reported the Commandante with diffidence. He explained briefly what had happened, ending with, 'My fault. I was careless.'

A low laugh came from d'Abreu. 'Knowing you, Vasco, I have my own thoughts about that. Not like you to be caught with your trousers down. But it's just as well he's gone. There could have been political difficulties with Pretoria if he had stood trial down here. Anyway, I wouldn't give much for his chances of reaching the border.'

'Who knows?' said the Commandante. 'And who cares?' It was a throw-away remark but he knew it was not true, for he cared. Not so much for Pienaar as for his own conscience. He doubted the morality of what he had done.

'That pilotcase you mentioned last night,' said d'Abreu. 'You'd better force the locks and check what's in it. Have one of the South Africans there as a witness.'

234

TWENTY-EIGHT

Patel had said that Gottwald and his guest – presumed to be Abdul Kahn – would be dining together at Beau Rivage on the Sunday night, and that between eight and nine o'clock would probably be the most suitable time; but he had given no indication as to what it might be suitable for. To this somewhat shadowy advice Luena had given a good deal of thought, during which various possibilities had suggested themselves, only to be rejected. But eventually one had come up which seemed practical and it was around it that he had formulated his plan.

Getting up late on Sunday he spent the morning in the hotel lounge writing a report covering his official duties in Mauritius, a task made difficult by the attentions of a fellow guest, a middle-aged and much-travelled lady, who was persistent in her efforts to engage him in conversation about Zimbabwe, a territory which, she said, she had known well in the 'good old days', an observation which struck him as unnecessarily offensive.

After lunch in the hotel he drove down the western side of the island to Tamarin, motoring on from there by the coast road past the salt pans of Les Salines towards Pointe du Sud. Not far along the road he found a beach, small and remote; changing in the car from T-shirt and shorts to bathing trunks, he swam in the cool waters of the Indian Ocean under a sky of intensely luminous blue; afterwards he lay on the white sand enjoying the hot sun. There were few people about: a handful of Creole fishermen, and two youths wind-surfing some distance off the beach.

From the road map be concluded that he must allow plenty of time for the journey to Soufflier since much of it would be over secondary roads which were, as he had already learnt, poorly signposted. With this in mind he took to the road again at sunset. Some distance on he parked in a lay-by under a grove of casuarina trees; there he ate the sandwiches he had bought in a café in Port Louis, washing them down with a bottle of Coke.

Though he planned to arrive at Beau Rivage shortly before eight o'clock that night, and appeared to have plenty of time, he decided to press on. Driving through a landscape of sugar-cane fields relieved by small towns and villages along the road, he passed the airport at La Plaisance ahead of time. With Mahebourg only a few kilometres away he turned off the road once more and parked. He spent the time rehearsing what he would do on arrival at Beau Rivage, the questions he would ask and the action he might take under various circumstances.

Finally he thought about the crashed Cessna; had it been found, had Trudi and Johnson survived? Both seemed unlikely since it would almost certainly have come down in the sea. So often since it disappeared he'd been made miserable by mental pictures of the crash and Trudi's last moments. She was one of the nicest white women he had ever known, direct and sincere, never attempting to patronise him, and absolutely free of racism.

He looked at the digital clock on the Renault's dashboard. It was time to go. He started the engine, engaged gear and drove on towards Mahebourg.

When the *Propriété Privée* sign showed up in the headlights he pulled off the road, released the Renault's bonnet-catch, got out, lifted the bonnet and went through the motions of examining the engine with the aid of a torch.

In the course of it he loosened a nut on the distributor terminal and pulled the lead clear. Unlocking the boot he took from it the Beretta and shoulder-harness and put them on under a lightweight denim jacket.

Next he took a pair of rubber gloves from the glove box, pushed them into a trouser pocket, and locked the car. He walked down the road, reached the *Propriété Privée* sign and started off up the drive. Set between high hedges of poinsettia, its bends concealed the house until he came to wrought-iron gates set in a stone wall, the name Beau Rivage worked into their rococo design.

The distant view of the house he'd had a few days earlier had not revealed what lay between the hedges, so the gates were an unexpected obstacle. He saw in the moonlight that they were secured with a bolt-lock; on one of the stone pillars supporting the gates there was a bell-push. Some distance beyond the gates he could see a part of the house where light came from a bay window. He knew from his reconnaissance that the front door lay to the left of the bay window.

He puzzled for a few moments as to whether he should ring the bell or climb the stone wall, but soon rejected the latter because it suggested stealth, the very reverse of what he had in mind. Masking his finger with a handkerchief he pressed the bell-push discreetly. A prolonged ring might upset Gottwald who was unlikely to welcome a visitor at that hour. When several minutes had passed without any response he rang again, this time less discreetly. But still no one came to the gate.

After a third unsuccessful attempt, and the passing of more time, he set about climbing the wall. It was high, over two metres he reckoned, but by using a gate-hinge for a foothold he managed to get over it.

Feeling the shoulder-holster in an attempt to bolster his confidence, he walked on towards the house where many lights were on including those of the covered verandah. A white Mercedes was parked near the front steps. He went up them, reached the front door and, using the handkerchief again, he rang the bell. Along the verandah to his left the sound of men's voices came through an open window. They were speaking French, a language he could not understand. He waited patiently but no one came to the door. Further attempts failed to elicit any attention; the front door remained closed and the two men continued their noisy discussion. To him it sounded like an argument.

Not sure what to do next, he approached the window, moving silently on his rubber-soled trainers. For some seconds he stood beside it, listening. The conversation in the room continued. He stepped in front of the window, looked into the room where the heads of two men showed above the back of the settee on which they were sitting. The settee faced patio doors set in the wall which faced the sea. Through them Luena could see lights along the foreshore, beyond them the white ridges of surf rolling in.

Knocking gently on the window he called, 'Excuse me, sir.' As with his other efforts that night there was no response. The noisy discussion continued. Assuming that he had been too timid he knocked again, very positively this time, and called, 'Excuse me, sir,' in a loud voice. With something of a shock he realised that the voices were coming from a radio on a coffee table near the settee; it occurred to him then that during the time he had been watching the two heads showing above the settee had not turned towards each other, nor made any other movement.

Putting on the rubber gloves he went back to the front door, tried the handle but found it locked. After a moment of indecision he went back along the verandah, climbed in through the open window and walked across the attractively furnished lounge to the settee.

Thanks to the briefing data he had no difficulty in recognising Gottwald and Kahn, notwithstanding the blood which had oozed from ears and mouths to saturate their shirt fronts. Both men had been shot through their ears, and from the dark colour of the congealed blood Luena thought they must have been dead for some time.

The Brigadier contemplated the plump, bespectacled face of Captain Le Roux with an expression which was a good deal more genial than usual. 'That is excellent news, Wilhelm,' he said. 'Three survivors, you say. Johnson's body found not far from the scene of the crash. So Pienaar, Wessels and the woman are safe. Due in Maputo in a day or so.'

'Yes, sir. That's what Carvalho said on the phone. Of course he spoke guardedly. He understands Pienaar and Wessels have had a tough time. Three days without food and water while they were drifting on the capsized boat, then a long trek through the bush. They must have come across the Cessna *before* they were picked up because the woman was already with them when they were found. Apparently Major Badenhorst – '

The Brigadier half rose to his feet. 'Pienaar,' he shouted with sudden fury. 'For Christ's sake, Le Roux, don't you make that mistake again. Pienaar has spent years building up that cover. There is no Major Badenhorst. He doesn't exist. You blow Pienaar's cover and you're out. Got that?'

'Sorry, sir. A slip of the tongue.' A deep flush suffused Le Roux's rotund face. 'It won't occur again.'

'It had better not.' The Brigadier sank back into his chair. 'Now let me see. Where were we? Yes. Carvalho told you the survivors were expected in Maputo tomorrow or the next day. Well, tell him from me that he's to see that Pienaar gets back here with the least possible delay.' The Brigadier rubbed his hands. 'He'll have a lot to tell us. Fantastic coincidence that he and Wessels picked up the woman. They must have come on the crashed Cessna during their trek through the bush. Found her there. Pienaar's no fool. He will have got plenty from her. He's always been a first class interrogator. And he'll have had

239

the opportunity of checking the wreckage. No doubt he's going to have some news for us.'

'Pity about Johnson, sir.'

'How d'you mean a pity?' Behind the steel-rimmed glasses the Brigadier's eyes turned on Le Roux like twin searchlights.

'No chance of catching him in the act now, sir.'

The Brigadier shook his head. 'You must think before you speak, Le Roux. Johnson was killed in the crash. If he was to have made a drop the parachute and the documents, whatever, would have been in the Cessna. If they were, the chances are that Pienaar has got them.'

Chastened, Le Roux pulled at the ends of his moustache, looked away from the penetrating stare. 'What I meant, sir, was that if we had caught Johnson in the act of making a drop we could have made arrests – him and the people on the ground. With interrogation we'd have got from them details of the ANC command structure on the Witwatersrand. Also, probably, the latest operational orders. With Johnson's death that opportunity has gone.'

'Not altogether.' The Brigadier picked up the crystal ball, cupped his hands round it, stared into the glittering facets. 'We should get a lot of important information from the documents he was going to drop. If Pienaar hasn't got them it can only mean that no drop was contemplated or that the aircraft caught fire and they were burnt. But that is unlikely since there were survivors.' He paused. 'We know that Johnson reported his onward flight plan as Maputo, Dullstroom, Grand Central. So it's odds on he was going to offload the woman at Dullstroom. That meant he was going to make a drop. Otherwise, why the Dullstroom stop?' The Brigadier replaced the crystal ball on its stand, leant back in the swing chair. 'What pleases me is that an operation that seemed to have gone right off the board now looks as though it's going to yield results. That is what's important.'

The Commandante told Wessels and Trudi that he had spoken to Maputo that morning. 'A military convoy will pass through Rio das Pedras tomorrow afternoon. You are to be there by two o'clock. Querrime will take you down in the Land Rover. He'll have three of his men with him so there should be no problems.'

'Hope you're right.' Wessels sounded dubious.

'There'll be an APC with you. Should be safe enough. It's about eighty-five kilometres to Rio das Pedras. Bush track from here to Pomene, then a dirt road on to Rio das Pedras. To be on the safe side you'll be leaving here at nine o'clock tomorrow morning. Okay?'

Wessels looked at Trudi. 'Okay by me.'

'I got down to River Island alone on foot,' she said. 'It'll be sheer luxury to complete the journey in a Land Rover with an APC escort.'

'So that's it.' The Commandante took off his combat cap and used it as a fan.

Wessels said, 'There's something that beats me, Commandante. How is it your outfit hasn't been attacked by Renamo?'

'They know we're looking for oil. Whatever government is in power, Mozambique must have oil. Importing it is a crippling burden on our economy. Renamo won't want to stop us finding oil as long as they hope to be the Government.'

TWENTY-NINE

Later that morning the Commandante took Trudi aside. She saw that he was carrying a hammer and cold chisel. 'I told d'Abreu about Johnson's pilotcase,' he said. 'He wants me to open it in front of a South African witness.' He looked at her with a half smile. 'Care to be the witness? You know the importance Johnson attached to it. And you're a South African.'

'Yes. Of course.' There was a strange look in her eyes. 'If it will help you.'

They went over to the Land Rover, got into the back where he unlocked a compartment under a bench-seat and took out the pilotcase. A good deal bigger than a briefcase, it had combination locks on both latches. 'Six-digit codes on those,' he said. 'Unless you know them it's a hammer and chisel job.'

Within a few minutes he had forced the locks.

'Glad poor old JJ's not watching this,' she said. 'His beloved pilotcase.'

'Yes. It's a pity. But let's see what's in it.' He stood it on end and raised the lid. There were three compartments; a large one in the centre, a smaller one on each side. In one of the smaller compartments there were a pilot's log-book, engine and maintenance records, and other flight documents. In the other, files containing correspondence, customs-forms, manifests and vouchers.

But it was the centre pocket which finally attracted their attention. When the Commandante had taken out a

242

waterproof toilet-bag and the folded linen hand towel beneath it, he peered into the centre compartment.

'Look at this,' he said.

She did, and laughed. 'How sweet! He told me about it. I thought he was joking. He said it was a present for his daughter, Clara.'

But for the hand towel and the toilet-bag, Clara's present took up the whole of the compartment. With a firm tug, the Commandante pulled it out, a brown teddy bear, about fifteen inches tall.

He frowned at it. 'Hell's delight,' he said. 'It's an overweight teddy bear, all right.' He passed it to her. 'See what I mean?'

She took it, tested its weight, looked at him wide-eyed. 'My goodness. What's in it? It's so heavy.' She gave it back.

With a pocket-knife he made an incision in its neck. A thin stream of white powder poured out. He sniffed it, tasted it. 'Funny,' he said. 'Wonder what it is?'

In an unusually subdued voice she said, 'Let me taste it.' She licked a finger, dabbed at the powder, put the finger to her tongue. 'It's heroin.' She looked utterly miserable. 'So Jake Motlani was right.'

'Who's he?'

'Just a man. But this is totally unbelievable.'

'Is it?' said the Commandante. 'After all, the stuff's there. Nothing unbelievable about that.'

She shook her head. 'But JJ wasn't like that. How on earth did he get mixed up in this sort of racket?' She sighed. 'There must be several kilos of the stuff in there.'

'Big money,' said the Commandante. 'I suppose that load's worth a lot at street prices.'

'You can say that again,' she said. 'A very large sum of money. And a lot more if you're doing the same thing two or three times a month. But why JJ?'

'Even nice guys sometimes do wicked things for money.' The Commandante pushed the teddy bear back into the pilotcase. 'I'd like to destroy the stuff but that's a decision for d'Abreu.'

'I suppose so.' She looked miserable. 'I just can't believe it. Think of the risks he was running. I know he was a pilot and well known to customs and immigration at Mutare, Maputo and Grand Central. But even pilots have their gear checked at times. A teddy bear in a pilot's case would have looked a bit weird. They might have pulled it out, felt its weight . . .'

'*His* weight,' corrected Ferreira. 'Teddy bears are strictly masculine.' His smile was sympathetic, as if he understood her feelings about JJ. 'But it wouldn't have been in the pilotcase at Grand Central.'

She looked puzzled. 'What d'you mean?'

He told her of the small silk parachute he had found in a locker in the Cessna. He'd not told the others about it at the time because he was suspicious of Pienaar and not sure of Wessels or her. 'To be honest I had come to the conclusion that Johnson was probably acting as a courier for Renamo. You'd told us of his special concern for the pilotcase. And I had found the parachute. He was flying over Mozambique territory at regular intervals. What could be easier when he was alone than dropping documents, orders, intelligence, from Pretoria, Malawi, wherever, to Renamo units in the bush? It all seemed to fit.' He smiled wryly. 'Couldn't have been more wrong, could I?'

'First Pienaar, now JJ.' She looked at him accusingly. 'Not to forget you, George Wilkens. So who in this outfit is actually who they're supposed to be?'

'Alfonso Querrime for a start,' said the Commandante. 'He's truthful, brave, unselfish and immensely loyal. A man can't do much better than that. And Gumede, for that matter. He's all those things, too.'

'Jan Wessels. What about him?'

'A good man, I think. Tough, intelligent, Afrikaans farmer. Dead honest, I'd say. Querrime told me how fed

244

up he was when he learned of Pienaar's real identity. I'm satisfied Wessels is one hundred per cent genuine.'

For some moments they sat in silence, each busy with their own thoughts. Trudi looked at him quizzically. 'Are you really doing a geological survey, Vasco?'

'Yes, most certainly. But of course I pass any worthwhile information to intelligence in Maputo. Things I learn, see and hear out in the bush. I'm a government servant.'

'I thought it might be like that.' She hesitated. 'Now I think I can safely tell you about me.'

'Oh,' He eyed her in surprise. 'What about you?'

She showed signs of embarrassment. 'I've had to lie to you in a big way, Vasco. I work for the Zimbabwe Government. In their anti-narcotics unit.'

'So your story of being ditched in Mutare by Greg the electronics salesman was eyewash.' The Commandante's expression was a mixture of humour and curiosity.

'Well I *was* ditched, but it was arranged. I drove down from Harare with Greg Nielsen. He's head of our new unit. On loan from the US Narcotics Bureau. We spent a couple of nights in the hotel together.'

'It was like that, was it?' The Commandante frowned.

'No, it was *not* like that. We had separate rooms,' she said defiantly. 'We were there on an assignment. We had to put on an act.'

'What sort of assignment?'

'To check on a drug supply line.'

'So that's how you know what heroin tastes like?'

'Right.' She fumbled in her shoulder-bag, found a tissue and blew her nose.

'What was the act?'

'We pretended to have a row after dinner on the second night. Before breakfast next morning he'd cleared out. JJ arrived late that afternoon. There was no reason at that stage to suspect him. All we knew was that there was to be a meeting at the hotel at noon on the Tuesday between a suspect already known to us and a contact who was not known to us. My assignment was to find out who the unknown was.'

The Commandante regarded her with new-found respect. 'How did you get into the anti-narcotics unit?'

Trudi explained that some of what she'd already told him was true. She *was* the daughter of German parents who'd settled in Johannesburg; her mother had died and her father had remarried. After working in Johannesburg for some years she had decided she wanted a new sort of life. So she went up to Zimbabwe where her brother, a mechanical engineer, was stationed. 'I got friendly with one of his Zimbabwean friends in Harare. A very civilised, well-educated man. Same age as me. He had just joined the new unit and he recruited me. His uncle is a cabinet minister, so he had some pull. He and I and a third guy, an African ex-CID, were given a short intensive anti-narcotics course by Greg Nielsen. After that I had simple briefs, mostly surveillance jobs in hotels like Meikles. Reporting comings and goings. That sort of thing. The Mutare job was my first really important assignment. That's just an outline, Vasco. There's a lot else I can't tell you because I'm not allowed to.'

'Of course. But I must say you're a convincing liar.' He eyed her severely.

'Have to be in my job, don't I? Hope you understand?'

'Naturally, I do. At least we're on the same side. There's one thing I'd like to ask you, Trudi.'

'What's that?'

'Until we opened that pilotcase you couldn't believe JJ was involved. Right?'

'Yes. That's right. I still find it difficult to believe.'

'But surely when the suspect you could identify turned up at the hotel in Mutare at noon he must have contacted Johnson. How was it you didn't spot that?'

'Oh, it's a long story, Vasco.' She brushed a lock of hair from her eyes. 'Just let me say that I got it hopelessly wrong. Jake, also on the assignment, got it right. I didn't realise JJ could be involved. Jake and the others were satisfied that he was. My job then was to check what happened when the Cessna arrived at Grand Central – and afterwards in Johannesburg. In other words I was to keep close to JJ.'

'Why didn't your people simply search, arrest and charge the suspect when he kept that noon appointment – and for that matter Johnson as well. In other words clobber them at the time?'

She shook her head. 'That would have wrecked the operation. We knew there was an organisation supplying heroin to South Africa. We knew it came from Pakistan via a certain country and we knew the names of several operators. The man who did the drop in Mutare was one of them. Our job was to find out who his Mutare contact was and keep him under observation. In that way we could trace the supply line to Johannesburg, the principal market. Once that had been done we'd have handed over to the South Africans to roll it up.'

'I see. That makes sense.'

She pointed at the pilotcase. 'So what happens to it?'

'It will have to go to Maputo. D'Abreu will see it gets into the right hands. I expect our Government will inform Pretoria. Nobody wants the drug racket to flourish. You'll be reporting to your people in Harare?'

'Of course. Poor JJ's wife. The South Africans are bound to want to find out what she knows. In fact they must,' she added, with professional severity. 'The fat cats behind this will soon repair the broken link.'

'JJ, you mean?'

'Yes.' She looked wretched and he changed the subject.

THIRTY

On the return journey from Soufflier, Luena found himself in a state of agitated confusion. Who had killed Gottwald and Kahn? Patel, the man who had confessed to Nielsen that to get even with Gottwald and Kahn had become an obsession? The visit to Beau Rivage had been on the day and at the time suggested by Patel; it was he who had provided the Beretta, ostensibly at Nielsen's request, but there was only Patel's word for that.

Although the air-conditioning unit in the lounge at Beau Rivage had been switched on, the window nearest the front door had been left open. Why? So that he could get into the house that way, leaving fingerprints as he climbed through? Fortunately, the rubber gloves had confounded that part of the plot to implicate him – if indeed there was such a plot. The telephone handset inside the front door had been on its cradle, the cable neatly severed at floor level. The bolt-lock on the gate could only be opened from the inside; whoever had done the killing must have climbed the stone wall surrounding the property.

As a youth, fighting in the bush war for Zimbabwe's independence, he had seen more than enough corpses to have a fair idea of how long the victims had been dead. Propped up shoulder-to-shoulder on the settee, Gottwald and Kahn appeared to have been dead for some time.

Everything suggested that he was intended to be the fall guy, the obvious suspect. Shocked at the revelation, he asked himself if Patel would really sacrifice him in such a bizarre, calculated way. The answer was yes, why not?

What did a young black from Zimbabwe, a complete stranger, mean to the Hindu if he could use him to dispose of the man with whom he was determined to get even?

Driving down the winding road through a landscape bathed in starlight he felt that he had lost touch with reality. It was as if he were in the grip of a nightmare, the two dead men on the settee its central focus, the other events of the night a misted background. He had all but reached Mahebourg when with sudden and chilling recollection he realised that he must get rid of the Beretta. He pulled off the road, consulted the map by torchlight. Beyond Soufflier the road hugged the coast in several places. He turned the car and drove back through Soufflier and on along the coast road until he reached a section where it ran close to the edge of a cliff high above seas breaking against rocky buttresses. There he stopped the car and got out. Kneeling in the Renault's shadow he threw the Beretta out over the water, the pistol glinting in the starlight as it twisted and fell. Further down the road he stopped the car again and got rid of the shoulder-harness in the same way. It was a remote stretch of coast, deserted by traffic at that hour, and he had no fear that he might have been seen.

Once back on the road to Port Louis his thoughts turned to the immediate future. He should reach the hotel before eleven, less than twelve hours later he would board the morning flight for Nairobi, one for which he had already made the reservation. For that, at least, he had Ranjut Patel to thank.

Mrs Gottwald would probably raise the alarm some time next morning, depending presumably on whether her husband had said he would go direct to the office or return home first. She might already have reported the villa's telephone as out of order, but repairmen would be unlikely to call there until some time on Monday. For these reasons, he felt reasonably sure that he would have left Mauritius before the alarm was raised.

Thinking then about his alibi some of his fears receded. He had little doubt that medical evidence would reveal that Gottwald and Kahn had been killed on Saturday night. He had spent the whole of Saturday with Jean Pierre, either on the beach or in the Lefroys' villa. In Port Louis that Saturday night Jean Pierre had been with him in the hotel, talking and enjoying a nightcap until well after midnight.

These more comforting thoughts were with him when the lights of Port Louis showed up in the distance.

Back in the hotel, the night humid and sultry, he lay awake for hours, his body and bedclothes moist with perspiration, his mind once again in a turmoil. Recalling the night's events he was appalled at the extent to which his plans had gone wrong. Had the front door at Beau Rivage been opened to him by Gottwald he would have explained that the Renault had broken down near the *Propriété Privée* sign; might he use the villa's telephone to summon assistance? He had had little doubt that Gottwald would have answered in the affirmative, if only to get rid of him.

The details of his plan after that had been uncertain, for he would have had to rely upon improvisation once in the villa. Central to his plan, however, was an intention to inform Gottwald in a quiet but direct way that he was investigating drug-dealing activities. He would have said enough about Kahn's recent visit to Mutare, and Gottwald's to Johannesburg and Zürich, to suggest that he had, and they might have, some knowledge of what was going on. Implying that he was an agent of the US Narcotics Bureau, he would have asked if they could help him; for example, had they any idea as to who might be involved in operations at the Johannesburg end? He would not refer to Johnson by name because he was still not satisfied that

Johnson was involved. He would, however, hint at the need for those concerned to repair a possible break in the line of supply. Could they suggest what might be done in that regard? His questions would not be accusatory, rather would they suggest that the Narcotics Bureau felt that these gentlemen might, fortuitously, have information which could be of assistance. Their reactions, the nature of their replies, would determine what else he might do, but he had been hopeful that something worthwhile would result; something a lot more useful than returning to Harare to report failure.

It had been his intention to use the Beretta only if forced to, either in self-defence or as a weapon of threat if they had refused to co-operate. As a tactic of last resort he had envisaged inflicting a flesh wound on Gottwald or Kahn in order to frighten them into submission. But he had thought of that as an unlikely eventuality; a little too James Bondish to earn Greg Nielsen's approval.

In the early hours of morning his last thoughts before falling asleep were of Ranjut Patel. Perhaps the man was innocent. Gottwald and Kahn could have been the victims of a gangland killing, his own presence at the villa that weekend a bizarre coincidence. The drug-dealing hierarchy tended to be Mafia-dominated, its occupational hazards high. Could it have been fear in the upper echelons that Kahn's appearance in Mutare, followed by the Cessna's disappearance and thereafter by Gottwald's sudden visit to Johannesburg and Zürich, might lead to revelations implicating them? It was a point he would discuss with Nielsen when he reported back on Tuesday.

The night before the survivors were due to leave for Rio das Pedras discussion round the camp-fire was restrained. Wessels, worrying about Pienaar's escape, was unusually subdued. Much as he now disliked the man, he felt an acute sense of responsibility; on his mind too were the

251

deaths of Scott and the others, for he knew that but for his determination to kill the big marlin, *Sunfish* would have run for shelter in Pomene Bay.

The knowledge of Pienaar's dual identity particularly disturbed him, for it meant that on arrival in Maputo he would be closely questioned on the point because he had organised the trip on which Pienaar had been his guest. How could he prove that he did not know the man was travelling under an assumed name and with an invalid passport? How could he prove that he did not know that Pienaar had been in the South African Police and, what was more, in the Security Branch of that force?

Whichever way he looked at it the situation likely to confront him in Maputo promised to be difficult and possibly dangerous. Upon reflection he had little doubt that Pienaar had done the right thing in making an escape, however slight his chances of reaching the Transvaal border.

Sitting by the fire, wondering what the next few days might bring, Trudi was silent. That Pienaar had gone was to her a relief; she had neither trusted nor liked the man, and in truth she did not really care what happened to him. It was evident to her that Wessels would have a difficult time in Maputo and that worried her because she liked him and she owed her safety to him. Even Pienaar had grudgingly admitted that the younger man had saved his life, though he'd not failed to emphasise that Wessels was responsible for the *Sunfish* disaster. Had it not occurred, reasoned Trudi, she would have had to trek down on her own through guerrilla-infested country from River Island to Pomene – and perhaps beyond.

She was not worried about what might happen to her once in Maputo. There would be no problem in establishing that she had only known Pienaar and Wessels for the few days that had elapsed since their chance encounter on

River Island. She would in any event telephone Nielsen on arrival in Maputo, tell him what had happened and ask him to ensure that the Mozambique authorities hastened her return to Zimbabwe. Harrowing and dangerous as they had been at times, she thought of the last two weeks as the most exciting and adventurous of her life, and she was sorry in an irrational way that they were coming to an end.

That made her think of the Commandante; she looked across to where he sat on the far side of the fire. What a strange, remote man he was. She wondered what was occupying the mind behind the dark sunglasses. Was he thinking about his wife and children? She assumed they existed though he had never mentioned them. Perhaps he hadn't got a wife and children. He could be a misogynist, though she didn't really think that likely. While often terse and uncommunicative, he had in their few days together treated her with consideration and with a good deal more attention than he had shown the Afrikaners. Finally, and most importantly, but for him the survivors' odyssey would, she knew, have ended very differently.

In the morning when she and Wessels left with Querrime and his men for the journey south, she would be saying goodbye to the Commandante, thanking him for all that he had done. They would drive off, she would wave, and that would be the end of a brief but, in its strange way, almost intimate relationship. She would never again see this strong, inscrutable man. It was a thought which left her with a sense of loss she could not explain.

First Johnnie Johnson, now Vasco Ferreira.

Two men she liked and admired, two very different men, yet both to her attractive despite the absurdly short time she had known them. Since it could not be the passage of time, she accepted it must have been both chemistry and the extraordinary flow of events which had determined her feelings for them.

As if echoing the moment of unhappiness, she heard in the distance the weird cry of a fish-eagle.

Shortly before they were due to leave for Rio das Pedras, the Commandante found her doing her face in the Land Rover's mirror.

'Making myself beautiful for the journey,' she said, pouting for the lipstick.

He examined her with critical eyes. 'When the scratches and bruises have gone and your hair's been fixed you shouldn't look too bad.'

'You're not supposed to notice things like that, Vasco Ferreira. Very ungallant of you.'

'Sorry. I was thinking of other things.'

She stopped doing her face, turned to him, the cool brown eyes challenging. 'Like what?'

'Like do you ever visit Maputo?'

'Not yet. But I gather you're sending me there in about an hour's time.' She got busy with her face again, speaking to him over her shoulder. 'Why do you ask?'

'Because I would like to see more of you.'

Surprised, she hesitated, turned to him once more. 'Would your wife approve?' It wasn't a very intelligent reply but it was all she could think of.

'Haven't got one.'

'Perhaps I'll visit Maputo again one of these days,' she conceded. 'But are you ever there, Vasco?'

'Quite often.'

'In that case, yes – I will come.' It was said impetuously and with a shy smile.

In an uncharacteristic gesture the Commandante touched her arm. 'Do that, please. It would be really nice.'

After Querrime and the survivors had gone there was renewed activity in the camp In the course of it, the

254

Commandante went over to the vehicles to check men and equipment. He had all but finished when he spoke to Mateus. 'Where is Gumede?'

Mateus repeated the question to the Africans gathered round the APC.

One of the men came forward. 'Gumede has gone,' he said uneasily.

'Gone?' The Commandante repeated. 'What d'you mean gone, Khosa?'

The African looked away. 'The rains begin, Senhor. I think Gumede has gone to his village to plant.'

'When did he go?'

'When the Senhor left the camp before sunrise with the Afrikaner.'

'He did not come with us,' asserted the Commandante.

'No, Senhor. But he was afraid for the Senhor's safety. He did not trust the other man.'

'What are you trying to tell me, Khosa?' There was a burst of anger in the Commandante's voice.

Khosa looked anywhere but at the fierce, dark face of the white man. 'The Senhor could not see Gumede, but Gumede was with the Senhor.'

'Did he have a weapon with him?' The Commandante patted the revolver at his hip for emphasis as he put the question.

'Yes, Senhor.' Khosa touched his forehead in a gesture of apology. 'The Kalashnikov. For the journey to the village.'

The Africans watched the Commandante with polite curiosity. He looked from Khosa to Mateus, shook his head. 'All right,' he said with tight-lipped weariness. 'Let's go.' He went to the truck, climbed into the driving-seat and started the engine. He signalled to Mateus, the APC trundled forward and the truck followed. For some time after the vehicles had been lost to sight in the distant mirage the sound of their engines could be heard in the camp.

*

The Commandante was angry, disturbed. Gumede had no village to go to, like his family it had been destroyed; the rains had not begun, one shower did not make the rains.

Gumede would return to the base-camp in a week or so with some improbable story about ploughing and planting 'in a new place'. And Pienaar? Pienaar with Gumede close on his tracks would not return to anywhere. How long had the Afrikaner survived? One hour, two hours perhaps — Gumede would not have wanted the sound of the Kalashnikov to be heard in the camp.

It was a rotten world, violence begat violence: Vietnam, Cambodia, Angola, Mozambique, Nicaragua, the Lebanon — the list was endless, the cruelty and terror mindless. Man's inhumanity to man; it would always be so. In a fierce gesture of despair the Commandante struck the steering wheel with an open hand.